Wheels

of Anarchy

Compiled by

Hugh Cooke & Paul R. Spiring

About the Compilers

Hugh Cooke was born in Cardiff in 1949, which was generally considered to be a bad wine year! Educated at Marling School in Stroud and University College, Cardiff, he has spent thirty-seven years teaching English and Philosophy. Hugh has written many plays and pantomimes, which have been performed both in English and German. He is the author of *Panto for Beginners*, a selection of his plays and pantomimes, and has published with Paul Spiring, an edition of Bertram Fletcher Robinson's essays, *Rugby Football during the Nineteenth Century*. Hugh is, at the moment, writing a detective story, in the series, *Sheepshagger Jones*.

Paul R. Spiring is a chartered biologist and physicist (UK). He is currently seconded by the British Government to work as a biology teacher within the English section of the European School of Karlsruhe in Germany. Paul is the joint author of three books: *On the Trail of Arthur Conan Doyle*, *Bertram Fletcher Robinson* and *Arthur Conan Doyle, Sherlock Holmes & Devon* and he has compiled a further four books. Paul also maintains a tribute website that commemorates the memory of Bertram Fletcher Robinson (http://www.bfronline.biz) and he is a member of The Sherlock Holmes Society of London, La Société Sherlock Holmes de France, The Conan Doyle (Crowborough) Establishment, The Sydney Passengers and The Crew of the S.S. May Day.

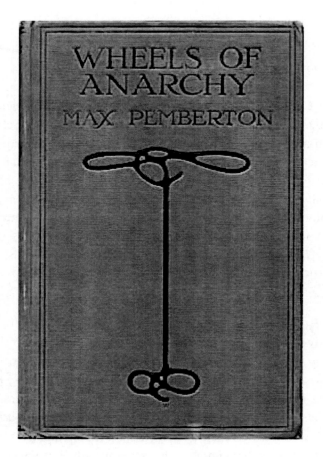

Frontispiece: The front cover of the first hardback edition *of Wheels of Anarchy* by Max Pemberton (London: Cassell & Co. Ltd., 1908). It features the Victorian hangman's rope set against a blood-red background. The story was based on notes that were compiled for the author by Bertram Fletcher Robinson (1870-1907) and it is dedicated to his memory.

Wheels of Anarchy

The Story of an Assassin

As Recited from the Papers and the Personal Narrative of his Secretary, Mr. Bruce Ingersoll

by

Max Pemberton

compiled by

Hugh Cooke & Paul R. Spiring

MX Publishing

First published in 2010

© Copyright 2010

Hugh Cooke & Paul R. Spiring

ISBN 978-1-907685-31-6

Published by

MX Publishing Ltd.,

335 Princess Park Manor,

Royal Drive,

London,

N11 3GX.

www.mxpublishing.co.uk

www.mxpublishing.us.com

Dedication

Bernard Davies visits the Sherlock Holmes Collection at
Marylebone library in London (1978).

This book is dedicated to the memory of Bernard Hurst
Davies (19 November 1923 – 21 September 2010). He was
born in Bath and he was educated at both King Edward's
School in Birmingham and Nottingham High School.
Bernard Davies became a professional actor and he also
wrote thirty papers on "the more neglected regions of
Sherlock Holmes topography". Between 1983 and 1985,
Bernard Davies served as Chairman of the Sherlock Holmes
Society of London, and in 1995, he was made an honorary
member, the Society's highest and rarest honour. During
2005, the actor, writer, journalist, comedian and television
presenter, Stephen Fry, gave a speech at the Sherlock
Holmes Society of London's annual dinner and he remarked
that "to be in the same room as Bernard Davies is a
remarkable honour."

Contents

Modern Preamble

Original Preamble

Wheels of Anarchy

I. Bruce Ingersoll Begins his Story   1

II. Good-Bye to Cambridge   7

III. We Meet Jehan Cavanagh   16

IV. The House of the Fen   24

V. The News in the Paper   35

VI. The Cry in the Night   43

VII. The Woman and the Child   51

VIII. Cavanagh's Destiny   62

IX. Prosper De Blondel   70

X. The Feast of Corpus Christi   81

XI. The Light in the Window   98

XII. I Hear Again of Pauline Mamavieff   114

Contents

XIII. The Prison at Bruges   122

XIV. The Prisoner   130

XV. The Second Interview   141

XVI. Root and Branch   150

XVII. The Red-Haired Man   159

XVIII. The Vienna Express   172

XIX. Upon the Plaza de Toros   177

XX. Dr. Luther James   194

XXI. To Barcelona and the Sea   208

XXII. At the Palazzo da Ponte   223

XXIII. Pauline is Afraid   231

XXIV. We Return to England   236

XXV. Feodor   246

XXVI. An Acquaintance at "The Bull"   257

XXVII. We go by Night to the Fen   264

XXVIII. I see the Lady of the Woods Again   278

Contents

XXIX. In the Library   283

XXX. The Boat at the Garden Gate   291

XXXI. Robiniof   301

XXXII. Her Own People   307

XXXIII. Pauline does not Answer to Us   315

XXXIV. The Miracle   324

XXXV. Jehan Cavanagh Remembers   330

Original Advertisements

Further Reading

Preface

This book includes a facsimile of the first hardback edition of *Wheels of Anarchy* by Max Pemberton (London: Cassell & Co. Ltd., 1908). The decision to republish this story was prompted by its link to Bertram Fletcher Robinson (1870-1907).

Until recently, Fletcher Robinson was rather a shadowy figure within the annals of English Literature, his major claim to fame being that he inspired Arthur Conan Doyle's, *The Hound of the Baskervilles* (1901). However, in recent years, it has emerged that Fletcher Robinson was a prolific writer in his own right and that his impact extended beyond that of Conan Doyle. For example, between 1904 and 1907 he also wrote four satirical playlets with a young PG Wodehouse the man that would later deliver *Jeeves and Wooster* to an appreciative global readership. Thus, Fletcher Robinson's influence upon Max Pemberton's work is a 'third thread' to his literary legacy.

There are two other reasons for republishing *Wheels of Anarchy*. Firstly, it is an entertaining story that is deserving of a readership that extends beyond those who can afford to pay US$300.00 for a good first hardback edition. Secondly, the story reveals that the fear of international terrorism has persisted for at least a century and is not a 'post-9/11' phenomenon. Hence, *Wheels of Anarchy* will prove to be of interest to fans of Sherlock Holmes, and to students of both Sociology and Twentieth Century literature.

Hugh Cooke & Paul R. Spiring

December 2010.

Introductory Notes

Max Pemberton & Sherlock Holmes

Max Pemberton is best remembered as a prolific writer of popular fiction. He was the son of a wealthy merchant and was born at Edgbaston in Birmingham on 19 June 1863. Pemberton was educated at the elite independent schools of St Albans School in Hertfordshire and Merchant Taylor's School in London. In 1881, he was admitted to Caius College, Cambridge to read Law. Whilst there, Pemberton 'elected for the river' and he became the captain of the successful first boat. Pemberton graduated in 1884 and then relocated to London to work as a journalist in Fleet Street. Between 1891 and 1931, he wrote forty stories including the best-sellers, *The Iron Pirate* (1896) and *Captain Black* (1911). He also wrote a number of plays and two successful biographies, *Lord Northcliffe* (1920) and *The Life of Sir Henry Royce* (1934). During 1920, Pemberton founded the London School of Journalism and, eight years later, he was knighted by King George V. Sir Max Pemberton died aged eighty-six years on 22 February 1950 at his London home following a long illness. He was buried in the nearby Kensal Green Roman Catholic Cemetery. Pemberton's life was commemorated at a requiem mass which was held at Brompton Oratory on 27 February 1950.

During 1891, Pemberton had his first novel published, *The Diary of a Scoundrel*. He also devised a plan to publish a penny newspaper to cater for the demand of the newly literate masses for popular fiction. However, he abandoned that plan due to lack of capital and instead, in 1892, he accepted a position with Cassell's as the editor of *Chums*, a socially elite magazine that was targeted at public school boys. He held that position for a year, during which time he also wrote his first best-seller, *The Iron Pirate*, which was first published as a serial. In around 1895, Pemberton was appointed by the *Isthmian Library* to edit a series of volumes about various *Sports and Pastimes*. The first of these volumes was entitled *Rugby Football* by Bertram Fletcher Robinson (1870-1907) and it was published in October 1896 (see Further Reading). Despite the success of this book, by December 1896, Pemberton had resigned his position with the *Isthmian Library* and accepted the editorship of *Cassell's Family Magazine* (later renamed *Cassell's Magazine*). Fletcher Robinson was appointed to succeed Pemberton and subsequently edited a further eight volumes for the *Isthmian Library* between 1897 and 1901.

Pemberton and Fletcher Robinson had much in-common. Both men had studied Law for a period at Cambridge University and each had won 'Rowing Colours' for their respective colleges. Their mutual respect developed into a life-long friendship and between 1897 and 1901, Pemberton commissioned Fletcher Robinson to write two books and thirty articles for two periodicals that were each published by Cassell & Co. Ltd. (London). These items included a series of six articles about major European cities for *Cassell's Magazine*. Later, Pemberton recalled in his autobiography, *Sixty Years Ago and After* (London: Hutchinson & Co., 1936) that during this assignment, Fletcher Robinson visited Livadia in the Crimea and was received by the entourage of Czar Nicholas II at 'The Old Grand Palace' (later renamed 'The White Palace'). He was entertained by the Emperor's Great Chamberlain and was subjected to persistent surveillance by the Russian Secret Police. Such experiences appear to have inspired Fletcher Robinson's literary collaboration with John Malcolm Fraser (later Sir John) entitled *The Trail of the Dead* (1902-03).

On Thursday 25 April 1901, Pemberton invited Fletcher Robinson to dine with him at his home at 56 Fitzjohn's Avenue, Hampstead, London. Pemberton's recollection of this event was later reported in an article that was published by the London *Evening News* (25 May 1939):

The late Fletcher Robinson who collaborated, with Doyle in the story [*The Hound of the Baskervilles*], was dining at my house in Hampstead one night when the talk turned upon phantom dogs. I told my friend of a certain Jimmy Farman, a Norfolk marshman, who swore that there was a phantom dog on the marshes near St. Olives (near Great Yarmouth, Norfolk) and that his bitch had met the brute more than once and had been terrified by it. 'A Great black dog it were,' Jimmy said, 'and the eyes of 'un was like railway lamps. He crossed my path down there by the far dyke and the old bitch a'most went mad wi' fear...Now surely that bitch saw a' summat I didn't see...'

Fletcher Robinson assured me that dozens of people on the outskirts of Dartmoor had seen a phantom hound and that to doubt its existence would be a local heresy. In both instances, the brute was a huge retriever, coal black and with eyes which shone like fire.

Fletcher Robinson was always a little psychic and he had a warm regard for this apparition; indeed, he expressed some surprise that no romancer had yet written about it. Three nights afterwards, Fletcher Robinson was dining with Sir [sic] Arthur. The talk at my house was still fresh in his mind and he told Doyle what I had said, emphasising that this particular marshman was as sure of the existence of the phantom hound as he was of his own being. Finally, Fletcher Robinson said 'Let us write the story together.' And to his great content Sir [sic] Arthur cordially assented.

The dinner to which Pemberton refers above took place on Sunday 29 April 1901 at the Royal Links Hotel in Cromer, Norfolk. Shortly thereafter, Dr. Arthur Conan Doyle (1859-1930) wrote a letter to his mother in which, he stated as a footnote that "Fletcher Robinson came here with me and we are going to do small book together 'The Hound of the Baskervilles' – A real creeper." Conan Doyle also wrote another letter to Herbert Greenhough Smith, the editor of *The Strand Magazine*, in which he offered this story to Greenhough Smith but insisted that "I must do it with my friend Robinson and his name must appear with mine." He also added that "I shall want my usual 50 pounds per thousand words for all rights if you do business." Conan Doyle later incorporated Sherlock Holmes as the central character into this story, which he completed in July 1901.

During December 1903, a group of six men founded an 'invited member only' criminology club in London. 'Our Society' or 'Crimes Club' would meet for dinner and to hear a paper that was prepared and read by one of the members. These events were intended to be 'strictly private' and so were usually conducted at a member's home. The original founder members included the author and journalist, Arthur Lampton, the physician and barrister, Samuel Ingleby Oddie, and the qualified barrister and actor 'Harry Brodribb Irving (eldest son of the famous Victorian actor, Sir Henry Irving). In around January 1904, a further six members were admitted to 'Our Society' and these included Max Pemberton, Fletcher Robinson and Conan Doyle.

On Thursday 18 October 1906, 'Our Society' met at Pemberton's home and he delivered a speech entitled *An*

Attempt to Blackmail Me. Two days later, Fletcher Robinson and Conan Doyle played golf together at Hindhead in Surrey. At about that time, Fletcher Robinson wrote a fourth playlet with PG Wodehouse and was also appointed editor of a weekly illustrated newspaper entitled *The World – A Journal for Men and Women.* This periodical was owned by Lord Northcliffe and managed by Pemberton. The latter man had resigned his position as the editor of *Cassell's Magazine* in around December 1905. It is difficult to conceive that Pemberton, Fletcher Robinson and Conan Doyle did not take the opportunity to discuss the plot for what would become the *Wheels of Anarchy* during this period.

On Monday 21 January 1907, Fletcher Robinson died aged thirty-six years from complications linked to enteric fever at his home in London. Three days later, he was buried at St. Andrew's Church at Ipplepen in Devon. Amongst the many floral tributes that were sent to the funeral service was a message that read "From 'Our Society', with deepest regrets from fellow members" and "In Loving Memory of an Old and Valued Friend. Arthur Conan Doyle." On that same day Pemberton attended Fletcher Robinson's memorial service at St. Clement Danes Church in London.

On Wednesday 18 September 1907, Pemberton attended Conan Doyle's wedding reception at the Whitehall Rooms of the Hôtel Métropole in London. The following January, he had *Wheels of Anarchy* published by Cassell & Co. Ltd. (London, New York, Toronto & Melbourne). The preamble to this book features the following 'Author's Note':

> This story was suggested to me by the late B. Fletcher Robinson, a dear friend, deeply mourned. The subject was one in which he had interested himself for some years; and almost the last message I had from him expressed the desire that I would keep my promise and treat of the idea in a book. This I have now done, adding something of my own to the brief notes he left me, but chiefly bringing to the task an enduring gratitude for a friendship which nothing can replace.

This statement is striking for several reasons. Firstly, it reveals that *Wheels of Anarchy* was based upon an idea that was devised by Fletcher Robinson. Secondly, it resonates with the acknowledgments that are printed in the various first editions of *The Hound of the Baskervilles* and attributed to Conan Doyle. Evidently, both Pemberton and Conan Doyle had valued the literary ideas supplied to them by Fletcher Robinson. Perhaps for this reason, it is not surprising that both Pemberton and Conan Doyle appear to have based a fictional hero on Fletcher Robinson. In Pemberton's *Wheels of Anarchy*, the heroic narrator is called Bruce Driscoll and like Fletcher Robinson, he is both a graduate of Jesus College and a noted Cambridge sporting

'Blue'. In Conan Doyle's *The Lost World* (1912), the heroic narrator is called Edward E. Malone and like Fletcher Robinson, he is a London-based journalist, loves a woman called Gladys, exceeds six feet in height and is a noted rugby player.

Introducing *Wheels of Anarchy*

Every age creates its own heroes. Villains go on forever. Watching the early James Bond films, despite Sean Connery, one is, frankly, embarrassed by the macho male chauvinistic attitudes of the hat wearing hero, but Goldfinger never goes out of fashion. Thrillers are the ultimate escape – they convince us that something can be done; that no matter how grim the situation is, or how invincible the enemy seems, right will prevail (i.e. us). The trend was seized upon first in 1903, by Erskine Childers in *The Riddle of the Sands*. Here the invincible enemy was an old favourite, the Germans. The French had somehow dropped off the radar, now only a historic threat. Whilst the Germans, so massively organized and ruthless with sharp, pointy helmets, gathered to attack, only two, ordinary British citizens stood in the way (who were they?). The poor Germans had no chance. The heroes were no Super-heroes, who could fly and bash down walls, but men with human frailties and limitations. They were like the ordinary Dr. Watson without the extraordinary Mr. Sherlock Holmes!

From this start, the protagonist, while still facing the dangers of the conventional hero like Allan Quartermain, seemed no better equipped than we, ordinary folk would be. When Richard Hanney strode onto the scene in 1915, we were ready to take to the heather with him, confident that those dastardly Germans (again) had no real chance against an ordinary Englishman (okay – actually a Scottish South African). Bruce Ingersoll (with a name like that he should be a newsreader) is the perfect hero for his time. He represents all that the age considered virtuous, honourable, brave and morally certain. Ingersoll is also clever and resourceful, but not in a suspiciously intellectual way. He is not tainted with aristocratic privilege, but is at home in the village pub or a Gentleman's club. Ingersoll has no "issue" or dark side. In short, he is the man that a mother dreams her daughter might bring home.

It is hard not to see Ingersoll as the product of discussions over brandy and cigars between Pemberton, Fletcher Robinson and Conan Doyle at meetings of 'Our Society'. Firstly, as previously mentioned, Ingersoll is a graduate of Cambridge University, and he shares Pemberton and Robinson's love of the place; secondly, the old device of the book's subtitle, "as recited from the papers and personal narrative of his secretary, Mr. Bruce Ingersoll" – a device that Conan Doyle had turned into a work of art with Dr. Watson's chronicles of the Sherlock Holmes adventures. Indeed, Ingersoll shares a great deal in common with

Watson, and he has no Holmes to minimize his efforts. He has no sexual ambiguity: like Watson, he has an eye for the ladies. Pemberton's description of the 'Fortune Teller' leaves no doubt on that score. Ingersoll becomes fascinated by Pauline Mamavieff, who, at first, gives him no encouragement. He is determined to play the 'White Knight' and rescue and protect, whether this is desired or not. Like Watson, he is sportsman – his love of Cambridge is not the ivory tower academia, but the rowing and rugby playing Cambridge. This element of his character brings us into the sphere of Fletcher Robinson, the likely model for the character. There is about Pemberton, as with Conan Doyle, an awkwardness when dealing with his female characters; they are either wet rags or clever and forceful, and devilishly attractive. Pauline is at her best as a character when locked up; it creates enough distance. As soon as she is out and available, she diminishes and disappears. To be fair, it is difficult to think of an action orientated male novelist who can create creditable female characters. Indeed, generations of young boys brought up on the *Biggles* books by Captain W.E. Johns became acutely aware that looking at girls put one in danger of walking into a propeller blade!

Where Pemberton is at his best is when our heroes hit the road. His description of a bull fight in Madrid is truly magnificent, as good as anything, Ernest Hemingway could manage. Even today in the age of budget flights, the glamour of rail journey to distant European show cities has not been lost in the same way that Vienna will always carry the shadowy figure of Harry Lime. Vienna, Venice, Madrid, Barcelona – these are cities of the soul – cities that each carry with them an underbelly of mystery, that cities like Los Angeles and Las Vegas can never achieve. The city that dominates the novel remains unvisited, Baku, which perhaps was just as well. Baku would have been perhaps too exotic, just lingering at the fringes of the imagination. To Pemberton, it was a mysterious Russian city, a sort of younger brother to both Moscow and St. Petersburg, and thus it should remain for the novel. The reality of the city is, of course, quite different.

While Erskine Childers had created the Germans as the major opposition to the might of the British Empire, the increasingly oppressive Russian state had led to a huge expatriate community throughout Europe. These carried with them the sinister imprint exploited by Joseph Conrad in *The Secret Agent* (1907) and *Under Western Eyes* (1911). Foreigners can always carry with them a threat of being different; not playing to our prevailing rules, but whereas the Germans may be portrayed as brutish, they basically were not that alien despite their tendency to wear lederhosen! The Russians, however, seemed to have another mindset altogether. They played chess, which Holmes would tell you is a sure sign of a scheming and devious mind. They were not all that far away from

Genghis Khan, or Taras Bulba. The British believed in their hearts that they were the only true candidate for world domination, and that the Russians, the Germans, the Yellow Peril, or the Belgians just didn't have the right credentials. As for the Americans, they were basically British, but didn't know it, and were too busy inventing games that only they played, so only they could win in the ridiculously entitled 'World Series'.

The threat from international terrorism, however, was as real as it is today. Bombs exploded in the cities and small cells plotted the downfall of civilisation. And like today, the real danger was not the physical destruction these small groups might achieve, but the massive loss of human rights and freedom that follow-on from the restrictions levied against the individual by governments. Ingersoll's boss, Jehan Cavanagh, accuses such governments as being too soft and too slow to respond to the threats that he foresees. So like a James Bond villain, he sets about using his money and his influence to deal with the situation. He feels that the biggest threat to democracy was democracy itself. It is not hard to see where this line of thinking comes from. Who does he pick as his right hand man? A Cambridge graduate, and former Jesus College man. In what other institution (except Oxford University), could one find a group of people so totally convinced of their right to lead? Public school and Oxbridge privilege ironed in over the generations. But Bruce is different because he actually has to work for a living. His sense of divine right has been distorted along the way, even if, unlike James Bond, he fights fair and by the rules.

In counterbalance to the hectic travel, is the intriguing 'House of the Fen'. Great Houses in fiction will always have Baskerville Hall looming in the background. The House of the Fen does carry a sinister feel about it, yet it also is a fixed point in the narrative. It seems to be a haven, yet of course, we know this is an illusion, just like John Ridd's farm in *Lorna Doone* or the jail in *Rio Bravo*. Pemberton creates a real sense of threat, but also a sense of moral uncertainty. Exactly who the attackers are remains as misty as the Fens themselves. As time goes on, exactly who the 'good guys' are becomes more and more confused. While Ingersoll remains our moral keystone, even he seems prepared to go outside the law to rescue his beloved.

The sad thing for this generation is that we have lost our heroes. What do our 'heroes' fight for today? We have little faith left in politicians; they are no longer serious, distant figures, certain of their values, but rather seedy, tainted figures plotting only for their own advancement. Not even the Queen seems a figure worthwhile to go out and die for, since we have become aware just how much she costs a poor nation. In America, the heroes are the figures fighting the establishment – the evil forces being the C.I.A., or the F.B.I. or even, at times, the President himself.

We may be faintly embarrassed when Richard Hanney preaches the virtues of the Imperial world for which he is fighting so bravely, but what exactly is James Bond risking his life so readily for? Ingersoll's motives are crystal clear. He has a set of values that even we, in our cynical cocoon, can relate to. He places love and friendship at the core of the world. Those that place 'the bigger picture' – no matter what that 'picture' is – before these central human virtues – are the true agents of destruction. The book's dramatic conclusion is full of shadowy figures that are symbolic of the moral confusion. Pemberton's description of the seduction of 'The Greater Good' that leads nations into wars of democracy, which destroy hundreds of thousands of the very people they pretend to be saving, is masterful.

Wheels of Anarchy could well be sub-titled, 'The First Global War on Terror', but Pemberton's vision goes beyond the black and white certainties of former President George W. Bush. His circle of violence is broken, and a resolution and redemption is reached. Jehan Cavanagh is saved and he then heads off to 'the great spaces and unbroken horizon' of Canada. He leaves behind the complexities of a Europe lurching inevitably towards the carnage of the First World War. Ingersoll is left with the dream of England's green and pleasant land – quieter and more civilized than the American Dream, but just as illusionary.

WHEELS OF ANARCHY

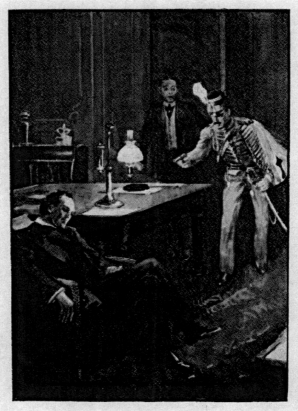

"I saw that he would shoot my patron through the very
heart " (p. 204).

WHEELS OF ANARCHY

*The Story of an Assassin : as
Recited from the Papers and
the Personal Narrative
of his Secretary,
Mr. Bruce
Ingersoll*

BY

MAX PEMBERTON

WITH A FRONTISPIECE BY
ROBERT B. M. PAXTON

CASSELL AND COMPANY, LIMITED
London, Paris, New York, Toronto and Melbourne
MCMVIII

AUTHOR'S NOTE

This story was suggested to me by the late B. Fletcher Robinson, a dear friend, deeply mourned. The subject was one in which he had interested himself for some years; and almost the last message I had from him expressed the desire that I would keep my promise and treat of the idea in a book. This I have now done, adding something of my own to the brief notes he left me, but chiefly bringing to the task an enduring gratitude for a friendship which nothing can replace.

MAX PEMBERTON

CONTENTS

CHAPTER I

BRUCE INGERSOLL BEGINS HIS STORY . . . 1

CHAPTER II

GOOD-BYE TO CAMBRIDGE 7

CHAPTER III

WE MEET JEHAN CAVANAGH 16

CHAPTER IV

THE HOUSE OF THE FEN 24

CHAPTER V

THE NEWS IN THE PAPER 35

CHAPTER VI

THE CRY IN THE NIGHT 43

CHAPTER VII

THE WOMAN AND THE CHILD 51

CHAPTER VIII

CAVANAGH'S DESTINY 62

CHAPTER IX

PROSPER DE BLONDEL 70

x   CONTENTS

CHAPTER X   PAGE

THE FEAST OF CORPUS CHRISTI   81

CHAPTER XI

THE LIGHT IN THE WINDOW   .   .   . 98

CHAPTER XII

I HEAR AGAIN OF PAULINE MAMAVIEFF   .   .   . 114

CHAPTER XIII

THE PRISON AT BRUGES   122

CHAPTER XIV

THE PRISONER   130

CHAPTER XV

THE SECOND INTERVIEW   141

CHAPTER XVI

ROOT AND BRANCH   150

CHAPTER XVII

THE RED-HAIRED MAN   159

CHAPTER XVIII

THE VIENNA EXPRESS   172

CHAPTER XIX

UPON THE PLAZA DE TOROS   177

CHAPTER XX

DR: LUTHER JAMES   194

CONTENTS

xi

CHAPTER XXI

PAGE

To Barcelona and the Sea 208

CHAPTER XXII

At the Palazzo da Ponte 223

CHAPTER XXIII

Pauline is Afraid 231

CHAPTER XXIV

We return to England 236

CHAPTER XXV

Feodor 246

CHAPTER XXVI

An Acquaintance at "The Bull" . . . 257

CHAPTER XXVII

We go by Night to the Fen 264

CHAPTER XXVIII

I see the Lady of the Woods again . . . 278

CHAPTER XXIX

In the Library 283

CHAPTER XXX

The Boat at the Garden Gate 291

CHAPTER XXXI

Robiniof 301

xii   CONTENTS

CHAPTER XXXII   PAGE
HER OWN PEOPLE 307

CHAPTER XXXIII
PAULINE DOES NOT ANSWER TO US   . . . 315

CHAPTER XXXIV
THE MIRACLE 324

CHAPTER XXXV
JEHAN CAVANAGH REMEMBERS 330

WHEELS OF ANARCHY

CHAPTER I

I AM asked to write the story of the strange events which have happened to me during the last twelve months, and to write it without reserve. The request is made with justice, and cannot very well be refused. In the name of my friend Jehan Cavanagh and of those who have judged him, I begin my task. May its recompense be the approval of many who have so greatly desired its accomplishment.

Let it be said that I have written but little before. The craftsmanship necessary to unravel the threads of this amazing mystery, and to lay them side by side upon my manuscript where all could count them, is not mine. I hardly know at what point the public interest in this recital would begin or where it should rightly be ended. For my own part, I can remember nothing which has any place in the story at all prior to the Fellows' garden party at Trinity College, Cambridge, in the month of June last year. And the garden party is no more than the tissue of pretty superstitions coming from a pretty woman's mouth.

B

My cousin Una and my aunt Lady Elgood were up for our mis-called May week. I had taken lodgings for them in Jesus Lane; other circumstances being forgotten, the ten days would have been jolly enough. But this was to be my last term at Cambridge. The world lay before me as a great sea upon which the mists of morning were rising. I knew nothing of my future; had little hope for it since my father's death. Even Una found me dull—and we were such old comrades in frivolity.

"You will never get me a husband if you look as solemn as that, Bruce," she complained.

I told her that the modern husband liked gravity.

"And marriage is no laughing matter—as he will discover by and by," I added, with that which she called my sardonic humour.

This was at the very Fellows' garden party of which I have spoken. Although I am a Jesus man, one of our dons managed an invitation for the affair, and we went there after a jolly lunch in his rooms. I think he was a little gone on Una, and would have had a chance but for his side-whiskers and intolerable habit of saying, "Eh, what?" in the middle of your best stories. When we arrived at the Trinity Gardens, we contrived to lose him near the door of a tent where an amateur lady palmist gave séances for the benefit of a local charity—as she said. My aunt insisted, however, that it was merely to hold the Fellows' fingers; and I told Una that she would do well to take the hint.

"Go in and have three-penn'orth, since you can't pitch a tent for yourself," I suggested to her. "You may see your future husband—like a snake in the grass. Don't tell the lady his name, or she may try to cut you out. Of course, it's all true. If these things weren't true, life wouldn't be worth living. Go in and capture an Indian rajah—he'd be cheap at threepence, Una."

She laughed at me, good, merry little Una, who is so very far from being clever, as I have often told her, but is one of the best little women that ever went spades with four aces in her hand. A man came out of the tent while we argued about it, and he, being a Dean—but not my own Dean—immediately exhorted her to do as I said.

"I do not remember when I was amused so much," said the Dean; "she actually told me of an illness I had when at school, and she detected that I was married. There must be something unusual in the shape of the hand which betrays our secrets. I intend to read the standard works upon the subject—and a remarkably pretty woman, too," he added, as he went bustling and smiling away. The advertisement was too much for Una. She whipped out her purse, and was inside the tent before you could count three. When she came out again, I saw her cheeks aflame with her heightened colour and her pretty blue eyes looking like

enraged turquoises. Her chestnut hair was all
awry, too ; and she was evidently very angry.

" Well ? " I asked her.

" A perfect little beast of a cat," she rejoined,
all in a breath. " She told me I was going to
die an old maid."

" Did you forget to pay the threepence, Una ? "

" No ; I didn't. But I snatched it up again
when I came out. It's nothing but a swindle ! "

" Oh, come," cried I ; " these things always
go by contraries. What can you expect for threepence, Una ? Husbands are booming to-day,
you know ; they're almost as dear as Kaffirs."

She was not to be mollified, but, my aunt
Mary coming up at the moment, they both insisted that I should try my luck before this
Pythia of the green baize table, and see if I
could do as well as the excellent Dean who had
preceded me. It was a jest at the best, and as
such we all treated it.

" Well," said I, " those who are born to be
hanged will never die by drowning ; " and, more
to amuse them than myself, I went into the tent
and discovered the lady.

She certainly was a pretty girl, and the dim,
religious light inside the tent helped one to forget
the unnecessary rouge upon her cheeks. A gold
chain, coiled about her neck, gave one the idea
that she habitually kept company with snakes ;
while upon a pretty hand some diamonds of
remarkable size glittered bewilderingly. Her

dress was of spotless white ; her arms, I noticed, were bared to the shoulder. She received me with a gracious dignity which she meant to be impressive; and instantly fixed upon me as mischievous a pair of eyes as I remember to have encountered.

" Have you ever had your hand read before ? " she asked.

I told her that fortune had never dealt so kindly with me.

" And you don't believe in palmistry, I suppose ? "

" Not a word of it."

We began pleasantly, you will perceive, and the continuation was in the same key. Her clients, I imagined—those of the male sex, that is to say—liked to have their hands stroked and pressed between her pretty palms. When she had done a lot of this, and looked into my face for a long time, she asked me if I had ever had an illness in my childhood.

" Measles," said I, " and plenty of them."

" Ah ! but were you not seriously ill, and did you not go abroad after it ? "

" I can remember an attack of mumps, and a journey to Boulogne."

This annoyed her, perhaps naturally ; and I could see that she was trying very hard. Presently she said :

" You have suffered a great loss lately—your father or your mother ? "

" That's true. My father died eight months
ago."

"And his death made a great difference to you?"

" Which might be obvious, or might be not.
I'll grant you the difference."

" You are of artistic tendencies, and have
written or painted ? "

" The front door railings—I once painted
them when I was a small boy. The writing's
better. Perhaps you saw my name in the
Fortnightly ? "

She blushed at this beneath the rouge upon
her cheeks—quite superfluous rouge, as the Dean
would bear witness. My antipathy appeared to
perplex her. I knew that she was determined
to impress me, and my obstinacy answered to
her persistency.

"You are going to meet a stranger," she
exclaimed presently; " whether he will bring
you good or ill fortune, I cannot tell you.   I see
that you will be married—after many troubles
and a great conflict between the head and the
heart.   Your life line is good, and the amative
faculty is not strongly developed.   Beware of the
man who is coming into your life.   That is all I
can say, Mr. Ingersoll."

She looked at me again with the keen, close
scrutiny of one who knew very much more than
that which my hand had told her.

And I left the tent remembering that I was
to meet Mr. Jehan Cavanagh to-morrow.

CHAPTER II

Una got engaged to Harry Relton at the Caius ball. I believe that she did it to spite the palmist, for I never thought she was partial to Harry, though I knew he was awfully gone on her. I told her that she was a lucky girl, and was glad that she had got a "First." Harry always had lots of money, and will have more now that his father has taken to making motor-cars.

He seems to have proposed to her on the kitchen stairs, just when the cooks were serving up the supper. This is a little ominous, and I hope that Una can cook as well as she can flirt. She tells me that she does not feel a bit different now that she is engaged. I had expected certain ecstatic expressions, and what the French style "a frenzy of rapture." Perhaps Harry will succeed in awakening those more serious views of life which Una has hitherto derided. Had he not a fortune, I should be inclined to say, God help them both. Certainly, there is no money in rowing as a profession ; while Una's little extravagances would ruin anybody but a Vanderbilt. As it is, they will make a pretty

7

pair, and drift through life as children upon a
sunny picnic.

I was glad to hear of her engagement—perhaps a little more melancholy because of it.
After all, this parting of the ways is a sorrowful
business enough, and not to be contemplated
lightly even by the most fortunate. To quit the
rooms one has loved so well ; to remember that
some beast of a first-year man will have them
next term ; to give up the offices you hold so
proudly, your cricket captaincy, your post as
president of the Union, your right to sit in the
chief seats ; to look out of your window upon
the familiar view, the old court wherein you
have almost counted the very blades of grass ;
that vista of tower and chapel and ivy-covered
turret, the distant panorama of the spires and
domes of Cambridge ; to know that you are
leaving it for ever—yes, that is a moment few
can bear to think of, few can face with courage.

And remember what a vague future I had
before me. Eight months ago, my father died
and left behind him a sum that scarcely satisfied
his many creditors. He survived my dear
mother some three years only; and I attribute his
misfortunes entirely to the grief with which he
bewailed her loss. Never afterwards was his
heart in the work he loved to do. I did not
know how poor he had become, but I pitied him
in poverty, and was glad to believe that it was
for my mother's sake. Such sums as remained

after all the creditors were paid hardly sufficed
to keep me at Cambridge until I could take my
degree. I had my two scholarships, it is true ;
but my debts grew apace, and when this fatal
May term came, I knew no more than the dead
how I should discharge them.

Needless to say, I must find some employ-
ment, and find it swiftly. It had been my
father's wish in the days of his prosperity that I
should qualify myself for a house-mastership in
one of our big public schools, where his influence
was considerable. A " First " in any good
Tripos would do that, especially for a man who
had some athletic qualification as well. Why I
chose the Moral Science Tripos I hardly know.
Perhaps because my father himself made much
of logic and philosophy ; and, although he was
but a lawyer in a big commercial practice, he
had read largely both in English and in German.
This choice of mine now appeared to be somewhat unfortunate. I could no longer hope for the
mastership, and who would go to the head of a
commercial house and say, " My logic is irre-
proachable, please make me your book-keeper " ?
To this point the University had done me a mischief and not a service. The fact was undoubted,
although the admission seemed treason to one
who loved Cambridge as I did.

So, you see I had to get my living, and to
lose no time about the business. I had written
a few articles for the more serious Reviews, and

had done well with them. A critical study of
Marx in the pages of the *Fortnightly* brought
me many friends. I published a long paper on
Individualism in the *Quarterly*, and had reviewed
books for some of the literary dailies. This
sort of work is not bread and cheese, as all the
world knows. I thought that it might help
me if I could add a secretaryship to it, and so
I inserted an advertisement in the *Times* stating
my requirements. The reply to this is the
beginning of the strange story I have to tell.

Now, I had expected something very different—a lengthy correspondence, perhaps, and
certainly the production of testimonials. Whoever took me into his service, I argued, would
want to know all about me from my tutor;
would discuss the question of my fitness for the
post, my capabilities, and the amount of salary
I required. I had imagined that I might snap
up a member of Parliament, or perhaps a diplo-
matist, for I spoke French and German, and
had travelled much with my father. What
must I have thought, then, when I received
two lines upon a sheet of mourning-edged note-
paper, addressed to me from Claridge's Hotel,
and informing me that Mr. Jehan Cavanagh
would be glad to take me into his service
immediately. Had one dropped a diamond
tea-pot into my lap it could not have astonished
me more. For was not Jehan Cavanagh the
great Canadian railway magnate, and was not

his name as familiar to me as that of Mr. Rockefeller himself? Please to note that there were but two lines of writing in all. *"Mr. Jehan Cavanagh presents his compliments to Mr. Bruce Ingersoll, and will be glad to avail himself of his services, beginning from June 15th next."* No references were asked for, you will observe; no salary was mentioned. I was without information as to where my services were required, or the nature of them. And yet the man's name was a guarantee which the most incredulous would have accepted. No figure stood more prominently than his before those interested in the future of Canada and her railway system. We had all seen pictures in the illustrated papers of his deer forest and of his yacht. When his father, the famous politician and financier of Quebec, had been killed by the fanatics at Baku some ten months ago, the event was treated in the newspapers as a world's tragedy. And this man asked me to be his secretary; was ready to take me without an interview, and did not stoop to bargain about my salary, or to ask me any kind of question whatsoever! Had he been less famous, or his reputation otherwise, the very circumstance would have put me on my guard against him. But I would as soon have questioned the solidity of the Bank of England, and I had no more hesitation in going to him than to my tutor's rooms across the court.

This, then, was the state of affairs upon that morning of my last day in Cambridge. Aunt Mary and little Una had already returned to St. Peter's, where they had a cottage. I had made my solemn obeisance to the Vice-Chancellor, and duly been numbered amongst the *doctissimi*. It remained to bestow my old gown and a handsome tip upon my bed-maker ; to arrange for the sale and disposal of my furniture ; and last, and most momentous of all, to settle with my tradesmen. All these were unwelcome tasks, but the last of them quite appalled me. I had about a hundred and fifty pounds in all the world, and owed nearly three hundred in Cambridge. Possessing no ability to make two sovereigns shine where one shone before, I could but go to my trades-men, and remind them that time is money and that it is more blessed to give than to receive. They might accept the dictum or deny it. In either case, the errand could not be a pleasant one, and I have never felt so shame-faced in all my life as when I entered the shop of Messrs. Warren and Fullerton, and asked to see one of the partners upon a private matter. To these people I owed nearly one hundred pounds. I had come to their shop to offer them forty pounds—and expectations.

Now, Mr. Fullerton himself responded to

my request, emerging from his private office
with his gold-rimmed glasses set high upon
his forehead and a pleasant smile upon his lips.
I had never known him to be more affable, and
yet the very fact seemed to add to my sense
of shame.

" It would be to make you some clothes for
the vacation ? " he put it to me.

I told him that it was something else
altogether.

" And not so pleasant, by a long way," I
added, " for it's about your account, Mr.
Fullerton ? "

" But your account is paid, sir. Did you
not receive our acknowledgment ? "

I stared at him as though he had flung a
bank-note at me. There he stood, a pleasant
white-haired old gentleman, telling me as
astonishing a fairy story as ever I heard in all
my life. Of course, it was a mistake ; the
very fact of it made my position more difficult.

" Paid ! " I cried in honest wonder. " Well,
who paid it, then ? "

" That I am quite unable to say. My partner is unfortunately at lunch. But I remember
the cheque, and that a receipt was duly drawn.
It is really most regrettable that you have not
received it."

" Are you positively sure of this, Mr.
Fullerton ? "

" As sure as I am of my own existence.

That is the kind of mistake we do not make in this office, Mr. Ingersoll."

He called to his head clerk, a man of the name of Humphreys, and asked him if my account had not been settled.

The worthy fellow, washing his hands in mythical waters, assured us that the cheque had been paid into the bank three days ago. I perceived in an instant that clerk and partner could not both be mistaken.

"Well," said I—for now it was necessary to cover my own retreat—"it is my solicitor's doing, I suppose, and there's an end of it. If I want any clothes in the ' vac.,' Mr. Fullerton, I will write to you for patterns. And, of course, if you still care to make for me when I am down———"

He interrupted me to say that the making of my clothes was the supreme satisfaction of his life, and that he had some patterns in fancy flannelling which would knock down an emperor.

This music of the shears found me deaf, however, and I left him to visit the rest of my creditors. Let it suffice to say that all had been paid. Jonas, the tobacconist in the Market Place; Wasgood, the bootmaker in Sidney Street; Tufnell, who makes the best racquets in all the world; Simpkins, whose cakes go straight to the hearts of blushing cousins; Wiseman, the bookseller—not a brass farthing

did I appear to owe any man among them
when I presented myself at their establishments.
To say that I was astonished is to convey no
impression at all of my feelings. I knew no
more than the dead what it all portended. I
neither rejoiced upon it, nor regretted it. That
a mystery had come into my life prevailed
curiously above any other emotion.

It would have been about three o'clock when
I returned to my rooms, and told the porter to
get me a cab. I had made up my mind to go
to London by the afternoon train, and there
to seek out Mr. Cavanagh immediately. By a
personal interview alone could I arrive at a
decision and determine whether I would accept
or reject his offer. Far from being overwhelmed
by his eccentric generosity, it alarmed me,
as I say, and even awakened some vague
suspicion.

For why should this man so befriend me,
and how had I, a mere undergraduate, become
so necessary to him that he was willing not only
to take me into his service without question,
but to pay my debts as a preliminary? These
questions I thought that I could answer in
London. You shall see how greatly I was
mistaken.

CHAPTER III

THE train was rather late, and I did not get to King's Cross until after six o'clock. People who live in the country often experience an odd sensation of bewilderment when they arrive at a London terminus; and that is a sensation I have never absolutely conquered. Upon this night in question a certain note of melancholy was joined to it. I seemed so very much alone; the future might have so much or so little in store for me. And to be candid, my would-be employer's generosity continued to perplex me even in the train. Why had he acted like this? Why did he deal so strangely with me?

These thoughts were in my head when I took a cab and drove to Claridge's Hotel. Let me admit, however, that a certain excitement accompanied them, and gave them a brighter turn. After all, I might discover that Mr. Jehan Cavanagh had excellent reasons for the course which he had taken. Far from being dissatisfied, I might yet say that I was the most fortunate of fellows, and bless the day which had brought me to the notice of such a patron. This I admitted when my cab

16

drove into the courtyard of Claridge's, and I asked if Mr. Cavanagh were at home. The intimation that he was then in his room added to my optimism. Face to face with him, I must hear the truth. Neither of us could have anything to conceal—the mere supposition was an absurdity.

Now the clerk at the hotel delivered me into the custody of a superb flunkey, and this man, owing something to his canary waistcoat and flaming plush breeches, conducted me with much dignity to the first floor, and there into a prettily furnished ante-room, where he asked me for my card and desired me to wait. The room was quite small, one of a suite ; and the door, which divided it from a larger apartment, stood ajar when I entered, and permitted me to hear a somewhat animated conversation which the appearance of the flunkey immediately interrupted. When a few words had been exchanged, a man suddenly appeared in the doorway, and peeped round a little cautiously as though to take a good look at me before I caught a glimpse of him. To say that his aspect was somewhat extraordinary is to give a poor impression both of his personal physique and the almost repulsive character of his face. I had travelled much, as I have said, and I named the fellow immediately for an Algerian. When he addressed me in somewhat peculiar French this opinion gained strength. He was

c

an Algerian in the service of Mr. Cavanagh, I
said, and perhaps a chauffeur, as his clothes
seemed to indicate. None the less, I thought
him an ugly-looking customer, and that impression was not easily effaced.

"Have you come to see Mr. Cavanagh by
appointment ? " he asked me.

I admitted that I had not.

" I will take your card to Monsieur Edward," he continued, " but I doubt if you can
see my master."

It was a little discouraging, and I waited
with a sickening feeling of disappointment. A
quarter of an hour must have passed before anyone else appeared ; and then I found myself face
to face with as mild mannered an individual as
there could have been in all London that day.
Very short, with lank black hair and the neatest
of black clothes, quiet in all his movements,
smooth in his speech, he addressed me with the
air of a man who would vanish into thin air
if anyone spoke to him in a voice above a
murmur.

" Are you Mr. Ingersoll ? " he almost
whispered.

I said that I was.

" Mr. Cavanagh did not expect you to-night,
but I think he will see you. Please to come
into his room."

He led the way through the adjoining
apartment where I had heard the sound of

voices, and thence to a comfortable sitting-room furnished as hotel sitting-rooms are, and remarkable in no other way. The apartment was empty, and the Algerian apparently had vanished. I did as the meek man told me, and took a chair.

"Perhaps you would like to see a paper, sir?" he queried.

I took a copy of the *Westminster* from his hand, and opened it at hazard. As if one could have read at such a moment.

"I will go and tell Mr. Cavanagh," he continued; "he is occupied just at present, but I will let him know that you are here, sir."

I thanked him, and he left me. Just as in the ante-chamber, so here—a loud hum of conversation from an adjoining apartment convinced me that I had intruded upon my future employer at an unpropitious moment, and would be better advised, perhaps, to postpone my interview until a later hour. This I might have done but for the appearance of Mr. Cavanagh himself, who entered the room almost before I had straightened out the paper. Be sure that I was upon my feet in an instant, regarding him with that close scrutiny we ever cast upon the faces of those who have our fortunes in their keeping.

Shall I tell you of Jehan Cavanagh, or have the newspapers said enough about him? There is no more striking figure in England or

America: a man of great height, of superb physique, and of that magnetic personality by which alone greatness is achieved. As all the world knows, he is a prominent Canadian; but few would guess that his father did not leave Ireland for America until his twentieth year. His mother, I have always understood, was a pure Parisienne; nor has he ever told me how he came to be called Jehan.

Certain it is that he has all the qualities of the Celts, their impetuosity, their tremendous capacity of liking or disliking people at a glance, their querulous moods, their broad good-nature, their artistic instincts. To these he adds, as everyone is aware, a mastery of the intricacies of finance and of the financial diplomacy of nations which has never been surpassed. There are few of the greater railways of Canada which do not owe something of their present prosperity to him. He has developed, almost to a fabulous extent, the working of the Baku petroleum wells which his father bored. He owns half-a-dozen newspapers in Canada, and three in America. His steam yacht is a fable of magnificence; his art treasures would be a gift that the greatest of nations might value. I had always believed that he was not married, and possessed no established home in Europe. But, then, I knew him but by hearsay, and set eyes upon him for the first time in my life at Claridge's Hotel on that unforgotten night of June.

Imagine a man six feet three-and-a-half inches
in height, with an oval face so dark that its com-
plexion might almost be called swarthy; give
him a figure square and well-shaped above the
ordinary; say that his eyes are a deep blue in
colour, his hair jet black and curly, his nose a
little prominent, his lips thick, his mouth large,
his hands as delicate in shape as those of a
woman; clothe this figure in a grey frock suit
with a grey tie to match; set a very small
diamond pin in the neck-tie and a plain gold
band upon the middle finger of his left hand;
brush the curly black hair high upon the forehead,
and let it come down upon the collar at the neck;
describe the face as quite clean-shaven; the
manner quick and all observing and restless; the
voice deep in tone and not unmusical: do this,
and you have Jehan Cavanagh before you as I
saw him at Claridge's Hotel and first heard
my fate from his lips. But the wonderful magnetism of his presence you will not understand
until you have known him as I came to know him
in the terrible months I lived through in his
service.

"Mr. Ingersoll, is it not?" he said, on
entering the room.

I replied that it was so, and that I had come
down from Cambridge, to see him in answer to
his letter. To be frank, I don't think he heard
a word of what I said. A newsboy's cry from
the street outside attracted his attention, and

turned his face towards the window. Then he
rang a little bell upon the table, and summoned
the meek servant who had been described as
Monsieur Edward.

" Why am I waiting?" he asked, in a tone
which conveyed impatience and almost anger.
" Do you not hear that?"

" I am sorry, sir; the paper is just coming
up."

Monsieur Edward withdrew, and left us alone.
I could still hear the newsboy crying the extra
special edition of a halfpenny evening paper, and
I thought it in no way curious that Mr. Cavanagh
should himself be anxious to see it. That which
did trouble me was the way in which he ignored
me while he waited for the paper. Not a word
did he address to me ; not a glance did he cast
in my direction; but, standing by the window
listening to the newsboy, he of a sudden pressed
both his hands to his eyes and remained in that
curious attitude until the man returned with the
paper in his hand.

" It was nobody's fault, sir. The boy forgot
to send it up."

" Give him nothing when we go away. And
Edward, Mr. Ingersoll is going into Cambridge
with me. We shall dine when we arrive. Send
a telegram and say so."

He unfolded the paper while he spoke, and
now fixed his eyes upon the leading column of
the news page. Whatever it was that he read, it

appeared to move him greatly. I could see his
eyes straining, as it were, to catch the meaning
of every word. His habit of tossing his massive
head in the manner of a great good-natured dog
may have added to the impression of his distress.
I could only conclude that the paper recorded
some fact of great moment to him, and confirmed
his worst anticipations. When he cast it aside,
a nervous hand had already crumpled it almost
out of shape. It lay torn and twisted at his feet
—and then, and not until then, he remembered
me.

"A man who reads newspapers and believes
in them is a fool," he exclaimed at length.
"Come, Mr. Ingersoll, we shall dine late enough
as it is. Let us go at once."

What could I tell him? That I had left my
luggage at King's Cross ; that nothing had been
arranged between us ; that I did not know whether
I could accept his offer, or must reject it ? In
truth, I said nothing of the kind, but, stopping,
when he had left the room, to pick up the paper
thus thrown down at hazard, I followed him to
the courtyard, and there entered the motor-car
with him.

CHAPTER IV

THE car was a large one, and a glance at it told me that it had come out of Holland and was a Spyker. There were two men upon the front seat, and one I recognised for the Algerian who had first met me in Mr. Cavanagh's rooms. Edward, the valet—for such I now knew him to be— opened the door for us and kept back the porters. I was the first in, for upon that Mr. Cavanagh insisted; and he was just about to follow me when he also remembered my luggage.

" You left it at King's Cross, of course," he exclaimed ; and then to Edward, " Let the second car bring Mr. Ingersoll's trunks, and don't forget his tennis racquets."

I opened my eyes at this, you may be sure, for how did he know that I played tennis ? He did not give me time, however, to put a question, but, taking his seat beside me, he went on to say—

" There is a covered court at my house, and we will have some games together. A 'Varsity blue should be much too good for me, but I may keep you in condition. I did not expect you until

24

the fifteenth—we could have picked you up in Cambridge, for we are going through the town."

I thought it wise not to be too curious, and to encourage him to talk—if I may use such a word. That he knew of my game at tennis convinced me that I did not come to him unknown, and that his enquiries concerning my 'Varsity career had been of a searching nature. What did astonish me was the complete change of manner which attended our departure from the hotel. Of his former emotion there was now no sign whatever. He talked with all that suave charm which those who know him so readily admit; and I began to feel as one who was sitting at the feet of a master and must not make light of my privileges.

" I have always regretted that I was not a University man," he said; " the mere making or losing of money is a paltry accomplishment, though made much of in these days. It is the whole manhood which the intelligent use of a University develops. Would you have written your paper upon ' The State and " Everyman " ' if you had not been to Cambridge? Impossible that you should have done it. Learning can no more flourish without its atmosphere than a palm without the sun. Every man in your society who thinks a great thought is the product of a thousand thinkers who have lived before him; every book that is written is the book not of the

individual, but of the living dead who breathe
upon its pages—I am of another world, and it has
moulded me in another shape. But I never pass
the gates of your splendid Academy without
longing for the philosopher's groves, and feeling
that I would sacrifice much to be able to say
quorum pars fui. Be proud of Cambridge, Mr.
Ingersoll; never forget what you owe to her."

I answered that he would not find me wanting
there; but I could not forbear to add that the
philosopher's groves were a little sleepy sometimes, and that some echo of the world without
would not be lost upon them in our day. This
reflection did not please him. He had built a
secret wall about our Senate, and would have no
man leap over it.

"There is too much of this thing called
modernity in the world," he exclaimed; "have
nothing to do with it, Mr. Ingersoll. Do not
listen to those who tell you that it is necessarily
a good thing. All that I have, any wholesale
grocer with a faculty for sanding his sugar can get
if he will give his mind to it. All that you have,
money cannot purchase. Time has dowered you
with this precious heritage. Credit time with
some discerning, and leave modernity outside your
gates. You have spent four years of such happiness as you may never find again. Be thankful
for them, Mr. Ingersoll, for by them alone you
have justified this phantasy we call life."

Much more he said to the same end, his

conversation illuminated by good learning and continued praise of my beloved Cambridge. This talk carried us almost out of London, and we had come to Finchley when a boy upon the pavement, taking advantage of a block in the traffic, ran across to the car, and offered us that very edition of an evening paper which Mr. Cavanagh had read with so much distress at Claridge's Hotel. From this moment I had a silent companion in the car. He waved the lad away with a gesture of positive anger, and sank back upon the cushions almost as though an attack of faintness had seized him. I think we must have travelled nearly thirty miles before he spoke to me again.

I had ridden to Cambridge several times on a motor-bicycle, and every inch of the road was familiar to me. Most people know it nowadays when motoring is so popular; but there were many cars, both met and overtaken, on that warm summer night. Say what we may, there is nothing so delightful as a motor-ride after dark, when the stars look kindly upon you, or the moon is up in a clear sky. This night the moon was in the last quarter, and of little service to us, but the sky had no cloud, and the air came cool and fresh as a sea breeze. I remember that we left the hotel just before seven o'clock, and that it was half-past seven when we passed through Barnet. From this place, as everyone knows, the open country is no longer blotted by villadom. Woods begin to bower the grand old road. You soon arrive at Hatfield Park, and catch a glimpse of the great house through the famous bronze gates. And so away to Welwyn, over Digswell Hill, and by such pleasant woodland scenery as you will find nowhere else but in this garden England of ours.

I say that Mr. Cavanagh lay back upon the cushions and shut his eyes as though he were sleeping. This was an example I had no desire to imitate. To me the experience was both exhilarating and delightful. I had eyes for every turn of that famous road. I could people the woods, and recall the figures of a hundred years ago; remember the very names of the coaches that had come galloping into London upon this famous highway; rebuild the inns; and espy the lurking figures of the highwaymen. The music of the splendid engine became for me but a murmur of phantom voices upon the summer breezes. An ever-changing panorama unfolded itself before me : towns and villages, woods and meadows, hills and valleys. As the darkness came down, and lights shone out from the windows of the cottages, I could imagine myself to be some king's messenger of the old days riding wildly to the North, and leaving the tocsin ringing in every hamlet I passed through. The grey shadows of twilight helped the illusion. Surely I was being carried into a new world, among strangers who had my fortune in their keeping. Even the lights

of Cambridge recalled me to my sober senses with
difficulty. I had surrendered wholly to the spell of
the night, and was like a man waked out of sleep
when Mr. Cavanagh suddenly spoke to me.

" Do you know the road to Huntingdon ? "
he asked me.

" A famous road," said I, " and very few
people upon it."

" It is for that reason I am taking it, Mr.
Ingersoll. We should be very thankful in these
days for roads with few people upon them. My
house is built on the border of the Fen—that is
to say, the house in which I am at present living.
Years ago, it belonged to the Chapter of Ely. I
believe that they own it still, though there are
many sub-tenants intervening. It's a queer old
place, and might well enough be haunted. If you
suffer from rheumatism, look out—but whoever
suffered from rheumatism at twenty-one ! I am
thirty-nine, and I speak soberly. Make much
of your health, and do not treat it lightly."

I made some trifling answer to this, and
pressed him to tell me more about the house to
which we were going.

" Of course, you are not often here ? " I said.
" You travel so much."

He did not resent my curiosity.

" The man who has not travelled has not
lived," he said. " If I desire long life, it is that
I may travel. The rest that follows upon travel
is the cigar that attends a good dinner. I have

taken this house that I may rest. I have asked
you to come with me that you may help me
to rest. Here I may hide from all the world.
Beyond my servants, whom I trust, there is not
a man, woman, or child in all the world who knows
that I have taken the House of the Fen. You will
keep my secret, for that is the first duty you have
to learn. Whatever is done here, whatever ex-
cites your astonishment, remember it is done
that I may be able to rest. You have only to
understand this, and many questions are already
answered. We are two who have fled the world
—for an hour at any rate. Our citadel is impreg-
nable. We can laugh alike at our enemies and
our friends. When we return, we shall have a
story ready. That is the evil day. Do not let us
think of it."

He leaned back upon the cushions again, and,
in spite of a certain forced gaiety of manner, I heard
him sigh deeply, and caught upon his face the look
of a man harassed by care to the last degree. To
say that the circumstance surprised me is hardly
to write the truth. I realised the immense re-
sponsibilities under which he laboured, the burden
of his riches, the loneliness of his life. Such men
as he, I had been told, rarely knew what happiness was. If I had any feelings at all, they were
those of pity; and I might have carried the
thought far but for the fact that the car suddenly
turned from the high road into a by-lane, and
there came to a halt, while my self-named

Algerian got down from the front seat and deliberately extinguished the acetylene lamps. Now, this was a curious thing at the best, and set me thinking deeply. Mr. Cavanagh's explanation, that the newspapers would track him to the North Pole if he went there, seemed to me quite unsuited to the circumstances. No one could follow a forty horse-power Spyker unless he had another forty horse-power car in which to do the business. We had turned out of a high road upon which no man, woman, or child had been seen since we left the outskirts of Cambridge. Here in this dark lane, where the hedges towered formidably above us and hardly a glow of the twilight could penetrate, the need of powerful headlights was tenfold. And yet the fellow out of Africa—for such I would call him—deliberately turned them out; and, more than that, went back to the high road and took a swift glance up and down it before resuming his place upon the front seat. These are the facts which set me thinking. I leave you to judge with what reason.

We were in a narrow lane, then, without headlights; our engine throttled down to complete silence, and not as much as a single blast of our powerful horn to warn any wayfarer we might meet. The next view I had was of a wilderness which looked like the common of a deserted village—an oval of green with cottages about it; but these cottages were all tumbling

down and empty, and a church close by seemed
in no better state of repair. By this we went
for a hundred yards or more, and then, turning
sharply, the car came to a halt, and I perceived
that we were at the gates of a lodge, and that a
man was opening to us. It was too dark to see
the fellow, or to take any notice of him, and, for
that matter, we were not detained thirty seconds
in all, I suppose. From this point a good drive
carried us a little way in the open, and then
through a close-set wood to one of the flattest
parks that can exist in all England to-day. I
know the district round about Cambridge very
well, but I had never imagined the existence of
such a cultivated estate upon the very flat of the
Fens; and when, after a little while, the house
came suddenly to my view, I thought it quite
remarkable that it had escaped the note-book of
the antiquary, and enjoyed a splendid obscurity
even in this twentieth century.

I say that the house came suddenly to my
view, and this is no ordinary manner of speaking.
So dark was the night that I should never have
seen it at all, but for an electric searchlight set
upon a tower some way from the mansion. This,
without any preliminary warning at all, burst
for an instant into a great dazzling arc of light,
revolving like the lantern of a warship, and showing me almost the very blades of grass by which
we passed.

As the house itself came within its aureole, I

might have imagined myself at the gate of a
mediæval château set upon the great plain of
Touraine or by the valley of the Garonne. A forest
of rounded towers declared their battlements
and lattices to the sky, and stood up menacingly
above a lake or river, I knew not which. Had I
made a guess, I would have named it for an old
Norman building, or perhaps have given it even
an earlier birth. There was no visible evidence
of modernity whatever; but, remember, I saw
it by the flash of a searchlight, and the whole
vision was that of an instant. Mr. Cavanagh
himself naturally heard my startled exclamation
when the light flashed out, and seemed pleased
that I should be astonished.

"That is my observatory," he exclaimed;
and added quickly, "It is also one of my fads.
We like to see who is about the place at night,
though my keepers do not altogether approve of
my methods. I shall tell you nothing about the
house, for you will criticise it for yourself in five
minutes' time. It is a very old house; in fact,
I may say that it was little more than a shell
two years ago. But builders have been clever,
and you will enter upon the possession at least
of as curious a habitation as there is in your
country to-day. To-morrow I will make my
apologies for taking out the lease in your
name——"

I looked at him as though he had slapped me
on the face.

D

" In my name, sir? "

" Certainly; in your name, Mr. Ingersoll.
Enter, and take possession—and quarrel with
me afterwards. There is Bain at the door.
We will not dress to-night. It must be after
ten——"

The car stopped as he spoke, and a bland,
and very English butler came out to meet us. I
had not a single word to say while I followed my
patron to the hall, nor afterwards when a footman
conducted me to my bedroom. The world had
changed, surely, since I left Cambridge this
morning. I was Bruce Ingersoll still, but who
could tell me what the amazing events portended?

CHAPTER V

Now, the House of the Fen was a house within
a house. The towers and battlements I had
seen from the park, the old brick walls, the
bartizan, the belfry: these were the shell which
contained within them as luxurious an habitation
as there is in England to-day. Naturally, I did
not discover all the detail of it upon the night of
my arrival. We learn little about a strange
country house until the daylight has helped us
to explore it. But the substantial fact, as I have
stated it, was evident the moment you entered
Mr. Cavanagh's mansion.

A house within a house: a fine suite of
rooms, built almost in the Italian fashion, about
an old garden, whence came the perfume of the
roses and the odours of sweet-scented shrubs.
This I perceived from the hall itself, and when I
mounted a broad oak staircase to my bedroom,
the plan of it appeared even more simple. They
had allotted me an apartment in one of the old
towers, it is true, but this room was to be reached
by a staircase decorated and panelled in the
modern fashion, and had windows on both sides
—mere loopholes towards the park, but wide

French windows towards the rose-garden, and
balconies before them.

When I had washed myself and gone down,
I found that we were to dine in the very gem
of a *salle à manger*, furnished so discreetly that
none but a great artist could have achieved it.
This was in the fashion of the private
rooms you find in the greatest of the French
hotels ; but it was decorated with priceless
furniture, and would have satisfied even a connoisseur.

I shall say nothing of this dinner. To be
candid, I was so tired and worn out both by
excitement and fatigue that I remember little
about it. Mr. Cavanagh, on his part, seemed no
less preoccupied, and our talk of commonplace
things would have been ridiculous had it not
been so natural. One moment of it, however,
stuck in my mind, and that was when he spoke
of the recent trial of the Belgian anarchist,
Norent, and laughed at the inadequate sentence
which a judge had pronounced upon the ruffian.

"There is no courage in Europe to-day,"
he said ; "if there were, one brave man would
exterminate these people as a terrier kills rats.
But our Ministers are afraid of them, and the
police shrink from overt action because of the
Ministers. Here in England you name
cowardice liberty, and plume yourselves upon it.
When the awakening comes—and it will be a
great awakening—those who perish will be the

victims, not of oppression, but of craven Governments. Remember it, Mr. Ingersoll, whenever
you read that this or that mad assassin is known
to the police. Say that the police are afraid of
him, because the Ministers are afraid. It is the
truth; but it is a truth for which a heavy price
will yet be paid by humanity."

He did not encourage me to make other
than a commonplace answer to this; and we
changed the subject almost immediately to
speak of modern athletes and of British
supremacy which other nations were challeng-
ing. I, naturally, was all for our own players,
while he, I discovered, believed that the
physique of the American would ultimately give
them the championships.

"Their climate," he said, "will beat you.
When they come here, you do not see them at
their best. I grant that you still keep your end
up at tennis and rowing and cricket. But I
don't like to think too much about the future.
I am sure it is their sunshine we have most
to fear. You know that I have always been a
bit of an athlete myself—I would sooner make a
hundred at the wicket than twenty thousand on
the Stock Exchange any day. Perhaps you will
be able to give me a thrashing at tennis; you
have nineteen years in your favour, but I shall
make you go all the way, and you will keep me
young. Here, at the Fen, I try to forget
every other interest but that of my own health.

I would play the boy's part, and play it
thoroughly. I strive to be alone and to live my
life free from the commercial tentacles which
hold me back. It is something to cast them
off for a few days. It would be much to cast
them off for ever."

I had it upon my tongue to say that he could
do so without much sacrifice if he had the mind;
but the same thing is said to rich men by fools
every day, and we know that a millionaire can no
more cast the skin of his wealth than a dog
change his paws. So I made some other answer
to Mr. Cavanagh, and, when we had talked a good
deal about American tennis and why they could
not beat our best men, the butler served us with
coffee and cigarettes. Almost immediately upon
this, my host bade me good-night.

"We have much to talk of to-morrow,"
said he. "If you feel like getting up early, I
will trot across the park with you at half-past
seven. We breakfast here when we feel like it.
Williams, the gardener, tells me that the courts
are very good; so come down in your flannels
when you do come. I rarely go outside the
gates when I am down here; there is more
to do in my own grounds than one man can get
through comfortably, and I do not profess the
smallest interest in villagers. Half-past seven,
then, for a trot; and when you like for tennis.
I am glad that you came to me to-day; it
has made things much easier, and there will

not be wasted days. Good-night, Ingersoll.
Ask for what you want, and see that you
get it."

He waved me good-night at the door of the
room again, and crossed the Italian garden to
his own rooms, as I supposed, upon the other
side. It would then have been nearly half-past
eleven o'clock, and without any more ado at all
I climbed up to my bed-room, and there enjoyed
the luxury of a pipe, denied to me since I got
out of the train at King's Cross that afternoon.
Until this time I had hardly examined my
bed-room at all, but now I found it to be a snug
place, and Edward, the valet, who came upstairs
presently, told me that my sitting-room was just
below, and that I could go from one to the other
by a narrow staircase let in to the buttress of the
tower. As to baths, he assured me that I should
find a swimming bath in the south wing, and
a Turkish bath, as well as others.

"It's a very old house, sir," he said; "but
Mr. Cavanagh has spent a great deal of money
upon it. I don't think you could find anything
nicer in the country—not more convenient, that
is, both for the servants and the gentry. Perhaps you would like a whisky-and-soda, sir,
before you go to bed?"

I smiled at the man's odd conjunction of
ideas, and told him that I would not take a
whisky-and-soda. Perhaps I might have been
more frank with him, and hinted plainly that my

vanity as a tennis player forbade me to do so.
A man, who would play any game well nowadays,
has enough to do to keep himself fit without
spirits ; but this is a purely personal matter, and
need not be discussed. When Edward had gone,
I smoked my pipe by the open window, and
began to think that I could guess the reason
why Mr. Cavanagh had brought me to the house.
I thought that his love of Cambridge and 'Varsity life chose me to be his secretary and companion in the country. He had made certain
inquiries about me, and discovered that I was a
pretty good all-round man, in addition to my
" First " in Moral Science and the open scholarship in mathematics I took at school. No other
explanation fitted in so well with the circumstances, and I had got quite into a comfortable
mood about it when I thought of the scene at
the hotel and the evening paper which had so
upset him. This paper, you will remember, I
brought in my pocket with me from London, and
now I searched for it eagerly, for I was keen
to discover what kind of news it was that could
affect a man like Mr. Cavanagh even in the
presence of a stranger.

Well, the paper was very much crumpled up
when I found it, and I must say that the laugh
was all against me when at length I smoothed
it out and began to read it. You know the kind
of thing there is in evening papers—so-called
racy gossip about horses ; some scandal, perhaps,

with a parson in it ; the story of a Countess and
her jewels ; and a lot of light-headed paragraphs.
These I read through that night, and then
wondered what on earth they had to do with
Mr. Cavanagh. As for the news, it could not
possibly concern him. There had been a pit
disaster in France, and a ship had gone down
somewhere off Vancouver. The rumoured
resignation of the Government filled a column
and a half. I read a long paragraph headed
" The Biter Bitten," and found it to contain an
account of a German anarchist who had blown
himself up in a laboratory in Paris and three of
his accomplices with him. The police imagined
that the men had contemplated an attack upon
the Prince of Brandenburg, then staying in
France, and had been killed by the very bombs
they intended for innocent men and women, and,
it might be, children. This was the whole story,
and certainly it had nothing to do with Mr.
Cavanagh. Why, then, had he been so
agitated ?

I pitched the paper from me — took it up
again and tore it into fragments. It may be
that I felt some sense of shame, and accused
myself of spying upon one who, so far, had
shown me nothing but kindness. After all,
what were the private affairs of such a man as
Mr. Cavanagh to me ? He had lived an honourable life, had made his money fairly, and had
done charitable deeds which every tongue

extolled.   Who was I to seek out a deeper
truth of his life or even to desire such knowledge ?
Indeed, I was ashamed ; and undressing quickly,
I switched off the electric light and must have
fallen asleep almost as soon as my head touched
the pillow.

CHAPTER VI

It was a heavy sleep that I slept, but far from dreamless. All sorts of vague ideas came floating to my pillow to mingle in a mad panorama of the past, the present, and even of the future. Now I would be with little Una in the palmist's tent ; thence flying headlong to London, to seek out an unknown enemy who had threatened me. Or again, I found myself at Claridge's Hotel, lifting Mr. Cavanagh in my arms, and, oddly enough, bearing him away secretly to a place of safety in the country. The searchlight in the park followed me everywhere—it flashed upon me in London, sought me out in dark lanes, was turned upon my bed to spy out my very bones. When darkness fell, I thought that I was abroad in the park looking up to the great gaunt house, and that someone called to me from its barred windows. This was a dreadful moment, for the cry had a note in it, which was not wholly human ; and while, upon my part, I strove madly to help the person, I could not move a step from the place where I stood nor utter a single cry for aid.

This latter dream awoke me—I do not know

at what hour. It was still black dark, and the
night at its zenith. I could not hear so much
as a whisper of wind beneath the eaves; a profound stillness reigned and yet, in spite of it, the
impression of the dream remained. Such an
hallucination of broken sleep almost led me to
believe that the person who had cried out stood
near my bed and waited for me to speak. This
will have been a common experience of many
who read these lines. Nothing is more real
than such dreams; none is more dreaded by
those who are bad sleepers.

Well, I sat up in bed, and fumbling for the
switch, I got a light at last and looked at my
watch. It was exactly half-past one o'clock, and
I remembered that the dawn would break in an
hour and a half at the latest. For the rest,
although my room looked a little ghostly as
rooms will at such hours, there was, needless to
say, nothing to affright me or to account for the
ridiculous ideas to which I have confessed. My
clothes, heaped anyhow upon an arm-chair,
remained undisturbed; my watch ticked at my
bedside; my money lay scattered upon the
dressing table; the fragments of the torn newspaper lay in the fender just as I had thrown
them down. Not a trace, you will perceive, of
any intruder, not a tittle of evidence that I had
not dreamed. So much I myself admitted
almost as soon as I switched on the light; and,
laughing at myself as I had often done before

when a nightmare plagued me, I dropped my head upon the pillow again and once more invited sleep. This time she refused me all her charities. I could not sleep a wink—I could hardly rest in bed.

Now, here was a circumstance which need not have troubled me at all. Good digestion in my case clearly had not waited upon good appetite. I had eaten a big dinner, and had eaten it after ten o'clock. The imps of wakefulness who held carnival in my head were imps begotten of *soles à la Victoria* and *soufflé en surprise*. This I told myself when I had suffered a good half-hour of it and still could not sleep a wink. A civil war raged where all should have been peace; and for that, one book, taken as required, could be the only remedy.

There were books in the room—so much I noted directly I entered it. A copy of " Famous Trials " had not escaped my vigilant observation, nor a well-thumbed edition of Thiers' " French Revolution." The latter can hardly be recommended as a bed-book, and yet, for some reason I do not pretend to divine, I took it up and read some pages of it upon this night in question. When I put it down I knew that I had heard my phantom cry a second time, and that it was no phantom at all, but a very real appeal, weird and human and awful, and plainly proceeding from the opposite side of the quadrangle to that in which my bedroom lay. Judge of my astonishment at this. Imagine how I lay and listened ; boy that I was amongst strangers, my suspicions awakened already, all my faculties quickened by the amazing events which had happened during the last four-and-twenty hours.

A human cry at the dead of night, an awful voice of woe and grief, this is what I had heard as plainly as a man can hear anything at all in this world and as unmistakably. You may be tempted to say that the dream still troubled me, that I was not quite awake, and far from being master of my senses. But I can answer that I had just been reading my Thiers and never understood him better. For the first time in my life I had formed the opinion that old Danton was the heroic figure of the Revolution, and I recollect that I had put the book down upon the bed to think of it when this fearful outcry startled me, and I lay listening to it in that nervous state of dread which the night alone can inspire. When silence came and I had the courage to get out of bed, I trembled like a leaf—the very first time such a thing had happened to me.

What could it be ? What did it mean ? Whose voice was it that I had heard ? I got out of bed to listen, I say, and the house answered nothing. Of course, I had slept with my windows wide open—who does not in the month of June ?—and so it came about that I heard the cry distinctly, despite the fact that my room lay, as I imagined, upon the opposite side of the quadrangle to that whence the voice came. Not a light, however, was to be seen anywhere when I stepped out upon the balcony and peered across the garden at the dark walls beyond. I did not detect as much as the rustling of a leaf or the creaking of a door—not a sound anywhere in fact, but blinding darkness and a black sky overhead, thick with cloud and moonless. A second attempt at the narrow windows overlooking the park rewarded me no better. I might as reasonably have looked into a well at midnight, and expected to see my face in the water. The so-called observatory, where the great lantern stood, gave no light at this hour. I could not distinguish even the shape of the trees.

I shall pass by the next hour, for that is of little moment to my story. How I spent it I hardly know myself. There would have been moments when I was in bed; other moments when I was at the windows; now upon this side, now upon that, vainly hoping that the darkness would lift or someone come to me. When dawn broke, no little child could have welcomed it with a finer rapture. I positively worshipped the sun as he rose that morning. Never had the country seemed so beautiful as when the cold grey light came stealing over the fens, and the earth was born again in all the glory of the fields and the river and the woods. Now, for a truth, I saw plainly that which the night had hidden from me. The House of the Fen was built in the very centre of a considerable lake fed by a little river. There

were bridges upon both sides from the island to
the mainland; but they resembled the draw-
bridges of the old time, and evidently were kept
raised after sunset. This I noticed at a glance;
but some minutes passed before I detected a figure
in the park, and many more before I recognised
the man. At last I named him for my self-styled
Algerian, and I saw that he was riding a black
horse toward the drawbridge.

I shall not tell you with what interest I
watched this man's approach, or how greatly the
circumstance probed my curiosity. So much you
will readily understand. That the fellow should
be abroad at all at such an hour seemed not a little
remarkable; but when, upon his coming to the
bridge, they allowed him to pass over and he went
through, as I imagined, to the inner garden, then,
I say, it was impossible not to link his business
to the cry which I had heard, and to believe that
he had come back to the house in answer to it.
This surmise I justified when I ran over to the
inner window and perceived that Mr. Cavanagh
himself waited for the man in the Italian garden,
and began to talk to him in gestures full of ani-
mation and of anger. Twice I saw him point to
a certain room in the western wing, and immediately afterwards turn and face his servant, holding
him by the lappel of his coat as though he must
hear every word. Then followed something even
more curious. For what should Mr. Cavanagh do
but take from the pocket of an enormous dressing

gown another copy of that very evening paper I
had seen him read at Claridge's Hotel. Beating
it with his hands, crushing it in nervous fingers,
he straightened it out at last, and invited the
Algerian to read a passage he indicated. Never
shall I forget the look of exultation that came
upon the fellow's face when he did so. To me
he stood as the very incarnation of evil awakened.
I had not the shadow of a title so to accuse him,
but the accusation remains. I thought him a
monster then, and I think him a monster now.

Let the impression pass, however. There I
stood at the window watching these two by the
cold grey light of dawn, and there I saw the sun
rise and put her golden spell upon the garden. If
I played an eavesdropper's part, my just curiosity
must be its own excuse. I knew nothing of that
which the men discussed; nothing of the reasons
which brought them together when all the world
was sleeping. Could I have overheard their words
they would not have enlightened me. Such odd
phrases as I caught came in a speech like to none
I had heard before. Their gestures wrote the
story of a mystery I could not even begin to
fathom. When they separated, the Algerian
going over to the stables, Mr. Cavanagh remaining
where he stood, I drew back from the window and
resolved to watch him no more. Another thought
had come to me, one more engrossing. Had I not
the shreds of the paper which the pock-marked
rogue out of Algeria had just been reading?

E.

Laboriously, and with blackened fingers, I gathered the pieces from the hearth and tried to put them together. It had been the news page to which Mr. Cavanagh turned with such interest, and the second column of the news page which he had invited his servant to read. How did that help me, you ask. I answer, not at all.

A trifling railway accident at Northampton, a borough council wrangle in some London suburb —these and the accident at Paris, where an explosion in a laboratory had killed four men supposed to be Anarchists—what had these to do with Jehan Cavanagh and his business ? The mystery remained incomprehensible.

And I gave it up at last, and tired and cold and greatly troubled, I crept into my bed and slept as I had not done since I was a child.

CHAPTER VII

THE WOMAN AND THE CHILD

THE tongue is generally in the cheek when we apologise for sleeping over late, and I confess that I am no champion of early hours. It's all very well to be up with the lark ; but a man who keeps such hours should be to bed with the fowls, and that's no gay proceeding, anyway.

None the less I was very much annoyed when I awoke at the House of the Fen, and discovered that it was nearly ten o'clock. What would Mr. Cavanagh think of me ? What should I say for myself ? Here was a nice recommendation for an untried secretary, that he should promise to be ready for a trot through the park at seven-thirty, and actually awake when ten had struck. Happily for me, Edward, the meek valet, quickly reassured me.

"Mr. Cavanagh did not think you would get up, sir," he said; "he was only joking about being in the park. He always says the proper time for getting up is when you can't sleep any longer. I don't think you will see him to-day. He was not very well after you went to bed last night."

51

I said that I was sorry to hear it, but the news brought back as in a flash a vivid memory of the scene I had witnessed in the garden, and all the wild events of an amazing night. If they appeared to me less terrible at dawn when I was dressed, let the glorious June day answer for that. I was young, remember, and when one is young impressions pass swiftly, to be forgotten on the instant and recalled in later years. I could give twenty explanations for Mr. Cavanagh's conduct now that the sun was up and all the house awake. Nothing seemed abnormal to me then ; certainly nothing had passed to make me afraid. And the day would make plain what the night had hidden, I said.

So I dressed myself; and, having been directed thereto by Edward, I took breakfast in my own little sitting-room which also overlooked the park, but not the Italian garden. I found it to be a perfect den, small and luxurious, and not unlike my own room at Cambridge. Monstrous arm-chairs upholstered in crimson stood on either side of the fire-place ; college pictures hung upon the walls ; old photographs of tennis teams with a certain Bruce Ingersoll among the players were all about ; a bookcase with cupboards in the Cambridge fashion jostled a cottage piano and a sofa upon which the War Office would have wept tears of joyful sleep. The kindly forethought of all this both astonished and delighted me. How could I fear to work for a man who had such con-

sideration for my personal comfort? Indeed, I
was all eager to thank him immediately, and I
heard of his indisposition with real regret.

"Has Mr. Cavanagh left no instructions;
nothing for me to do, Edward," I asked the
valet.

It was a positive pleasure to receive an
affirmative answer.

"There is something in the library, sir, which
Mr. Cavanagh would be glad if you would see to.
It's a list of streets and houses in some foreign
places. He wants you to search them out in the
guide-books, and write him a report about them.
After that, he thinks you would like to ride round
the grounds, and you are to order a horse at any
time you like."

To this I answered that I would ride when I
had done the work which Mr. Cavanagh desired
me to do; and going down almost immediately
into the library—a spacious room built the whole
length of the eastern wall, and promising some
day to topple over into the lake beneath—I there
found the lists of which Edward had spoken, and
a pile of guide-books to aid my task. It did not
become me to question my patron's motives; nor,
to be honest, did I reflect upon them at all. He
had business with many men in many cities. It
would be very natural that considerations of
locality should arise.

This was all very well, but as the work went
on I discovered some curious facts. And first, so

far as I could judge by the guide books, all the
streets about which Mr. Cavanagh had desired me
to make inquiries from the guide books were
mean streets, the very slums of America and continental cities, of Chicago and Paris and Naples
and Rome, the worst streets, as the books said,
and rarely safe for foreigners to enter. More than
that, in the few cases where I could lay hands
upon an official directory, I found that the people,
nominally living in the houses, were not those
upon Mr. Cavanagh's lists; for the latter were
full of Russian, Spanish, and Italian names, and
there were curious dots and signs and marks after
each of them; while in one case someone had
written in pencil, against the name of a certain
Paolo Canza, an intimation that he had been tried
at Rome in the year 1903, and sentenced to ten
years in the mines. This sentence apparently the
man had not served, for the bald word " escaped,"
and the date of the escape, " November 30th,
1904," were noted in the margin. A little later on,
I read an Irish name in the list; that of a certain
Michael Keating, then living in Illinois Avenue,
at Chicago. Here, again, a marginal note stated
the simple fact that the man had been sentenced
at Chicago to imprisonment for fifteen years,
and was then undergoing his punishment.

These were odd things to read, you will
admit; and when, later in my work, I came upon
a woman's name, I confess that my curiosity did
get the better of me. The entry to which I refer

concerned a certain Mademoiselle Mamavieff;
and she, if the note were trustworthy, had recently visited many cities. A minute inspection
of the writing led me to the conclusion that the
lady had fled from Baku just seven months ago;
had been traced to Vienna and a house in the
Market Place there; had gone back to Buda;
thence down into Bosnia, when she had passed
to Venice, and lived for a few weeks at a poor
house by the Merceria. Again upon the road,
this restless Mademoiselle Mamavieff is next
heard of at Rome, in a shabby street near Santa
Maria, in Cosmedin. I find her again at Monte
Carlo, where she put up for just five days at the
Hôtel Belle Isle. She goes thence to Paris, and
there is lost, but not without lasting efforts to
trace her whereabouts; for I read many endeavours in this place and that, and always without
result. Thus the conclusion comes to me that
my patron is greatly interested in the travels of
Mademoiselle Pauline Mamavieff, and as anxious
as a man could be to discover the city which
harboured her.

Now, some people, I suppose, would have
grinned about all this, and found it mightily
amusing. I don't know why it should be so, but
the fact is there, that we laugh at a lover whose
secret is discovered, and think that we ourselves
are altogether above such weakness. We have
too much common sense, or believe that we have,
to descend to any such folly, and we make fine

faces over the poor devil who has been caught in
the trap, and are ready enough to mock him. I
will grant you that I did begin to think it possible
that Mr. Cavanagh was very much in love with
Pauline Mamavieff; but I had too much respect
for him to pry into the affair, and I hope that I
did what I could to follow the instructions with
which he had honoured me. Carefully and
minutely I made my researches in the books, and
recorded them upon the paper. This street, I
would write, had houses of some respectability—
that was a mere slum. My own travels helped
me everywhere to a degree beyond belief. I could
often describe the localities concerned from my
own memory of them. I flattered myself that 1
knew the slums of Paris even better than the
touts and rascals who frequent the Folies
Bergères and the Moulin Rouge. And where
this was the case, be sure I took advantage of it.
Indeed, I thought the work well done, and was
in no way ashamed of it.

It would have been nearly two o'clock when
I put down my pen, for that was the hour at
which Edward carried a light lunch to my
room; and immediately afterwards, accepting
Mr. Cavanagh's kind offer of a ride, I mounted a
very likely-looking chestnut cob and set off for a
canter round the park. A brief inspection, as I
passed through it, showed me that the hall of the
house was in reality the armoury, and that it
contained many suits of rare armour, and not

a few ancient weapons of a kind I had seen nowhere but in the Tower of London. This hall
opened upon a terrace facing the lake ; and you
crossed thence by an ancient drawbridge, bolstered
up by modern girders and a modern turnstile ; so
that, while at first you would have said that the
bridge lifted up and down, you came, in the
end, to see that it really swung about on a pivot
as some of the river bridges both in England and
America.

The lake itself had a breadth of sixty yards,
perhaps, on this side of the house. I judged
the water to be both deep and running, for it
was very clear, and the bottom appeared to be
of gravel. The terrace engirdled all the house,
as it appeared ; but the wall of it rose at least
twenty feet above the water, and was sheer
and formidable. The further bank had a cor-
responding terrace, with gravelled paths and
some pretty beds of common flowers ; the
scarlet geranium giving welcome colour, and
calceolaria helping the contrast. There were
no trees for some distance beyond this garden ;
and I perceived that the woods, through which
we had passed last night, lay quite a mile from
the house ; while the observatory stood out, as
it were, on a great grassy prairie and had a
gallery at the summit of its detached tower in
the manner of a lighthouse.

I have told you something about the house
itself, and this is no place to add a long account

of it. Very old in its outward aspect, just a
jumble of crooked walls and crazy turrets and
broken battlements, you would have named it
for an early Tudor mansion, long neglected and
wholly meretricious from an architectural stand-
point. Few of its windows were worthy of the
name, save the great stained glass window of
the hall and the lancets in the library. A
chapel, built out on piles in the very centre of
the lake, gave a note of pure perpendicular, and
appeared lately to have been restored ; but the
whole edifice conveyed an impression of decay-
ing antiquity ; nor would the shrewdest observer
have guessed that it merely served as a shell
for a modern structure within—a veritable
pavilion of roses, which would have won upon
the imagination of the dourest philosopher.
This I had discovered immediately upon my
arrival, but I liked to remember it as I went
cantering away, leaving the battlements behind
me and content to imagine myself a cavalier
of the old time riding abroad.

And it was hot, to be sure, upon those low-
lands of the park. A June sun burned up the
very earth. All animate nature moved drowsily ;
a shimmer of intolerable heat tired the eyes,
and set one longing for the shadows. The very
bees moved from flower to flower as though
labour were a burden hardly to be borne.
Myriads of gnats floated in clouds above the
lake ; the sky above was without a cloud ; every

object stood out in a glory of primitive colouring which we rarely see in England. For myself,
I pitied the poor devil of a cob I rode, and let
him go almost whither he would. But I remember that he carried me by the observatory,
and this I discovered to be exactly what Mr.
Cavanagh had described it. Not only was it an
observatory, but an exceedingly well-equipped
one to boot. The great telescope mounted in
its dome has few rivals in any country. There
is a finely-fitted scientific laboratory adjoining,
and a plant for the electric light. The latter
was Mr. Cavanagh's installation; but Professor
Rainham, of Cambridge, erected the observatory,
and my patron introduced little except the great
telescope. As to the monster searchlight, Mr.
Cavanagh had named it one of his fads, and as
such I consented to regard it. They had placed
it upon an extension of the gallery which runs
round the tower of the observatory; and when I
rode by it the lantern was very carefully covered
by a tarpaulin, and not to be examined.

You will imagine that I made no long stay
in this place, for to do so would have been an
impertinence. Mr. Cavanagh would show me
the house in his own good time. I had no
desire to go to him and to say, "I have seen this
or that, and will you tell me about it." Half
the things we own in this world give us pleasure
because we may show them to others and ask
for admiration when so doing. I thought of

this as I rode away from the observatory, and, striking a bridle path through the woods, found myself in a thicket which might have been a thousand miles from anywhere, so remote the place seemed and so silent. Here was such a wood as existed, surely, in the days of Merrie England. Never were such oaks, such yews, such avenues of elms—boled every one, and telling of the centuries. The sward below could not have been finer if they had laid it for a pleasure garden. Daffodils had died here by myriads in the springtime; there would be violets when October came, and lilies abundantly at the seasons of the rains. Even more delightful to me was the stillness of the scene, the sense of Nature's mysteries with which it inspired me. Is there not in every man this stooping to mother earth, something of the prowling animal which loves to creep out alone, nostrils distended to the perfumes of the grass, ears intent, eyes open, worshipping Mother Gaea to Uranus wedded? Such homage I paid that day, lingering in the pleasant wood, knowing that I lived, and grateful for my life. And here I saw the woman and the child.

I had ridden down a fine open avenue, and turned aside between the brambles to a little path that should have carried me back to the park again. Here I discerned a delicious pool and a ring of bushes all about it. And by the pool stood the child, floating a little boat in the water, while the woman watched him with restless eyes, now bright as with a passion of love, and then, as suddenly, aflame with a great hate that nothing could conceal. A more beautiful creature I have never seen in all my life. Her hair, I do believe, was the fairest that ever fell upon gentle shoulders ; her skin was as white as ivory.; her figure so perfect that an artist would have stood amazed. Nor had I less praise for the child who played by her side. Impossible but to believe that he was her son. For he had curls of the very golden hair which coiled its silken tresses about her pretty neck ; his skin was no less white ; his beautiful eyes as blue. Her son, undoubtedly ; and yet this mother, by whose side he knelt, knew moments when love had withered in her heart, and nothing but a passion of hate remained. The terrible truth of it all flashed upon me as I watched her. Good God, I said, a mad woman ! And then I remembered the cry I had heard in the night, and it was no longer a mystery.

The woman had lost her reason, and the man, who watched within a step of her, was the fellow I would still call my Algerian.

CHAPTER VIII

CAVANAGH'S DESTINY

IT was very distressing to see the way in which
this poor lady started to her feet at my approach,
and instinctively clasped the child to her breast.
She was wholly the mother in that moment,
passionately agitated for the child's sake and
thinking of nothing else but its safety. The
look of terror that crossed her beautiful face I
shall never forget. It needed no seer's voice to
tell me that she had been the victim of some
great sorrow, and that her troubled reason associated me in some way with those who had
persecuted her. When I lifted my cap to her,
she trembled pitiably. I was ashamed to have
discovered her, ashamed to go away without the
exchange of some civil greeting. In the end I
rode on aimlessly, afraid to speak, and yet railing
upon my silence.

A mad woman at the House of the Fen, and
this savage African for her keeper. Such, then,
was Mr. Cavanagh's unhappy secret—such the
true story of his seclusion. If the facts were
very terrible, I perceived at the same time that
they called rather for the pity than the judgment
of his fellow men. And to this reflection there

was added a sense of regret and humiliation for that which I had done last night—watching him from my window and imagining a hundred absurdities. Of these I repented deeply in that moment; and I resolved to confess the whole story to Mr. Cavanagh should the opportunity rise. When I returned to the house, I was astonished to discover into what a state of excitement this encounter had thrown me. Had I ridden at a gallop over miles of country, my sense of fatigue and personal distress could not have been keener. But this I attributed to the shock of it all; and chiefly to the vision of that sad face, which followed me to the house and even to my room.

You will remember that I had not seen Mr. Cavanagh since I watched him in the Italian garden at sunrise. When I returned, however, he was waiting in my room for me; and this greatly to my satisfaction. We had exchanged but the briefest word as yet concerning my own position in the house, and all my attempts to thank him for his generosity had failed ignominiously. I thought that it would now be otherwise, and was not wholly disappointed, as you will see.

"Well," he said, speaking from the depths of a great armchair as I entered, "and do you permit it, Mr. Ingersoll?"

"Sir," said I, "there could not be a more welcome visitor."

He smiled softly, and reminded me of our appointment at half-past seven that morning.

"Your judgments are not retrospective, Mr. Ingersoll. Come, a man who was up at six o'clock and waiting at half-past with a racquet in his hand——"

We laughed together while he rang the bell for Edward and the cigars.

"Mr. Ingersoll will take some tea," he said; "tea with very rich plum-cake of the kind that he always buys at Matthew's in Trinity Street."

"Did you really know that I dealt with Matthew's, Mr. Cavanagh?"

"My dear boy, I know everything that it is my business to know. You, for instance, paid me the compliment of imitating me last night; you could not sleep, I remember, and were watching at your window."

Be sure that I went as red as a turkey-cock at this. His manner invited no humiliating confession; I was dumb before his kind sarcasm.

"Make no apologies," he continued, taking pity on my embarrassment, "you are our creditor in the matter. Indeed, Mr. Ingersoll, I am saying that you paid me a great compliment in coming here at all. I should have been frank with you at the beginning—I intend to be quite frank with you now. Help yourself to tea and then light a cigar, for we have much to talk about."

I obeyed him, drinking my tea in silence, and

fearing to intrude upon his thoughts. When I
had lighted a cigar, he went over to the window
and looked across the park, as though in search
of the lady and the child whose discovery had
caused me so much distress. I knew that he
was thinking of them even before he spoke, and
could have anticipated his question readily
enough.

"You met a lady over in the woods by the
high road, did you not?"

"That is so, Mr. Cavanagh."

"I would tell you that she is my wife. There
was a little lad with her; he is my son."

I can see him now, standing there in the
warm glowing light, his black hair twisted upon
his fine forehead, the handsome face white and
convulsed, as though a story of tragedy had just
been written upon it. No woman's voice had a
truer ring of music in it than that which named
his son. Fame, fortune, the applause of men,
the glory of success; what were they when set
against this precious heritage? His son! You
had but to hear him to know how this man
loved.

"My wife and my son; yes, Mr. Ingersoll,"
he cried, turning about and facing me with flashing eyes, "yonder is my destiny; the woman I
love more than anything on earth, as you see
her; my son in the arms of a mother who has
forgotten how to embrace him. That is Jehan
Cavanagh whom men envy; there is your

F

millionaire who can command all that the world
has to give.   Remember it, when you would
judge me ; husband it, as the confidence which
you share with the chosen who are my servants.
Do that, and to-day you will become my
friend."

He stood beside me waiting for me to speak.
God knows, I knew not what answer to make to
him.   I am capable of deep sympathy, but often
unable to express it in so many words.   How
should I tell this man among men that I was
sorry, how best express the overwhelming sense
of pity with which I heard him ?

"Mr. Cavanagh," at length I rejoined, "there
could be no greater privilege than to call you
my friend."

"You speak very earnestly, Mr. Ingersoll."

"I speak from my heart, sir."

"I am sure of it ; men never deceive me.
You are telling yourself at this moment how
difficult it is to say anything at all, and are
saying words which are precious to me.   I am a
man who never forgets those who are willing to
suffer because I suffer.   Let the shadow lie as
lightly as may be upon us both, for we have our
work to do, and it is for a woman and a child that
we are labourers at all."

I did not understand him, had no idea at all
of his meaning ; nor was this the moment when
he chose to enlighten me.   I perceived that he
had his own way of going to work and would

not question it. None the less, curiosity whispered odd things into my ears, and I shut them out with difficulty.

"Mr. Cavanagh," I said briefly, "it was to be of service to you that I came here, and it is unnecessary for me to say that I will begin when and where you please."

"You have begun already, Mr. Ingersoll."

"You refer to the lists you left for me to make out?"

"To nothing else. Will you permit me to see them?"

I passed them over to him and he examined them with a close scrutiny, while he appeared to approve of that which I had done. When next he spoke to me, he had my papers still in his hand, but he made no mention of them.

"Do you remember an essay you wrote in the *Fortnightly*, concerning the rights of the individual as against the limitations of the law?"

"Perfectly well; it was a paper which cost me a great deal of trouble and not a little silly ridicule."

"It would have done so. The greater the truth, the wider the door by which fools pass in. You took up your stand, I remember, upon that large question of private wrong as against State incompetence or indifference. You conceived a position wherein a Dictatorship became in fact a National Directory. The State failing the individual becomes the law maker. A clever paper, I have read it many times recently; I shall read it many times in the days to come."

"It would have been more carefully written if I had known that."

"Do not say so. You wrote what your mind told you to write; your heart chose the words. What we call style is sometimes a cloak to cover a barren theme. Let the man speak, and the style is there. You must treat of that subject again when we have the leisure, and develop it. I am greatly interested—so much interested that I propose to help you in such studies. Would you care to travel with me, Ingersoll?"

I liked to hear him drop the prefix to my name, and responded that I should like nothing better.

"When my father was alive," said I, "we always spent part of the Long abroad. I suppose I have travelled a good deal in a way—that is to say, I have done the stock things, and come home to bore my friends about them. You would laugh at me—but I have seen some of the capitals of Europe, Mr. Cavanagh, even Belgrade and Constantinople."

He smiled not unkindly at this candid limitation.

"How little you have seen, my dear lad, time and I will show you. Do you know Antwerp, by the way?"

" I was there last Easter for three days."

" We will be there to-morrow, also for three days. I had not meant to go ; you remember that I promised you some tennis. But it cannot be. We shall return to London by motor to-night. Are you glad to go with me, Ingersoll—quite sure that you are glad of this visit to the Continent ? "

" Mr. Cavanagh," I said, " you know that it is so, for no one can hide anything from you."

He was greatly pleased, I could see, and when he laid his hand upon my shoulder, the gesture was full of kindness and perhaps of gratitude. All the loneliness of that splendid life made its sure appeal to me at such a time. Why had I been chosen for his confidence? How came it that he stooped to me of all the millions at his command, this master of fortune and of riches, to bid me serve him faithfully ? I knew not, but the act won my friendship as nothing else could have done.

CHAPTER IX

I was not in the least surprised to find myself in Antwerp. All that I had read or heard about Jehan Cavanagh told me of his extraordinary passion for travel. Never to sleep more than four nights together in the same bed became a rule of his nomadic life ; men told me of the way he would rush from place to place upon the shallowest pretext, coming to London one day, and leaving the next morning for America. When he took me to Cambridgeshire and spoke of rest, I don't think that he deceived himself. As for me, the perplexities of my own position drove such thoughts from my head. I hardly remembered his words.

But if I was not surprised by his sudden resolution to travel, the method of it certainly set me thinking. Just as we had entered the House of the Fen stealthily, so we left it secretly and by night. It is true that the Algerian did not accompany us, and that it was left to the valet, Edward, to examine the high road before we ventured upon it, and to leave the great lamps unlighted until we were almost in the town of Cambridge. From that place, going back upon his own intention, Mr. Cavanagh determined to drive straight to Harwich by way of Newmarket and the Bury road; and so we never called at London at all, but were on board a tug before midnight and in the River Scheldt next morning. I thought it somewhat unnecessary to charter a steamer to take us across, but, as he put it to me, his own yacht lay in the Solent and could not be round in time, and he never set foot upon a passenger ship.

"Why should I?" he asked me; "if money can buy anything at all, let it buy me privacy. Shall I lie awake at night listening to the agonising groans of the lady who 'knew that she would be ill'? Certainly not, when a few poor counters with the King's head upon them can deprive me of her society. That is the best use of money, Ingersoll—to let us live our own lives undisturbed by our curious neighbours."

I agreed with him altogether. It was a new experience to me to travel so luxuriously, and, to be candid, I enjoyed every moment of it. When we arrived at Antwerp, a private carriage awaited us on the quay, and we drove at once through those fine old streets, not to an hotel as I had expected, but to a suite of rooms almost opposite the great cathedral itself. These appeared to have been furnished in much haste; but everything in them was of the best, and Mr. Cavanagh settled down at once, as he is able to do whatever his environment.

I should tell you that we arrived in the city almost before the working day had begun at all. There were very few people in the streets when we drove through, and the doors of the cathedral were not open. None the less, we found a splendid breakfast prepared for us in Mr. Cavanagh's new apartments, and two French servants whom he addressed almost familiarly. Oddly enough, the voice of one of these reminded me of a conversation I had heard at Claridge's Hotel in London two days ago, when I had been waiting in the ante-room; and I came to the conclusion that the servants had crossed over from London while we had been upon our way to Cambridge; but this, be it said, was only my idea, and could not be accepted as a fact. The main thing appeared to me that they had excellent hot coffee for us, and a very pretty breakfast; and when we had made a hearty meal, Mr. Cavanagh himself proposed that we should lie down for an hour.

"There will be nothing to see in Antwerp to-day," he remarked significantly; "my interest begins to-morrow. Go and sleep, Ingersoll, and let other people sweep up the dust a little. If there is one thing on this earth more than another which I find depressing, it is the spectacle of a housemaid shaking a mat out of a window. Go and sleep, my boy, and wake up hungry."

I promised him that I would do so, and went to a beautifully furnished bedroom which adjoined his own. Broken as my night had been, I found it quite impossible to sleep; and when a full hour had passed, the bells of the cathedral made any further attempt a mockery, and I determined to take a bath and go out upon my own account. In this I was disappointed, for I discovered presently that Mr. Cavanagh himself had made no attempt whatever to practise his excellent precepts; and when I returned to the sitting-room, I found him in animated conversation with one of the queerest looking men I have ever set eyes upon in all my life. Bald as an egg, ferret-faced, his mouth awry and misshapen, his ears enormous, his hands long and thin and browned by the suns of many lands, his dress that of a French gentleman who is also something of a dandy—such was the Chevalier Prosper de Blondel, as Mr. Cavanagh introduced me to him.

"You must know each other well," he said, as I held out my hand to the Frenchman; "the Chevalier's work will also be your work, Ingersoll, when things are settled. Speak your worst French to him and see if he survives. He is one of my friends; let that be sufficient."

"And one of Mr. Ingersoll's friends as well," the Chevalier rejoined in a voice that was delightfully musical and soft. I cannot tell you why it was, but when I touched this man's hand it seemed to make the blood course in my veins as though I had been running a race. Such a

thing I have never experienced before or since.
And his eyes; surely they were looking straight
through my head at the wall behind me, just as
though my body did not impede his vision at all.

"I am always at the Chevalier's service,"
said I, "and at least my intentions are better
than my French. Is there anything I can do
this morning?"

He laughed and exchanged a quick glance
with Mr. Cavanagh.

"To-morrow," he said to my patron, as though
in question, and added almost in a whisper, " the
eyes are young; they will be useful."

I thought that the suggestion did not please
Mr. Cavanagh altogether, and he dissented as it
were with a gesture of the head. When the old
Chevalier had taken leave of us, no further mention of him was made; and I fell in very readily
with my patron's suggestion that he should be
my guide for an hour or two, and show me something of Antwerp. That was a delightful walk
indeed. I think that it made me ashamed of my
own poor scholarship to listen to this wonderful
guide as he recalled to me the part which the
Netherlands had played in the story of modern
Europe, and how little her art reflected the
sovereign victories she had won.

"It would have been impossible," he said;
"Art can only deal with the humanities when
Faith inspires her. We complain of the re-
ligious dominance in art, but our complaints are

not logical. Inspiration, which breathed upon
Rubens' canvases, breathed also upon the humblest masons who built this house for them. The
perfection of form as attained by the Greeks has
not the soul which these things have. I would
burn a Grand Inquisitor cheerfully, but Art has
no quarrel with him. He compelled men to turn
for their ideals to a faith in which they believed.
Few believe nowadays, and so we have fashionable
portraits at a thousand guineas apiece, and enough
nonsense written about impressionism to fill a
library. Look at the face of the Christ in the
Descent yonder. Did impressionism paint it
or the figure of the Virgin beside Him ? An age
which cloaks its deficiencies in cant—that is our
century. We have but one reality, money, and
there lies faith."

This will tell you that our first visit had been
paid to the great cathedral, which has always
seemed to me one of the most impressive Gothic
buildings in Europe. It goes without saying
that such a man as Mr. Cavanagh cared nothing,
as a rule, for the common sights of cities ; but
we passed through the cathedral upon our way
from the Place Verte towards the ramparts, and
he had the idea to see Rubens' famous pictures
of the Descent from and Elevation to the Cross.
Afterwards, I remember that we visited the older
quarters of Antwerp, especially that which is
called by the police " the Spanish quarter,"
where are veritable descendants of the soldiers

who came to Antwerp with the Duke of Alva. These fearful alleys and courts appeared to interest my companion profoundly. He studied the faces of those we passed by with an interest I found it impossible to explain.

" If you would study the life of a city," he said to me, " go first among its criminals. Are not they to be our masters to-morrow—the assassins and robbers and malefactors who are to rule us in the name of humanity, and to begin by slaughtering our wives and children ? Look at these old houses, Ingersoll, and remember that the Spaniards ran from door to door more than three hundred years ago, torturing and burning. They spared no man, woman or child. Have we progressed so far since their day ? We have called them every name that can decently appear upon the pages of our histories. But has our civilisation carried us so very far after all ? Look up yonder to that window where the glass is broken, that crazy attic with the dead plant on the sill. There Morivert lived a year ago—Morivert who threw a bomb under the wheels of the Vienna express and killed twenty of its passengers. You say he was a madman, for that is the way authority must excuse such crimes ; but is it not to confess that in practice we are where we were four hundred years ago ? Take your soldiers away from this city for a single day, and I will promise you a thousand dead before the morrow. The Spaniard is here as he is in every city ; and the children are in his keeping. That is why I say to you, go first among the criminals, for the day is at hand when they will be our masters."

Now this was wild talk, and I could not take him altogether seriously. The great god Anarchy has never had any terrors for me, for I have always believed in the sanity of the British people ; and I confess that what went on in other countries had been of little concern to my mind. At the same time, it was impossible to forget that his father had been killed by the anarchists of Baku ; and now it suddenly came to me that his wife had lost her reason in the terrible hours of that mad revolt. Should it be so, I could well understand the morbid curiosity which drove him to the meaner and more dangerous quarters of the city.

" Mr. Cavanagh," I said, " you are not speaking of our own time, surely? " It was impossible to believe that he did, and the heat of his reply altogether astonished me.

" Come," he exclaimed, " I'll put you to the proof. There will be, here in Antwerp to-morrow, the public procession with which these people keep the Feast of Corpus Christi. Ministers are to walk in the procession, and one of the Princes. The barracks of the city are crowded with troops to-day ; there is not a gendarme who will know an hour's rest. Will you say that the children are safe because of them? Would you be quite at ease if children of your own were to watch the

show from the balconies of the Place Verte?
Oh, a fine cry this of authority and order and the
sanity of the people! Tell me, Ingersoll, would
you be quite at your ease? I'll not believe it.
You have too much sense; you know too well
that which Messieurs the Assassins are doing in
Europe to-day."

I could make no fair answer to this and, in
truth, I knew not how to meet it. To my re-
joinder, that I had never heard of any great dis-
content among the workmen at Antwerp, he
replied, almost impatiently, that the workmen
had nothing whatever to do with it.

"There is nothing nobler on God's earth,"
he said, "than the man who works patiently and
without complaint for his daily bread. Leave
such out of your category, for we have nothing
to do with them. I am telling you of a new race
of assassins, ten times as powerful and twenty
times as numerous as the followers of the Old
Man of the Mountain, who ate hemp at Alamut.
I am asking you to remember that these people
flourish in spite of the Governments of Europe,
who are too cowardly to deal with them. These
monsters kill and slay at their pleasure. Neither
reason nor pity restrains them. They have
no compassion for women, none for little children.
The sanest among them does not know what he
wants or how to get it. We are asked to believe
that a certain sanction of liberty should make
some apology for them. Ministers and Parlia-

ments speak of them almost in whispers. There
never has been a man courageous enough to
stand up and say that they should be extermin-
ated like vermin, trodden under foot, shot upon
sight, hanged from the windows of their own
houses, hunted remorselessly, ceaselessly, to the
end. I say that it is abject cowardice which dictates this common truce. The Ministers are
afraid, the police are afraid. One strong man
would save the world from this visitation. But
he is not yet born, and while we wait the
women suffer, and the children die in their
arms."

I had never heard him speak with such
vehemence, and you will imagine in what a
frame of mind I listened to this recital. For the
first time since we had left London the episode
of the evening newspaper and its account of the
supposed anarchists at Paris recurred to me, and
I could not but associate it with this almost
incoherent confession. He had suffered greatly,
more than the closest of his friends would ever
know ; and out of this suffering a creed of destruction was born. So much I perceived at the
beginning ; but that which followed after, no
man, I make bold to say, would have foreseen,
whatever his powers of perception.

"You cannot make war upon madmen, Mr.
Cavanagh," I said at length ; "you cannot shoot
down the insane. Our common humanity for-
bids it. Is not this the truth rather than your

story of men's cowardice ? There are some wise heads left—even in the Governments."

" Ingersoll," he cried, taking my arm in an iron grip, " if the woman you loved turned from the son she had borne you, would you preach that doctrine ? "

I could not answer him. We had emerged from the narrow thoroughfare at the moment, and calling a passing cab, he bade the man drive us to the gardens.

" Old Prosper will be there," he said, his whole manner changing instantly when the sun shone upon us again. " Oh, I like old Prosper ; he has a sound head on those ugly old shoulders. Let us go and see him eat, for that is the most horrible spectacle in Europe."

CHAPTER X

THE Feast of Corpus Christi is celebrated with much pomp and circumstance in Antwerp, as all the world knows. Had I been in ignorance of the fact, an incessant hammering under my windows at bedtime would have been a sufficiently unpleasant argument. Standing upon my balcony at eleven o'clock, I watched a very army of "blue blouses" working by the light of monstrous flares. These conjured stands and bambinos, as it were from the very earth; while gendarmes and cavalry looked on in contented idleness. In truth, I heard the laughter and ribald songs of crowds far into the night, and when Edward brought me my coffee next morning, the day of the feast itself, the Place was hardly to be recognised.

For now a thousand ridiculous banners fluttered boldly upon the gentle breeze of day. There were stands everywhere; scarlet tapestries hanging from the windows; balconies ablaze with bunting and lanterns; while a vast concourse moved restlessly to and fro as though still in quest of a vantage ground. Mr. Cavanagh himself had already made mention of the procession

G
81

to me, and excited a certain curiosity; but I will confess that I had quite forgotten his gloomy prophecies, and regarded the scene with that pleasant interest which spectacle rarely fails to awaken. To me it was just a procession which had become famous the whole world over; even the appearance of the little brown Chevalier in my room did not bring a new view of it.

He was faultlessly dressed, I remember, in a grey frock suit and patent leather boots polished to such an absurd degree that a man might have shaved by them. Even browner than yesterday, as seen in the veiled light of my bedchamber, I found his voice not less musical, his touch not less repulsive to me. He had come, as he said, to beg a favour, and for Mr. Cavanagh's sake I heard him patiently.

"Our friend is not very well this morning," he began, his English being quite wonderful to hear; "we must take good care of him, Mr. Ingersoll—it is our business and our privilege. You have entered into his service, I understand, and henceforth are one of us—in a cause, I venture to say, which is noble above all words. Am I wrong in this; do I misrepresent your convictions, Mr. Ingersoll?"

He took a cigarette from his pocket as he spoke, and offered me one from his case. It was absurd to watch his ferret eyes twinkling incessantly, and to remember that they might be evidence of genius—or madness. I was not

afraid of him—let that stand at the beginning;
but I have met few men whose society so dis-
tressed me, and for reasons I am utterly unable
to define.

"Chevalier," I said, coming 'over from the
window towards the chair where he sat, "what
is this cause, and how can I help it?"

He shrugged his shoulders until they seemed
to touch his very ears.

"You are here to help our friend, are you
not?"

I admitted that it was so.

"Then that is the cause, sir. If your ears
have not told you anything——"

"Come," cried I, "this is not honest. I have
heard much of this vague talk, and it has not been
altogether a pleasant thing to hear. Mr. Cavanagh's father was killed at Baku, and the incen-
diaries tortured his wife until she lost her reason.
Is that true or false, Chevalier?"

"It is quite true," he replied, and yet with
no more emotion than a man speaking of a disaster in the street.

"And, being true, Mr. Cavanagh asks my help.
What form is that help to take, Chevalier?
Name it, and we shall begin to understand each
other."

He nodded his head as who should say, you
put it very plainly.

"Mr. Ingersoll," he said, taking a packet of
papers from his pocket and choosing a photo-

graph from them, " would you recognise that
lady if you met her in the street, the theatre, or
the church ? Should she pass these windows in
the crowd to-day, would you be able to pick her
out, and call our attention to her ? "

I took the photograph he offered me, and
looked at it as one may look at a beautiful picture. To me it represented a mere child, a little
schoolgirl still in her teens, yet with eyes so
wonderful that even the camera could not hide
their light. Deep set in a sweet round face,
wide open, nay almost staring, they were such
eyes as a man may carry in memory to his life's
end, and die because of them. This was my
belief when first I saw them in that house on
the Place Verte, at Antwerp. It is my unshaken
faith to-day.

" Am I to know the name of this young
lady ? " I asked, falling to a commonplace.

The Chevalier grinned until you could see
every tooth in his cavernous mouth.

" Certainly. She is Pauline Mamavieff, who
shot Mr. Cavanagh's father at Baku."

I did not let him see what it cost me to
hear this story. No doubt he remained convinced that the dramatic force of it would
make its own appeal, for he nodded and grinned
just as though we two were in the possession
of some great secret which we would share
with no others

" Who shot Mr. Cavanagh's father at Baku,"

he repeated, dwelling upon each word as though
his tongue were loth to part with it. " That's
why we're watching her, Mr. Ingersoll. That's
why we shall trap her if we can ; trap her, hang
her, shoot her, or, better still, send her to the
police in her own city who have the whips and
the branding irons. Will you watch the crowd
for her face now? Certainly, you will. Are
you not my friend's friend? Certainly, you
will begin to help him to-day ; we cannot begin
too soon, can we? To-day and every day while
there is work to do. Shall I tell him that I
found you very willing ? "

I said that he would find me willing.
Looking back upon it all now, I wonder that
no clearer perception of Mr. Cavanagh's strange
mission had come to me before that moment ;
and yet I do not think that I was to blame.
Brick by brick the house of his mad dreams
was built up before me. Day by day he pressed
his logic upon my awakening imagination and
trained it to bear its greater burdens. In Antwerp that morning I added but one fact to my
knowledge, that he had left England in the
hope of tracing a mere child who had killed his
father in the riots at Baku. The fact, and
nothing more! But a leaf from the tree of
knowledge I must presently discover! But
a grain of sand from a vast and arid
desert !

" I am perfectly willing to do as Mr. Cavan-

agh decides," said I. "If this child did indeed
shoot his father——"

He interrupted me sharply, nibbling his
words as a rat nibbles a straw

"There is no doubt of it. She was seen by
twenty people. A revolver, Mr. Ingersoll. They
train these girls to use it, and then cry, ' Have
pity on our daughters!' She is very clever,
Mademoiselle Pauline Mamavieff. The police
of five cities are asking for her, and she snaps
her fingers so. Of course, she may not be in
Antwerp at all to-day. It is mere surmise.
Should there be an accident while the procession
is passing——"

"What kind of an accident?"

"Oh, there will be no mistake about it:
horses down in their own blood, people running,
smoke and noise everywhere. Yes, yes, you
have read of it all; and if you see it to-day,
Mademoiselle Mamavieff will not be far off.
We know it; we know that her cousin Georges
arrived in Antwerp last night. They are
French, born of French parents in the Caucasus,
Mr. Ingersoll; the father has been twenty years
at Saghalien, the mother, I believe, was flogged
to death because she would not let a general
make love to her. Not an amiable family, you
see, and now it has come to this. But we
shall trap them; we shall trap them yet. I
have not served my friend Lepine fifteen years
for nothing. You did not know that I was a

policeman ? Ah, then I shall begin to say that
I have some manners, after all."

Upon my word, it was horrible to hear him
chattering away like an excited ape, and no
more moved by what he said than any stone
statue in the great cathedral opposite. So far
as I understood him at all, he meant to say
that the great procession might be attended by
one of those mad and senseless outrages to
which Europe has become so accustomed in
later years. And he plainly hinted that if it
were so, this little schoolgirl, whose wonderful
eyes had looked out at me from the picture,
would take a part in it. A more monstrous
fable could not have been recited. For my
part, I would not believe a word of it, and I told
him as much before I left the room.

" Of course I will do what you want—that
goes without saying. But you seem to me,
Chevalier, to be out on a very strange errand.
Suppose that your witnesses were mistaken.
Say that this child did not pull the trigger, and
what then ? "

He snapped his teeth as he answered me.

"Impossible, Mr. Ingersoll. She has confessed it. Do not take us for madmen."

" Confessed it—to whom ? "

" To me."

He stood up as though to impress upon me
the dramatic nature of this admission ; and,
in truth, I was impressed. The bravest advocate

could not have found a word to say thereafter,
and certainly I made no attempt of the kind.
The girl had confessed she was a murderess,
and that was the end of it. I neither asked
pity for her, nor would have shown her pity.
The man himself, secure in his knowledge of
her guilt, confronted me with that proper
authority he had the right to exercise, and I
saw that if my young eyes could discover the
girl for him, this should be the last day of
her liberty.

It was now about the hour for the advance
guards of the procession to pass our windows,
and we all went out to the balcony prepared
for us. Here an awning had been arranged
against the sun, and seats placed in what had
become a tent before the front windows of the
house. We could, I remarked, see the procession, and ourselves remain unseen. That
lavish hospitality for which Mr. Cavanagh is
famous had half filled the available space with
bottles of wine and boxes of cigars; but there
were low arm-chairs for a front row, and a very
wall of flowers to cover the iron railing. Mr.
Cavanagh himself I discovered to be in a mood
both thoughtful and restless. He rarely noticed
me, but conversed from time to time in a tongue
I did not understand, with the brown-faced
Chevalier who shared his confidence. When
a distant trumpet-blast announced the approach
of the procession, his face lost all its colour as

in a flash, and he drew the curtain aside and peered down into the serried ranks below with eyes so keen and watchful that nothing could have escaped his notice.

They do these things on the Continent with a fine relish for the picturesque, and their true artistic sense rarely rubs shoulders with the ridiculous. I have seen few pageants in my own country—the Englishman has but lately mastered their secrets, and his colour schemes are apt to be as substantial as his beef—but this religious pageant in the streets of Antwerp is certainly to be named as the finest thing of its kind I have ever seen. Mediæval if you will, cowls outnumbering the cassocks, soldiers at the head of it, cavalry to whip it in, monks and nuns, priests and bishops, all the cathedral dignitaries, the municipality, the big wigs of the town looking as though piety were the chief business of their lives—truly a heterogeneous company which linked the centuries to the point of marvel. And remember that it passed slowly through streets which were a blaze of triumphant colour; of colour stolen from the very bowels of the sun; a heaven and earth of colour, all embracing and all victorious. Not a house, I say, that did not contribute its quota of flags and tapestries and glorious blooms; not a window that should be named a lack-lustre ; but everywhere a vast wall of clinging stuffs, primitive and satisfying and

worthy of the day. Upon the pavements, it is
true, there might be some complaint. Many of
the women wore black veils ; the tones were
altogether more sombre, the religious note more
pronounced. But against this, it should be said
that we were present for an act of worship, not
of joyaunce. These people had kept their faith ;
even a cynic could not have denied it.

I remember that the procession was headed
—when the soldiers had gone by—by a hundred
little children, in dresses of spotless white, each
scattering roses in her path. They were followed
by the bearer of an immense banner, symbolical
heaven knows of what, but gloriously blue. At
the banner-bearer's heels came sisters of mercy
uplifting lighted tapers ; and then a thurifer,
and again cowled monks each with a lantern upon
a pole ; then other thurifers and acolytes and
abbots in copes, and bishops in mitres—a great
gold snake coiling its way through the city's
streets to the cathedral doors thrown wide open
to receive it. Solemn music, tender and plain-
tive, litanies as the Gregorians knew them,
the dwelling chants you might have heard the
Benedictines sing in Italy before the gentlemen
from over the mountains came down, these we had
from trumpets and horns and trombones. The
drums rolled majestically ; the voices rose and
fell in harmonic cadence as though Melancholy
sat in the sunlight and the heaven was hid from
her. But such, to my mind, is ever the mental

response to the liturgy as monks will chant it ; and emotionally it is far superior to Anglican intricacies.

They were very slow afoot, these good monks and fathers, and they well understood that haste and dignity rarely go arm in arm. To me the novelty of the spectacle and the people's attitude towards it stood for more than any mere merit of its own. I shall say frankly that I had, for the moment, clean forgotten the Chevalier's monitions, and Mr. Cavanagh's ill-defined anxieties. That which passed in the street, the reverent attitude of very humble folk, the jaunty bearing of the scoffer, the little human asides between lover and mistress, the maternal anxieties shared by devotion, and the natural assumption that Master Pierre or young Jean would dirty his new frock—that, I say, engrossed me completely. When I looked up, I think an exclamation from Mr. Cavanagh recalled my attention. I can only tell you that our eyes met for an instant, and that, upon this, I was hurled backward against the stone wall as though some great rushing wind of heaven had struck me down and blackest night had come upon me. This, I say, is all that I can tell you of the circumstance. It may be, as others have put it, that a thousand terrors inflicted my mind at the time ; I may have believed myself on the very threshold of death, maimed, blinded, hurled to destruction. I do not know. I shall not say that it was not

so, for recollection answers nothing—nothing but
that one impression of awful overwhelming force,
of a rushing air and then the darkness.

Of course, a man is not to live through such
a tragedy as this and recollect no phase of that
which follows after. Pen in my hand, I can look
up from the paper and see the Place Verte once
more ; shaping slowly from a shadow land to
sunlit reality. Now a pit vomiting smoke and
cries of human agony ; then houses above the
wraith, bunting, tapestries, the balconies of
flowers ; and so down to the very ground, whence
the black cloud is drifting and the figures of the
people are to be seen, and there are soldiers with
quaint helmets, and hussars and gendarmes ; but
not the dead I had expected to see, nor any
sign of that human woe of which the wailing
voices speak.

This is to come after, when the people are
driven back, and the officers dismount, and little
groups are formed, and that which, an instant
gone, was a living man is a dead something
over which a sergeant's cloak is thrown,
and that which was a child is lifted in strong
arms, and carried by one, who sobs as he goes,
to a friendly house near by.

For the moment there is nothing to tell me
that the glory of the summer's day has been
assailed by this mad outrage. The people are
so many stricken animals, bending abjectly to
the coming storm. Many of the women have

fainted ; the children cling to their skirts and
wonder that they are not answered. Those who
race to and fro upon excited horses are officials
at their wits' ends ; masters of the tape which
has been trodden underfoot ; lovers of rotund
phrase and portly document ; little tyrants whose
cheeks have been slapped by a hand of fire. I
can hear their frantic cries as I write. Once
more the pompiers come thundering down the
Place ; they uncoil their hoses, and set the
pretty brass engines to work. There is no fire,
however. The very smoke has drifted away ;
and but for that great cavity in the wall of the
restaurant next door, the powdered mortar and
sagging beam, you would have laughed to hear
that a bomb had been thrown at all.

Whoever had done this damnable thing had
done it from above. If I had not guessed as
much for myself, the searching glance Mr.
Cavanagh turned upon the upper storeys of the
restaurant, the words he spoke to the Chevalier
—in English this time—would have been
suggestion enough. The assassin had thrown
the bomb down ; it had struck the iron rail
of an awning above the porch below, and
immediately exploded at a height of six feet
or so from the pavement.

Local in its action as these explosives are, all
the damage had been done within a circle not
more than twenty feet in circumference. Herein
the dead and dying fell, horribly mangled ; about

this the soldiers grouped. Of the assassin himself no one appeared to think; that is, no one in the crowd below. But Mr. Cavanagh thought of him. Justice, for the time being, lay in the hands of this cool, unemotional man beside me; of him and his quick, all-observing lieutenant. No general upon the field was ever cooler than Jehan Cavanagh when he spoke to the Chevalier Prosper de Blondel—almost before the smoke had drifted above the awning.

" Dubarrac has arrived then. What were they doing in Madrid? "

" I have no explanation to give, sir, if it is Dubarrac."

" I am convinced of it. Does that smoke tell you nothing? It is Dubarrac, and he has come from Madrid. What then, Chevalier? "

" They are searching the house, sir. It would be the third floor and the little front room with the bed in it. He was not there last night, nor at eight o'clock this morning. But Dubarrac —he is a miracle ! "

They said no more,' but watched the room above with the curious gaze of men who believe that a tragedy is happening therein. I could only assume that they themselves had been expecting this outrage, and guessed its authorship. When the Chevalier had declared that the house was already being searched, he seemed to be telling a fairy story. Searched, and by whom? I had not seen a living man re-enter it

since the awful moment of the crash. It was
the other way about. Those within came tumbling into the street, as though fire pursued
them. There they went, pell-mell, waiters
and guests, men and women, crying, screaming, imploring the soldiers to save them. And
the Chevalier spoke of search. By whom?
I repeated to myself. Must I suppose that
these two were the masters of an organisation
already at work in European cities? The very
magnitude of the idea forbade belief in it.

Be it repeated that if Jehan Cavanagh's
agents searched the house, the evidence of that
fact was slight enough. I had but the man's
word for it ; and presently, to put an end to
further speculation, the police themselves went
in, and were shortly to be seen at every window.
And not the shattered house alone, but those
upon either side of it, and our own particularly
they searched. I heard their swords clattering
upon the stairs, the tramp of heavy boots above
and below ; they even intruded, but not to
remain. The Chevalier had but to speak a single
word to the officer in command to earn a salute
and an immediate withdrawal. Was it because
of Mr. Cavanagh's name, or the little brown man's
former occupation ? I could not tell you then ;
I did not know at that time that there was no
figure more cordially welcomed in every police
bureau in Europe than that of Prosper de
Blondel.

For our part, then, we had no share, no
overt share, that is to say, in this quest at all.
The few words which passed between Mr.
Cavanagh and his friend were often incomprehensible to a stranger, rarely excited. And
their very silence—imagine it—was almost a
torture to such a youngster as myself.

Why did they not recite every circumstance
anew, debate it in hot words, press out into the
street to see the damage done, and hear the
soldiers talk ? You know what youth is in the
presence of its first tragedy. Death—what
fear he strikes, how he sets the mind going. All
the dire imagination of it, the clinging visions,
the dreadful questions! I went through them
all, standing out there on the balcony. Would
that wretched man, whose face a sergeant's cloak
had covered, would he never see the sun again ?
had he passed from all existence into the black
void so to dwell through eternity? What had
been the sensations of that instant of death ?
Had he suffered?   Had he known ? and by
whose hand had he fallen ? Not the guess or
surmise, but the truth. Was the madman still
regarding his handiwork from some garret
above ?

Such speculation dumbfounded me. I stood
aimlessly by the railing, peering at the crowd
below, but not thinking of it at all. When I
picked out a face therein many minutes must
have passed before I could have said why it held

me, or what was the fascination of it. At last,
however, I knew, and, starting up eagerly, I
took the Chevalier's arm, and bade him look
with me.

"The woman," I said; "your Mademoiselle
Mamavieff! She is down there, just behind that
officer of Hussars at the corner. Do you not see
her, Chevalier?"

They lifted their glasses together, and
remained for many minutes gazing at the place.
The Chevalier, I thought, made some sign to
someone upon the opposite side of the way, but
of this I could not be sure.

"Young eyes are certainly good," he exclaimed
at last. "But, my friends, why should we forget
to breakfast?"

H

CHAPTER XI

IT must have been about four o'clock in the afternoon when I found myself alone with Mr. Cavanagh. The little brown Chevalier, strangely silent during the excellent breakfast we had eaten, spent a full hour afterwards, writing at a table in the window, whence he could look down upon the street below. From time to time, it is true, he uttered certain observations I could neither explain nor understand. His remark—in an interval of resting—that Dubarrac had certainly escaped to England seemed but an opinion at the best. No messenger had come to us, no letter been delivered. If he were not a wizard, he knew no more about it than I did, and that was little enough, heaven knows.

What astonished me more than anything else was the way in which these two men mastered an excitement which they could not wholly conceal. Their words were rare. When I pointed out to them the presence in the street of that very Mademoiselle Mamavieff whom they had come to Antwerp to discover, not for an instant did it appear to divert the current of their thoughts, or to provoke any overt action. We

sat to breakfast as men who have witnessed an
unfortunate accident and do not wish to discuss
it. The confusion below our windows had no
meaning for us. Soldiers went galloping by,
officialdom had its glasses on, the police per-
spired as men who have run a race—it was all
nothing to us. Just silence or the occasional
meaningless phrase; and this notwithstanding
Mr. Cavanagh's drawn face and the restless eyes
of the silent Chevalier. No longer, I thought,
was it possible to believe that these men had
come to Antwerp better informed than their
neighbours. You shall see how greatly I was
mistaken.

Now, the Chevalier left us alone at four
o'clock, and shortly afterwards Mr. Cavanagh
proposed that we should drive through Antwerp
before we thought of dinner. This was a propo-
sition very welcome to me, and for two hours or
more I enjoyed a delightful outing with him. If
he seemed not to remember the events of the
morning, I discovered later on that he had not
wholly forgotten them. Following immediately
upon a visit we paid to the famous church of St.
Paul, with its grotesque Purgatory in the porch,
he asked me if I had not the intention to write
something about that which I had seen upon the
Place Verte.

" Yours is just the pen," he said, " give them
a word picture of it. Tell them in England how
the women and children die—because there are

laws. That would make a fine sequel to your
paper on Individualism Gone Mad. Justify the
authorities if you can, Ingersoll. I think we
should all take some share in this work—you
could do much for those who believe in repression,
as I believe in it—war *à outrance*, no truce by
night or day with these fellows. Say something
upon the other side; there is far too much cant
about liberty in your country and in mine."

I told him that I would try to do as he wished,
but frankly confessed my difficulties.

"They will say that a nation might as well
make war upon Broadmoor; that is quite sure. It
is an affront to humanity to call these people
sane, sir. Preach extermination as an antidote
to homicidal mania, and you set going something which will move your altruists to frenzy.
Of course, you have foreseen that."

" I have foreseen everything, Ingersoll. Your
country shelters these people because she is afraid
of them."

"I do not believe that, Mr. Cavanagh."

" My dear boy, what right have you to
believe or disbelieve? Did you not have your
first lesson this morning? Be a student yet a
little while, and then tell me what is faith and
what incredulity. The time will come when I
shall have no stouter champion than Bruce
Ingersoll. I have known it from the beginning,
and I am more than ever convinced of it."

He changed the subject very quickly, and

went on to speak of the comparative indifference
of great cities to that which should concern them
most nearly.

" When the battle of Sedan was fought, men
ploughed in the neighbouring fields ; here, not a
man or a woman diverts the course of habit by
a hair's breadth because of the affair on the Place
Verte. It is nothing to them ; their own children
might have been among the dead, but while
they are not—well, shrug the shoulders and
pass on. We must bring it home to the people,
Ingersoll ; show them the thing in their own
houses. That is my mission ; be sure I am not
neglecting it. To teach the people what this may
mean to them—what it has meant to me."

He spoke very earnestly, and was evidently
much affected by his own words. For a little
while, indeed, he appeared to be suffering as I
had seen him suffer at the hotel in London.
The fit abated, however, as quickly as it had
come upon him, and I found him almost in a gay
mood at dinner, while his humour was almost
sardonic.

" The Chevalier is preparing a little surprise
for us," he exclaimed capriciously, when we had
returned from a restaurant to our own rooms,
" we must not disappoint the Chevalier, Ingersoll.
It is in the Rue Anglais, I believe, at about nine
o'clock. Will you care to come with me ? are
you afraid ? for I must tell you that there is some
little risk in it. We are not exactly at the Fen

in our own snug rooms. Will you come with me,
knowing that, Ingersoll ? "

I answered that I would go, whatever the
risk. My hesitation in accepting his amazing
view of these people must not let him believe me
to be a coward.

"And I am very glad to go—with you, Mr.
Cavanagh," I added, for this was nothing but the
truth. He appeared to be pleased I thought, and
at once summoned his valet, Edward.

" Mr. Ingersoll and I are going where they
do not like fine coats, Edward," he said ; " please
bring something that will disguise our beauty,
and quickly—for Monsieur de Blondel is awaiting me."

He was obeyed without any question, and
ten minutes had not passed when we emerged
from the Place Verte, two as characteristic
" blue blouses " as you would have found in all
Antwerp that night. For my part, I do not
believe my oldest friend would have recognised
me, even had he held me by the shoulders and
stared into my eyes. Mr. Cavanagh himself
looked just like some burly workman who had
spent an unprofitable evening at a café, and was
being taken home by his son under protest.
Why these disguises should have been necessary,
what was the meaning of them, I knew no more
than the dead ; but I could not forbear to ask
a question, and that surprised my companion
greatly.

" Do you hope to arrest Mademoiselle Mamavieff to-night, Mr. Cavanagh ? "

He swung round upon his heel and faced me
almost while I spoke.

" What makes you think that, Ingersoll ? "

" Oh, the Chevalier asked me to keep my eyes
open for her."

" Did he tell you why ? "

" He told me what he thought, sir."

" And what I intend to do ? "

" He said nothing of that."

" He was wise ; come on, Ingersoll."

I thought it a strange answer, and the tone
in which it was uttered boded little good to this
wretched girl wherever he might find her. Our
walk had now carried us down toward the Scheldt,
and we followed the bank of the river some little
way, by the wharves and the docks and the
towering shapes of the ghostly ships.

Once, when a lad, I had stayed a few days at
the Hôtel Anglais on the quay, and I remembered
the place when we passed it ; but our destination
was not here, but in a little narrow street some
quarter of a mile further on. Down this we
turned boldly, and halting without any pretence
before the door of a house on the left-hand side
of the way, Mr. Cavanagh produced a latchkey
from his pocket and instantly admitted me.

You are to imagine this street running at
right angles to the river, straight toward the
Cathedral and the heart of the city. The houses

—for they still stand as they stood when the
Spaniards lit their fires in Antwerp—are of
immense height, some of them wooden, the eaves
bulging, and very old ; the lower stories often
open to the winds of heaven. The pavement is
of flags worn by time and the sabots of many
generations almost flush with the sodden earth
below. Those who are abroad might be named
for sailors in peg-top breeches, or flashy women
of the worst kind a Continental city can show
you. This, I say, was the general aspect of the
street; and the house into which we turned
seemed no more fortunate than its neighbours.
The very staircase quaked under our footsteps as
we went up ! there were not three whole panes
of glass in the room upon the second floor where
at last we halted. I saw no man, woman,
or child ; I heard no voice in all the house. It
might have been neglected since Alva came to
Antwerp for all it spoke of occupation ; and when
Mr. Cavanagh told me that it was his house,
then, in truth, I thought the jest a little flat.

" Your house, sir ; but you don't mean
that ? "

" My house, Ingersoll ; and I am going to
have supper here. No, don't strike a light, please.
We must have cat's eyes to-night ; cat's eyes, aye,
and tongues of velvet. Now please to feel your
way with me, and come across here. There are
chairs in the window ; I do not expect my guests
to stand, Ingersoll."

We felt our way across the room, and, sure enough, there were two chairs in the bay of the window. When my eyes had become a little accustomed to the darkness, I perceived a table before the chairs, and the ill-defined shapes of bottles and glasses.

" Schnapps, Ingersoll," he whispered, " pay a compliment to the Dutchman, even if you are in Flanders; there is no better drink in or out of the Netherlands than Schnapps. When you want to smoke, keep your cigarette below the window. And don't strike a light here, unless you would like to know who lives in the house opposite, and what he is doing there."

I looked across the street and perceived a light in the window of the house opposite, and this so near to us that an outstretched arm might almost have touched it. The bulging eaves bridging the street so sagged upon their beams, that a man with a good head might have stepped from our window to the other with no more risk than a child who walks upon a gate. The fact was too patent that it should have escaped me at such a moment. One glance at the room opposite told me that it was occupied ; a second convinced me that the men who occupied it were not less alert than we, not less vigilant, not less fearful.

There were five in all in the opposite room, three playing dominoes at a table in the centre, one asleep upon a crazy sofa, the third writing by the candle's light. Curtained at the sides, the

lattice in the centre had no curtain for a reason
presently to be disclosed. The men themselves
were apparently of diverse nations, a Russian, a
Spaniard, and three Germans—for so I placed
them by light of my own insufficient experience.
That they also dreaded espionage their quick
movements and frequent questions made as plain
as day. There were not two minutes together
when one or other did not open the casement,
and peer down very cautiously into the street
below. I wondered now that Mr. Cavanagh had
been able to come to this house at all; I could
not understand it.

" My house, Ingersoll," he whispered, as he
drew me toward the window—but not so near that
we ran any risk of observation—" the house I
have owned while those gentlemen have honoured
this street with their presence. Do you recognise
Jean Ferrers, sail-maker, and his son, Michael ?
Well, we are that pretty pair ! the originals being
where their friends will not soon discover them.
There's a good reason to try some Schnapps
before the damp gets into our bones. Try some,
Ingersoll ; tell me that it keeps your spirits up,
and that you are just as comfortable here as in
your nice little room upon the Place Verte."

It was odd to hear him speak in this tone, but
I came to see that some natural excitement of
the situation prompted it, and I do not doubt
that the bottle of Schnapps had really belonged
to the old sail-maker from whom his agents took

the house. Of course, we never opened it, or thought of opening it. Nor was I insane enough to think of smoking; but just sitting there in the black dark, I watched the men with him and waited, I knew not for what. If danger threatened us, I did not realise its presence. The mystery of the house itself, the clear figures of the hunted men—all this and our situation, the suspense and the oddity of it, kept me as engrossed as a man at a play. Why had he brought me here, and for what? That I might take a second lesson from him? Indeed it appeared to be that.

This view I had quite accepted when I settled down to watch the men and to try, of my own intelligence, to frame some answer to a riddle so perplexing. That the gang was connected in some way with the outrage I had witnessed upon the Place Verte I never doubted. It even came to me that one of them might be the notorious anarchist Dubarrac; and this conviction growing, I put it bluntly to Mr. Cavanagh.

" Which is Dubarrac ? " I asked, the question escaping me almost involuntarily. Evidently it pleased him that I should have asked it.

" Ah, you are learning, I see," he exclaimed. " Well, Dubarrac is writing a letter to his friends in Spain, telling them of this morning's success."

" Why did you not let the police know that he is here ? "

" Because the police are not clever enough to

catch him ; or if they catch him, they would fail
to convict him."

" Then you hope to do that for them ? "

He did not answer me. The man Dubarrac
had ceased to write, and was listening intently as
though his quick ear caught an echo of footsteps
in the street below. Again he came to the
window and peered down into the shadows.
Then he whistled very softly, and the whistle
was answered from some room above our own.

Here was a surprising discovery if you like ! I
had believed that we were quite alone in the
house, and you may imagine what it cost me to
correct this impression. Not only were there
others watching with us, but they must be
Dubarrac's own friends, since they had answered
his signal.

The discovery, I say, set my blood tingling as
a blow might have done. I fell to a kind of panic
which prompted me to fly the house at any cost ;
to escape to the light and the life of the streets ;
or, failing that, to face the peril and have done
with it. From this cowardice Mr. Cavanagh
himself saved me. Not a thought came into my
head that his amazing mind did not instantly
anticipate.

" Is not the Chevalier musical, Ingersoll ? "

" Then it was the Chevalier who whistled ?
What a fool I have been ! "

" You did not think of it—that is all. The
Chevalier can whistle very nicely, it appears, but

his notes do not altogether please our friends
opposite. Observe that they are far from being
at their ease. Look at the man Dubarrac—he
has actually forgotten to finish his love-letter, and
is loading a pistol instead——"

It was as he said. A whisper of alarm ran
along the street, and brought these men to their
feet in a flash. Away went the dominoes; out
went the light. I had an instant's vision of five
terror-stricken faces, and then the scene was
hidden from me.

"Back, Ingersoll; back," Mr. Cavanagh
whispered. "We have no longer the protection
of their light. Did you bring the pistol that
Edward bought for you? Very well; you may
need it presently. Now wait and watch."

He drew me back into the darkness, and there
stood at my side waiting. What was happening
in the street, I cannot exactly say; but presently
I heard the shuffling of many feet, and quite
suddenly, without any preparatory warning whatever, a great shout as though a mob had collected
beneath our windows, and clamoured for a
prisoner. This fearful cry, like the yell of a
hundred human wolves, was dreadful beyond
imagination to hear. I stood aghast at it; afraid
of the sound of my own voice.

"Do you hear, Ingersoll—the good burghers
of Antwerp have come to know why Dubarrac has
killed their wives and children! They are good
burghers, and some of them have been in prison.

If our friend over yonder falls into their hands, they will tear him limb from limb. I do not exactly know how much our friend the Chevalier has paid them, but it is a considerable sum, and— good God, what voices they have ! "

The mocking tone, you see, could not support this new evidence of his own handiwork. The brief talk had told me much, but this was not the time to reflect upon it. There was a mob below our windows, and this mob waited to avenge the poor creatures who had been murdered on the Place Verte that morning. To me the moment was one of an excitement surpassing anything I have ever known. The truth came as upon a beam of light. We were here not to catch these men, but to kill them ; not for the law's justice, but that of a rabble paid for their ferocity, lusting for blood. The fact was indisputable ; as indisputable as it was terrible.

My friends have often asked me how I came to be the silent witness of such a scene as this ; why I neither uttered a protest, nor accused Mr. Cavanagh of dealing unfairly by me. The answer lies, perhaps, in the absolute justice of that which was done, and in my own conviction, not then understood, but latent in my mind, that he acted in the interests of humanity, and by his fellow men, must be judged.

If this be not so, and cowardice was at the root of it, cowardice and curiosity, fear of him and fear of myself, then let the record stand, and

with it that appeal to circumstance which alone
remains to me. For how could I have interfered?
what could I have done? There we stood in the
room, no light anywhere, yells and hooting from
the street below, my conviction firm that Jehan
Cavanagh's agents were in this very house; there
we stood and waited, I say, and what strength was
mine either to save the assassins or to respite
them? As much as that of a man who, single-
handed, would go out against an army; the
strength of a child in the presence of a master;
the authority of the humblest soldier who has
heard his general's order and fears to obey it.

No, for a truth, I held my tongue as any man
among us would have held it. The swiftly
changing scene caught me in a potent grip of
curiosity which no argument might shake off. I
listened to those fearful cries in the street below
with a dread and an expectation I may never
define. My eyes seemed glued to the darkened
windows opposite; I feared to avert my gaze
even for an instant.

What was happening within that house? Had
the men escaped, then, that they gave no sign?
Were all our cunning plots in vain? To this, I
would have answered yes, but for the appearance,
wholly unexpected, of one of them upon the
window-sill I had been watching. There he
stood as plain to be seen as any mouthing figure
upon a theatre's stage. And I bear witness that
it was awful to hear the yells with which the mob

discovered him ; a ghastly spectacle to look upon
his face as he turned his swift glance below or up
to the heavens, or across to that very room in
which we were waiting. I discerned his purpose
now ; a child would have guessed it. He would
bridge the gap between the eaves, and boldly
come across to us. So much evidently he and
his had long contemplated doing, for willing
hands aided him to thrust a pole at our lattice
and to break it in. Answering the mob with a
defiant curse, I saw him take a revolver from his
pocket and deliberately fire at the people. Thrice
he fired before passing over, and then flung the
pistol behind him that others in the room behind
might not be without a weapon. So much at
least the imagination suggested for I could hear
the outposts of the mob thundering at the doors
of his house and the crashing blows they rained
upon it. When, at last, he ventured the crossing,
I knew that the rabble had forced the house
and was almost upon his heels.

So there he was—clinging to our crazy lattice,
and feeling his way into the very room in which
we stood. For my part I had no courage even
to lift a finger against him. A touch of Mr.
Cavanagh's arm upon my own set my heart
beating and every nerve at a tension. The man
was on the sill ; he had his arm about the lattice ;
he was coming in. And then he rested for a reason
I could not see ; rested and uttered a loud cry, and
implored those behind to come over and help him.

If my eyes told me the truth, it was this, that the lattice had swung open a little way and refused to budge farther. Whether it had been so contrived, or were an accident, I know not to this day ; but you will see the man's position, unable, as he was, to force the window ; unable to draw back ; the rabble yelling below him ; his friends urging him on ; the door of the room behind them splintering beneath the blows that were rained upon it. Thus it was, and·thus the end came. For the man at length released his hold and fell : and the yells of the mob ceased upon that instant, and a dead silence ensued.

I had no courage to go to the window, nor would Mr. Cavanagh permit me. The low murmur of sounds now coming up to us was that of human dogs fighting for a carcase. In the room opposite I heard a fearful outcry, the report of pistols, the thud of heavy blows, the crashing sounds which attend a *lutte pour la vie* such as that must have been. That some figure was hurled out to the people below I know full well ; but whose figure I cannot tell you. Mr. Cavanagh bade me follow him from the house, and I went willingly down the crazy staircase and out to a narrow street wherefrom I could see the river again. There were police here, but they paid no attention to us. Our disguise was sufficient, and they regarded us simply as two workmen making their way home. We walked in silence back to our rooms in the Place Verte, and there Mr. Cavanagh left me alone.

ɪ

CHAPTER XII

MR. CAVANAGH first spoke to me of a regular engagement at the end of the month of June, nearly three weeks after I had gone to his house in Cambridgeshire.

We left Antwerp on the morning following the Feast of Corpus Christi, and going to Paris were five days there at the Ritz Hotel. During this time I found my employer to be a man so changed that I should never have known him for the Jehan Cavanagh of the Fen, and certainly not for the self-styled owner of the house in the Rue Anglais. All that had passed in the city appeared to be completely obliterated from his mind. He lived the life of other men, shared their pleasures, and could stoop to the most trivial amusements.

Here, in Paris, we might have been two youngsters just down from Cambridge, and embarked upon the grand tour. Dinners at Armenonville, dinners upon the islands in the Bois, loitering about the shops during the afternoon or speeding headlong for Chartres or Beauvais or any place that had something to show us, we became tourists without a redeeming feature

114

if it were not our own enjoyment of our liberty.
Never had anyone a better guide to frivolity
or one who so delighted in it. I found Paris a
very fairyland, and quitted the city with real
regret.

And so we returned to London, and staying
the night at the Carlton—for rarely did Mr.
Cavanagh visit the same hotel upon consecutive
occasions—he took me next day to a suite of
offices in Victoria Street, ostensibly owned by
a certain Bertrand and Co., emigration agents,
but in reality devoted to a very different purpose, as you will presently see. The whole of
a considerable house appeared to be required
by these very busy agents, and I thought it
not a little strange that the largest room upon
the first floor should be reserved for my employer,
and placed absolutely at his disposal, as I
quickly discovered it to be. Here, as elsewhere,
furniture of a luxurious kind decorated the
apartment, and comfort seemed the first consideration. Whatever Jehan Cavanagh will do,
that he must do as luxuriously as money will
permit him.

So it was a very fine room, and furnished
with almost a feminine profusion. Mr. Cavanagh alone appeared to keep the key of it, and I
noticed that a commissionaire at the door received him with great respect when we entered.

His business in the house I had yet to discover ; but he quickly set me to work writing

out certain commonplace documents for him ; and I was in the middle of these when he interrupted me to speak of my engagement.

" By the way, Ingersoll, what am I paying you for all this ? "

Well, I suppose I looked up very sharply, as most men will do when there is any talk of money about.

" I never thought of it, Mr. Cavanagh."

" Oh ! come now ; you mustn't expect me to believe that. You have been thinking of it almost every day since we began. ' What's the fellow going to pay me ? ' you have been asking yourself ; and then saying ' I believe he's a swindler, for he never mentions it.' "

" Oh, no, I haven't got so far as that yet."

" But you'll soon arrive there. Come now, a man doesn't live on promises, or on another man's hotel bill. You have your future to think of ; it's in my keeping, Ingersoll, but you have to think of it. Now, suppose I give you a thousand a year until you get married."

" A thousand a year——"

" I said so. A thousand a year until you get married, and then we'll talk about it again. You are to do for me all that you feel able to do ; I emphasise that, Ingersoll, all that you feel able to do, and I am to pay you a thousand a year. Shall we say that it is a bargain ? "

" But, Mr. Cavanagh, I shall never be able to earn a thousand a year."

" I think that you will—from my point of
view. Come now, could you not write to-day that
article on the business at Antwerp—I mean
something about the affair in the Place Verte?
Give yourself up to it, and try to tell the English people exactly what happened. Don't mince
matters or exaggerate. Neither would serve our
purpose; but I want you to go a little deeper
down than the descriptive writer who has head-
lines to dish up; and you must ask your old
question again as to the Individual right where
the State has failed. What am I, the Individual, to do? What are my rights when the
law is either powerless or afraid? Shall I let
these madmen murder my children, or, being
influential enough, shall I take up arms against
them? You will not put it quite so bluntly,
for that would be indiscreet. But encourage
the idea of private initiation; bruit it abroad,
let men discuss it. That is what I want for a
beginning, and you will do it better than any
other."

I reflected upon the matter for a little while,
and did not hesitate to express my difficulties,
as I had already expressed them at Antwerp.

" There would have to be altruistic assump-
tions," I said at last; " you cannot glorify
lynch law in civilised countries, Mr. Cavanagh.
You cannot give men, however powerful they
are, the right to be both judges and executioners.
This would be the English view; I am sure of

it. But I think you might very well demand
drastic measures on the part of the law, and
claim the individual right should those fail."

"Exactly, Ingersoll; and since it has been
demanded, and they have failed, what is your
authority against the man who comes to the
law and says, 'I can do what you have failed to
do; I will be the master of these people; I will
devote my life and my fortune to that end; I
will save your children from them'? You
must have that in black and white, you know;
not as fact, but as a supposition. Just ask what
the State would have to say to such a man.
Put the idea abroad, and let it germinate."

I told him that I would certainly do my
best to set out the whole idea logically and
fairly. Two or three days would be needed to
search authorities, and especially to substantiate
that fundamental moral basis upon which such
a hypothesis might rest. That he himself had
read much upon the question his sagacious
observations soon convinced me. This gospel
of Retaliation had become the gospel of his
life. When he consented to forget it, he did so
only by a great effort of will which was often
attended by dangerous reaction. Nor shall I
omit to say, here and now, that when the
safety of helpless people depended in any way
upon his principles, he acted with a courage
beyond anything I have ever known.

Let the justification of this bold statement

be deferred to another place. I have but to tell you that Mr. Cavanagh interviewed many odd people in his offices in Victoria Street, and that I took down notes of what they said. Much of this information must be regarded as confidential and cannot be divulged here. But I clearly perceived that those who came to us were at work in many cities, and principally the cities of the south. From Odessa, from Naples, from Barcelona, from Geneva the emissaries came with their monitory tidings of plot and counter-plot, of secret meetings by night and lone vigils by day. And for each Mr. Cavanagh had a patient hearing, jotting down notes in addition to those which I myself took, and often uttering some sapient criticism. In truth, the task occupied us the whole of the morning, and he had just suggested that we should go to lunch when who should come in but the little brown Chevalier, who hailed us both in his own mild way, and declared immediately that he had news of the greatest import.

" Messieurs," he said, dragging a chair to the table and speaking so rapidly in French that I had the greatest difficulty to catch his meaning, " they have taken the woman, and she is now in the jail at Bruges. Please to read the telegram for yourself. She was taken at the Café Americain at ten o'clock last night by my agent, Sennival. She will be charged with complicity in the affair of June 14th. If we wish it, there can be no doubt about her conviction ; but do we wish it ? It is for you to say, maître ; I have given no instructions until I hear from you. Shall she go to prison in Belgium, or back to her friends at Baku ? They would be very glad to see her in Baku ; the Chief of the Police has told me so, and there is a pretty place prepared for her. Is it your wish, then, that she remain or return ? I have come here as fast as ship and train could carry me to tell you this. It is great news, maître ; the greatest that it has ever been my good fortune to bring to you."

I knew that he had been indiscreet, and Mr. Cavanagh's quick glance at me confirmed this opinion. He should not have spoken before me ; at least, not yet. But the words were out, and the story told, and none could doubt their meaning. The girl criminal, who had shot Jehan Cavanagh's father, lay in the prison at Bruges, and would speedily be put to her trial. My employer had sufficient influence with the police at Brussels either to secure her conviction or to ensure her deportation to Russia, where a fate, horrible beyond all imagination, must await her. And this was the little dimpled schoolgirl I had seen upon the Place Verte ; hers the eyes which had looked at me so wondrously from the picture.

I had not believed her to be guilty then, and I did not believe her to be guilty now. The story of her arrest seemed to be a terrible one. And yet what could I do? what could I say upon her behalf? I had but to look at Mr. Cavanagh's face to read the deep satisfaction with which he had heard of the Chevalier's news, and his unflinching purpose of revenge. This girl, child that she was, had accomplished the supreme sorrow of his life. She, little schoolgirl that she might be, had armed him against the world of revolutionaries. And now she had come to justice and must repay.

"To Russia, Chevalier!" he said, almost reverently. "Let her own people judge her; let them punish her."

CHAPTER XIII

I HAD come to consider the fate of Pauline Mamavieff to be fully determined upon when the news came to me that I, myself, must go to Belgium and see her. This request reached me by letter from Cambridgeshire just five days after I had paid my first visit to the offices of Bertrand and Co. in Victoria Street. Mr. Cavanagh, himself, had gone down to the Fen upon the night following our return to town; but I remained at the Carlton Hotel, visiting the offices daily and working upon that newspaper article he so much wished me to write.

I shall not tell you how often, during those long and quiet days, I thought of the child in prison at Bruges, or the fate which had been prepared for her. Perhaps those " strange involuntary thoughts " of which Byron speaks in " Mazeppa" are never to be defended logically, nor sympathy itself to be reckoned wholly as a virtue; but the fact remained that in my deeper heart I believed Pauline Mamavieff to be innocent, and would not abandon this conviction whatever the circumstances. In vain the Chevalier repeated his story of her alleged

122

confession; I heard Mr. Cavanagh with indifference when he assured me that there could be no doubt of her guilt. My own opinion remained unshaken. She had not fired the pistol which killed Jehan Cavanagh's father; or, had she done so, it had been by accident. To this belief I held tenaciously, and no college of logicians would have turned me from it.

And then came Mr. Cavanagh's own word, that I was to go to Bruges, and to hear the girl for myself.

"I am anxious to remove all doubt from your mind," he wrote. "Go to Bruges, and ask for Count Marcelli at the Palais de Justice there. He will procure you admittance to the prison. See Pauline Mamavieff, and hear her story. It may help your work for me. It will certainly convince you that I am doing well to leave her punishment to her own people."

The letter reached me by the first post of the day, and ten o'clock found me in the Ostend express upon my way to Bruges. I had become accustomed by this time to the nomadic life which Mr. Cavanagh desired me to lead in his service. But I recollect no journey of them all upon which I embarked with such a heavy sense of responsibility as this. I had believed Pauline Mamavieff to be innocent, and I was going to Bruges to hear her tell me that she was guilty. I was going to ask her by what mad teaching, what calamity of association or idea she had come to commit this crime, and to stand unashamed before the world because she had committed it. At the best it seemed impossible to accomplish anything in her favour; at the worst I must go back to Mr. Cavanagh and say, " You have done well ; let her own people judge her." These were the alternatives which no argument could hide from me. I was going to destroy my own ideal of her girlhood, and to destroy it willingly.

We made a poor passage to Ostend, a stiff easterly gale blowing in the Channel, and the sea running high beyond the Goodwins. To me, a deck hand always where a Channel passage is concerned, the crossing was memorable only for the unwelcome attentions of a doleful individual in a blue cape-coat, who took many opportunities to tell me that he doubted if the ship would make the shore, or that, if she made it, we had done better to be all drowned. A more pushful, tenacious, and generally disagreeable companion in travel I have never met with. Even at Ostend I had to bribe a guard to keep him out of my carriage, and when I alighted at Bruges, this bearded disciple of an unknown nation was the first person who addressed me.

"Do you go to the Hôtel de Londres ? " he sidled up to ask me.

"I go to any hotel that you are not going to," said I, for it was time to be rude.

"Ah," he said, " you English haf no

manner"; and I was glad to see him slouching off in as fine a huff as even my disgust could desire.

Ten minutes later, my cab set me down at the Hôtel de Flandre, and within an hour I had called at the Palais de Justice, and asked to see Count Marcelli. He, however, was, as a small man with a big sword informed me, "absent," and would not be at the Palais until eleven o'clock on the following morning. There was clearly nothing for it but to spend as pleasant an evening as might be possible in my solitary circumstances; and this I set out to do without any loss of time whatever.

So here I was in Bruges, that wonderful old city of the Counts of Flanders; with its canals everywhere to remind me that it was not Venice; its ponderous old porches to speak of gorgeous interiors and angelic Dutchmen; its superb Hôtel de Ville; its general air of being everything and nothing in the perspective of fame—this Bruges which all praise and few remember, this mart of the Hanseatic League, this bauble in the tawdry crown upon the head of Burgundy. Viewed as I viewed it after many years, the moon at the full, the hotels resonant of the remoter West, a dull, hushed modern world rubbing tired shoulders against the mighty buttresses of the past, I thought it a gem of the Netherlands thrice unfortunate in its past, its present, and its future.

For me I confess the supreme interest centred in a more human aspect. For was not Pauline Mamavieff in the gaol behind the Hôtel de Ville, and should not I see her in the morning? The reflection kept me to the streets as a tired dog that has forgotten a new doorstep. I passed the prison twenty times, and asked what the child was doing; what were her hopes and her fears, her secret thoughts in these lonely hours when none might share them, when night alone was her confidant. A romantic speculation, you say! Truly so, but not a speculation apart; for who should tap me upon the shoulder as I passed the prison for the twentieth time but the bearded man of the steamer ; and he insisted upon a hearing.

"Good-evening, sir ; you take the air."

I looked the fellow up and down very sharply, and saw him cringe at my gaze. So far as I could make him out at all, he would have passed for an unmistakable son of Palestine desiring to sell me a diamond ring as a bargain. And yet not a needy Hebrew, for his clothes were good and he wore a watch-chain like a ship's cable. Why he should have singled me out for his attentions I had not the remotest idea. To say that I was suspicious of him would be to write an absurdity.

"Yes," said I, "like most of my country-

men, I take everything I can get. Is that
what you want to know?"

He shuffled down the street after me, just
like a beggar who has five starving children and
only a box of matches for sale to support
them.

"I know Bruges; I know Bruges very well,"
he said. "If there was any place you like to
see—the thing that the Englishman all want
to see, but don't know where to find him——"

"Look here," said I, "if you follow me any
further, I shall certainly kick you."

"But you want to see the curiosities,
sir?"

"And I am seeing one. Now, what is it?
what do you want to say to me?"

We had come to a dark place of the street,
and, greatly to my astonishment, this nimble
old man suddenly clutched my arm as we
walked, and began to whisper into my ear
almost as though I had been his brother.

"Save the life of Pauline Mamavieff, sir;
you can do it. I know why you have left London. Do not listen to the Chevalier; he is in
the pay of the Governments, and will show no
mercy. Save the life of Mademoiselle Pauline.
I know it is no good that I ask for myself; I
shall be like my comrades—there is death everywhere; but for Mademoiselle Pauline pity, for
she is not your enemy."

And there he stood, cringing and shivering;

the very picture of an abject coward. It goes
without saying that I would have questioned
him if the opportunity had come to me; but a
patrol approaching at the moment, he turned
and disappeared instantly.

"Do you know that man?" I asked the
sergent in the best French I could muster.

He did not understand me, and I returned to
my hotel greatly wondering.

It was known, then, that I had left England
to visit Pauline Mamavieff in the prison at
Bruges! It was known, or thought to be
known, that the Chevalier de Blondel had sent
me. I perceived instantly that the Chevalier's
risk in this discovery was also Mr. Cavanagh's
risk. If these men had discovered him, he
should know of it without the loss of a single
instant. This was my first impression, to be
corrected in my own room later when I reflected
upon Jehan Cavanagh's insurpassable foresight
and the magnitude of that organisation whose
outposts I had seen, but of whose active and
militant army I knew nothing. Could it be
possible that such a man would put his life into
the hands of the first old Jew whom I chanced
to meet upon a steamer's deck? The idea was
preposterous; I could not entertain it for a
moment.

This was well enough in its way, and re-
assuring; but when I went to my bedroom
that night, I think that there came to me for

the first time some true idea of my own part in this gigantic drama that men were playing in the cities of Europe, of the tremendous moment of it, and its universal significance. For if it were war, as already I imagined it to be, then must such a war be waged, and waged in secret, as the world had not known since the beginning.

But, after all, it was but a boyish and perhaps a futile supposition; and I went to bed to dream that I had released Pauline Mamavieff from her prison, and was crossing Europe with her, to some haven of refuge, I knew not whither.

CHAPTER XIV

I was early at the Palais de Justice upon the following morning, and there discovered that Count Marcelli expected me. A man of diminutive stature, florid in his gestures and animated to the point of absurdity in his talk, he received me with a courtesy wholly French, and a disposition to oblige me that was wholly English. Indeed, I had not been two minutes in his private room before I felt in some way that I had known him all my life.

"Mr. Ingersoll, is it not? Yes, it could be no other. One glance at the face and I know that I am speaking to my friend's friend. You have passed a good-night, monsieur, slept well, found your hotel quite comfortable? Then I am content and shall make my apologies for being absent yesterday. Pray tell me at once just what it is that you wish me to do."

I took the chair he offered me and lighted a cigarette as he had done.

"Mr. Cavanagh has written to you about my visit, Count?"

"Not written; when does Jehan Cavanagh write? No, no, it is not he at all—my friend

130

the Chevalier—you know the Chevalier?—well, I have a telegram from him and it is here. To put myself at your disposition; and here I am, very ready to accept your commands. You know Bruges, perhaps?"

"As the man who gets seven days from Cook knows it. Let me tell you at once, Count, that Mr. Cavanagh wished me to see a young Circassian who is in prison here; at least, she is called a Circassian, though I believe she is of French nationality—a certain Pauline Mamavieff."

"Ah, the little Anarchist."

"No other, Count. I am to see her and to see her alone, if you can be so kind as to permit it?"

Well, he answered me by jumping up and declaring that nothing in the world was easier.

"You shall go there at once," he said; "I guessed it would be that when I heard you mention Mr. Cavanagh's name. We all know the very natural interest he takes in these people; I am delighted to be of assistance to him; who would not when Jehan Cavanagh is the man! Of course, you recollect the great friendship he showed my Government in the recent emigration decrees at Quebec. He has only to ask in Belgium, and there is nothing—but here is Captain Richard, and he will go with you. Mes compliments, monsieur; you are about to visit a charming young lady, I assure you. If it were

possible to believe that she had not gunpowder in
her pockets, I would have made love to her long
ago. But they tell me she is a monster . . . and,
my dear sir, we make no love when we are up in
the air like the flying machines of our friend
Santos-Dumont. Beware of Mademoiselle ! . . .
Remember that there is a story."

It was all very good-humoured, the persiflage
of a man who had given no thought to the matter.
Captain Richard, the military governor of the
prison, I found to be a different personage altogether—padded, laconic, reticent. I don't think
he spoke a word while he crossed the open court,
behind the Palais de Justice, to the door of
the cell, wherein Pauline Mamavieff awaited her
sentence of deportation. Here, however, he
asked a question which it puzzled me to answer
in a fitting manner.

" How long will you be with the prisoner ? "

" I don't know, Captain . . . "

" Then I will give you fifteen minutes."

He opened the door upon the words, and
showed me into a great stone cell of the old
prison—an extensive apartment built below the
level of the court, but airy for all that, and lighted
by gas jets placed in cages high upon its walls.
For an instant the change from the brilliant sunshine of the courtyard to this artificial light of
the cell tried my eyes, and left me a little confused ; but that passed in an instant, and then I
saw that the room might have been some fifteen

feet square, that it had no decoration upon its
walls but a crucifix, and that its furniture con-
sisted merely of two chairs, a table and a bed.
Upon the table, a tin pannikin and half a loaf of
coarse bread spoke of breakfast; the bed had
been stripped of its blankets; an open book lay
by the side of the pannikin, and Pauline Mamavieff's little white hand rested upon it.

I had seen her, remember, once before, upon
the pavement of the Place Verte at Antwerp on
the morning of the tragedy. Here, in the cell,
my first impression of her beauty was that it had
suffered not a little by confinement; but this
passed quickly, and I returned to my own original
opinion that the picture did her less justice, especially to those amazing eyes which I have never
matched in all my experience. Even upon the
threshold of her cell, I was conscious that they
looked me through and through. Every step
toward her was a new invitation to praise them
—the matchless eyes of the little convict in the
prison at Bruges.

And so it comes I can say nothing of her
dress, tell you little of her height, her look,
her gesture, her attitudes; I saw but a young
girl before me, her brown hair tumbled upon her
shoulders, her red lips parted, her ears decked
out with admirable turquoises. A ruby ring upon
a finger of her left hand caught the garish beams
of light and played with them. I believe that
her dress was of plain black cloth, but cannot be

sure even of that. The eyes forbade that I
should notice it. Very shame could not turn
my own from them.

"Mademoiselle Mamavieff," said I in English
—for Mr. Cavanagh knew that she spoke our
language—"will you allow me to talk to you a
little while?"

She did not move from her seat; did not take
her hand from the book.

"You are an Englishman," she said, . . .
and I thought that she uttered the word with
satisfaction.

"An Englishman, who is anxious to help
you if he can."

"To help me! Oh, no, there is no one in
Bruges who is anxious to help me, I am sure."

"I shall convince you to the contrary if you
will listen to me."

"But who are you? Why should you be interested in me, sir?"

"I am an Englishman, as I say, and I am
much interested in your case—for a simple reason
—because I believe you to be innocent."

"Innocent of what, sir?"

"Of firing the pistol which killed the father
of the man who sent me here."

"You come from Jehan Cavanagh, then?"

"From Jehan Cavanagh, as you say."

She began to tremble at this, and all her
resolution did not help her. For my part, it was
now coming into my mind that I had but to

mention my employer's name to bring this abject fear and humiliation upon those who heard it.

"Mademoiselle "— I rejoined quickly —" I am your friend, whatever Mr. Cavanagh may be. I am here to prove that you are innocent."

"It is not so," she answered with a new calm, "you have come here because the police sent you, monsieur."

"You do not believe that, mademoiselle; look into my eyes and tell me that it is true," I said.

She tried to do so, but tears stood where I had discerned nothing but courage and resolution when first I entered the cell.

"You do not believe it, mademoiselle, you cannot tell me so to my face?"

"And if I cannot, monsieur?"

"Then I shall be able to talk to you."

She did not answer me immediately, hiding her round, babyish face upon a naked arm, and allowing many minutes to pass before another word was spoken. When she looked up a sweet smile had taken the place of her tears, and she remembered that I was standing.

"Won't you sit down; prison chairs are very hard, but please sit down. I am quite ready to be questioned. They have asked me so many questions since I came here a few days ago."

"But not the question that I am going to ask you."

" I must hear it first and then, perhaps, I will answer it."

" What is the name of the man who killed my friend's father at Baku ? "

She looked me straight in the face again, and without a blush, a word of self-befence, or any argument whatever, she quietly and simply said :

" I killed him, sir."

" You ; what had he done to you ? "

" He was the friend of the General who had my father flogged to death."

" And you shot him in revenge . . . just because he was the friend ? "

" Just because he was the friend."

" Saying which, you expect me to believe your story ? "

" Why should you not believe it, sir ? " she asked sharply.

" Because, mademoiselle . . . I do not."

She laughed at the words, but instantly checked herself.

" What reason have I for telling you an untruth ? "

" You wish me to repeat it to Mr. Cavanagh ? "

" You are clever . . . shall I not know your name ? "

" My name is Bruce Ingersoll."

" Bruce . . . Bruce . . . I like that, sir.

I will remember the name of Bruce Ingersoll when I go back to Russia."

"Then you know that you are going back to Russia?"

"Count Marcelli told me so yesterday."

"To be tried for this crime there?"

"To die there, sir, as my father and my mother died."

"My poor child, I had forgotten that—and they did not tell me that your father was dead."

"Why should you remember it, Mr. Ingersoll?"

"Because it is impossible that I should forget you, Mademoiselle Pauline."

"Me; oh, no, no, no. Don't say that. You come from the police. You are to go back to them and to say, 'She told me this and that, and here are the names of her friends for Mr. Cavanagh to remember.' So many have come to me as you have come. The law asks so many questions, Mr. Ingersoll, and hears so many untruths. I have told them none, and they do not know what to make of me. In Russia we flog people until they tell as many lies as we wish to hear, and all that has got to be because of the law, without which the world would come to an end. Oh, let me tell you that I do not think so, that your law of man is hateful to the law of God; that in the days to come there will be no law but that of the human soul looking upward

to the light. Yes, yes, that is my faith. Looking
upward to the light. I do not fear death, Mr.
Ingersoll, I fear to live."

I listened with ears which tingled as she
spoke. Here, in an instant was the little schoolgirl transformed . . . a child no longer, but a
woman confessing her whole soul as in a rhapsody,
unafraid and undaunted, knowing nothing of
right or wrong, of guilt or of innocence ; but this
supreme consolation of her faith.

" Mademoiselle," said I very quietly, " if there
were no law, Pauline Mamavieff would not suffer
for another man's crime."

.   " Shall I never convince you, Mr. Ingersoll ? "

" You will never convince me, mademoiselle."

" Why is it that you doubt me ? "

" The truth written in your eyes ; the sure
knowledge that you are all kindness and gentle-
ness and love ? "

" No one has ever spoken to me like this
before."

" I shall hope so to speak many times in the
days to come."

" You ? but you will never see me again. I am
to go to Russia in a few days now. Count Marcelli told me so this morning. Why are you so
certain that you will see me again ? "

" Because I am determined to do so ; and
when a man is determined under such circum-

stances as these, he generally gets his own
way."

"No"—and this she said very firmly—"determination will not help you, Mr. Ingersoll.
Besides I wish to go."

"Knowing what they will do with you
there?"

"I saw my father flogged," she said; and at
that her face lost all its colour in an instant, and
left but the black rings about her wonderful
eyes. Upon my side I had nothing new to
urge upon her; I neither knew how to persuade
or to coerce her; but I still had a question
to put.

"You do not really believe that I come from
the police, Mademoiselle Pauline?"

She laughed in my face.

"You would have brought me chocolates if
you had been a policeman," she said; "they
used to bring me many, but I have had none now
for nearly a week."

"All eaten, mademoiselle?"

"Every one of them, Mr. Ingersoll."

"I'll bring you some to-morrow when I come,
if you will begin by being sorry for your opinion
of me."

"I'll try," she said—just as a child might
have said it—a laugh upon her lips, the light of
childhood in her eyes. The moment would have
been one of signal advantage could I have
profited by it, but such was not to be. The

laconic Captain appeared in the cell while we were laughing together, and informed me that my time was up.

"Good-bye, mademoiselle, until to-morrow."

"It will be never," she said . . . and so I left her.

CHAPTER XV

I HAD not breakfasted when I went to the Palais de Justice; but my first visit upon leaving it was to the telegraph office that I might send a cable to Mr. Cavanagh. His private code—an exceedingly ingenious one, by the way—it had been my business to learn at the offices of Bertrand and Co., and I now employed it to tell him both of my visit and of my strange encounter with the old man who had travelled from Dover with me. A staunch sense of duty impelled me to keep nothing from one whose willing servant I had become; a belief, no less profound, in the justice of the case recorded my positive conviction that Pauline Mamavieff was innocent of the crime with which they charged her. The rest I left to him, and going to a café for my breakfast, I tried to tell myself that nothing remained but that Oriental ejaculation " Kismet," which is so often our welcome substitute for unpleasant obligation.

It seemed so easy . . . and yet how difficult it came to be. Out there in the sunshine, the influence of a mediæval somnolence all about me,

141

great grotesques of churches and of buildings,
sombre Flemings in round black hats, Rubens
women in bulk and sabots, Bruges of the bridges
and the dark canals ; and I at my ease amid it
all. What perversity forbade me to take my
leisure contentedly, to forget why and whence,
to be other than a lazy tourist thankful for the
sunshine of that summer's day ? A story old as
Eve perchance. The eternal story of the heart
rebellious, of the man who turns his back upon
the sun because another wills that he shall not
see it. For so had my little Pauline commanded
me. I said that I must forget her, and, saying
it, I perceived her image upon every glass that
imagination turned to me ; heard but the music
of her voice whenever voices echoed about me ;
dwelt in my thoughts but upon her brave confession and the unspeakable misfortunes that
might attend it. It may be that I loved her
already ; I cannot tell you truly. The desire to
believe that she was nothing to me, to forget her
words, to mock her faith—these were enemies of
the truth as an observer might have written it.
And they were my own enemies also, blinding me
when I had need of my eyes as never before in all
my life.

Indifference, I say, and from that restless-
ness and again impatience that was almost a
fever. Why did not Mr. Cavanagh reply at once
to my telegram ? I had told him as plainly as I
could that in my opinion the prisoner at the

Palais de Justice was innocent of the crime with which they charged her. Why did he not come over that I might fully explain my reasons for this belief? Not for a moment would I hold him guilty of a wish to condemn one who was little older than a schoolgirl just because the police of Baku held her to be guilty. But he answered me nothing ; there was no cable that day ; none next morning when I called at the Post Office almost before the porters had swept it out. And, remember, that if I would save Pauline the hours were precious. Count Marcelli himself had hinted that she was to leave Bruges before the week had run. Let that befall, and no human power could save her from the devils of the Black Sea who had put perpetual shame upon her mother and flogged her father to death. Is it any wonder that I was at the prison gate by ten o'clock asking for the Count, and determined to see the prisoner again, and have another interview, let them say of me what they might ?

To be brief, they said nothing whatever. The Count was again absent, and the laconic Captain Richard did such honours of the Palais de Justice as were to be done. I could see the prisoner, he said, for fifteen minutes as before. "But, Mr. Ingersoll," he added, "they will be fifteen minutes and not thirty."

To seek argument with such a stiff-backed tool of authority would have been futile beyond all words. I bowed to him, and expressed laconic thanks to match his own.

"You know that they have decided to remove the prisoner on Sunday," he went on. "It is good. Let them all go back to Russia, and blow each other up. We have no room for them in Belgium."

"Is it quite certain, Captain, that this girl is one of them?"

"She has never denied it. The affair at Antwerp owes something to her gang, be sure of it. They are everywhere, monsieur. If I had my say upon it, I would shoot them down like rabbits, and leave the judges to try them afterwards——"

"The innocent and the guilty, Captain Richard?"

"The innocent and the guilty—as if there are innocent among them! Let us think of honest men first; that is my opinion."

We were at the cell door by this time, and I would carry the matter no further. I thought that he watched me a little curiously as I went in; but this perquisition did not distress me. Mademoiselle Pauline herself, already dressed, lay upon the mattress of the bed when I entered, and for a moment I thought that she would be asleep. But this was not so, and she started up presently to show me a laughing face and heavy curls of thick brown hair about it.

"I am very surprised to see you," she said.

" But I told you that I would come."

" That is just why I am surprised. Did you bring me my chocolates ? "

" They are here ; enough to make you ill for a week."

" It is very nice to be ill for a week if you know that you will get better afterwards. Why did you come back, Mr. Ingersoll ? "

" To ask you some questions."

" Why question a woman who never tells the truth ? "

" You are not a woman ; you are, or should be, a schoolgirl."

She became serious at this, and looked at me very earnestly.

" Have I not suffered enough to be a woman ? "

" Perhaps. I am here to save you from suffering. We have fifteen minutes, you and I, to tell each other many things. I shall lose none of them."

" Very well ; then I will not open my chocolates. One might tell the truth with one's mouth full."

I drew a chair near to the bed, and watched her a moment before I began to question her. A lace chemise showed me how rapidly her heart was beating. I had known her already to be a splendid little actress; but that which acting cost her, both in resolution and mental suffering, this moment first revealed to me.

K

"We are going to talk about Baku," I began.

"Yes," she said.

"And the late Jehan Cavanagh. Did you know him personally ? "

"I never saw him but once in my life. It was the night I killed him."

"The night upon which he died. Why did he go to Baku at all ? "

"He owned the petroleum mines ; many of them. That is why he went to Baku."

"And your father was in his employ."

"Oh, not at all. My father was secretary to the Black Sea Transport Company. He knew all the Englishmen who came there. That is why I speak English."

"How, then, and why did your father become a politician ? "

"When General Seroff came to our house he——"

"Came for what ? "

"To see my mother."

"I understand ; your father had a wrong to avenge ? "

"He never avenged it. My friends will do that."

"And the sum of all your charges against old Mr. Cavanagh was that he was General Seroff's friend."

"He protected the General from my people. He saved his life. That is why I shot him."

" In the French café at Baku ? "

" In the French café at Baku."

" Who was with you at the time ? "

" An old Dalmatian servant of my father."

" No one else ? "

She flushed crimson.

" I will tell you," she said ; " there was another."

" A friend ? a relative ? "

" A friend ? "

" Shall I say that he was your lover ? "

" Yes," she answered in a low voice ; " my lover."

" Were you going to marry this man ? "

She laughed, a little hardly, I thought.

"No one thinks much of marriage in Baku."

"Yes ; but you had thought of it."

" I shall not tell you ; you have no right to question me, Mr. Ingersoll.   Why do you trouble me like this ? "

" The desire to set you free ; to save you from going back to Russia."

" But I wish to go back to Russia."

" To meet this man ? "

"You are jealous of him already, Mr. Ingersoll.   Of course I am going back because I wish to meet him."

" Then there is nothing more that I can say to you ? "

" Yes," she said, leaping to her feet with all the impetuous agility of a child ; " there is some-

thing still to be said, Mr. Ingersoll. Why did
you come here? I will tell you. Because my
pretty face attracted you. If I had been an old
and ugly woman, would you have come then?
Oh, don't say so, for I would not believe you if
you did. You came because you thought I
would like you if you came. Now you know that
I love someone else, you are sorry for your interest
in me. That is why I shall not call you a friend,
Mr. Ingersoll. You help me because I am
Pauline, not because of truth or justice, or anything else at all. Be honest and say so, Mr.
Ingersoll. I shall like you a little if you will."

She stood before me, panting with excitement, her eyes wide open, her thick lips parted,
her short blue skirt caught up to show her
brown stockings and the bright buckles upon her
worn shoes. Her raised left arm was bare to the
elbow ; she nursed my chocolates to her breast
with her right hand ; her face was flushed and
angry ; the pretty hair all tumbled about her
shoulders. Such a picture in a prison cell a man
will never see again. It needed all my resolution
not to catch her in my arms, and tell her that I
loved her.

"It is all true," I said at last. "Please like
me a little because of it."

She took a step across the floor, and looked
into the very depths of my eyes.

"You came here because you wished to love
me ? "

"I don't know. I thought you were the prettiest girl I had ever seen, and I didn't believe that you had done what they said. So I came, because I wanted to save you."

"For whom, Mr. Ingersoll?"

"I did not know then; I know now. For myself, Pauline."

"And why, Mr. Ingersoll?"

"Because you have taught me to love you."

She stood quite still. Then, leaning back against the wall behind her, she hid her face with her hand and burst into passionate weeping.

"You cannot save me," she cried.

"Will is better than cannot, any day."

"For my lover in Baku——"

"Time will prove. I am going to save you. Good-bye, little Pauline. If they send you to Russia, I will follow after. Good-bye."

She stood an instant quite irresolute. I could hear the laconic Captain at the door, and, caring nothing for what he might say or might leave unsaid, I took her in my arms and kissed her.

CHAPTER XVI

ROOT AND BRANCH

I KNEW directly I stepped out into the passage that he had seen me, and his first words confirmed a gloomy assumption.

"At any rate," he said, "the lady is a Frenchwoman."

"Then you discriminate, Captain?"

"Not so in such a case. The question should follow dissatisfaction. It is for you to complain of her, Mr. Ingersoll. Since you do not?"

"I believe her to be absolutely innocent, Captain. You must have imagined that I did."

"Most people would at such a moment. There is another of the gang here!"

"Another!"

"I will show him to you. Not a very savoury specimen. I do not think he will receive many chocolates. This way, Mr. Ingersoll!"

He turned abruptly from the corridor, and led me down a narrow tortuous staircase to a deep circular cell in the lower of two basements. A tremendous door, ribbed and barred with iron, spoke of ancient centuries and modern degeneration.

"This was the 'dripping cell' when Alva came to the Netherlands," he said quietly; "they tied their man in a chair, and let the water fall drip by drip upon his forehead. For an hour he laughed; the next he raved; the third he was in agony; and the day after found him a shrieking maniac. A little of that sort of thing would be a good antidote to the Terror. I will show you one of its apostles."

He raised a flap in the door, and invited me to look in. I had half-expected to see what I saw, but the fact startled me none the less. For there, crouching upon a bench in a corner of the cell sat my old friend of the steamer and the market-place; the nameless, bearded importunist, who had asked me for God's sake to help little Pauline.

"When did they arrest him?" I asked. The answer was, "Last night."

"But we have been looking for him since our friends were blown up at Antwerp. There are three more of his kind still at large between this city and Brussels. When we have them also under lock and key, we shall be able to sleep in our beds without dreaming."

"Do you know the name of the man?"

"No name—that is to say, a name which means nothing to us. He calls himself Andrea, of Sebenico, a town upon the Dalmatian Coast. God knows where he does come from. They say in Paris that he is an Italian Jew. Barcelona

would like to lay hands upon him; Geneva has
something to say to him."

"And what are you going to do with him?"

"To ask him to work for the rest of his life;
and when he doesn't do it, to flog him until he
does. I thought you would be interested to hear
the news; and, Mr. Ingersoll, while you are in
Bruges, be a little careful. We cannot follow
you everywhere, remember."

I thanked him for the hint and returned
immediately to the hotel, wondering all the way
what I should do if Mr. Cavanagh did not answer
me at all. Happily, there was no need to push
this speculation very far, for he was the first person
I met upon going up to my room, and with him
there sat the little brown Chevalier as talkative,
as optimistic, and as self-reliant as ever. This,
however, did not altogether deceive me. I perceived that both the men were anxious and not
a little glad to see me back.

"My dear Ingersoll, so the jury could but
agree?"

"Absolutely agreed," I replied dogmatically.

"Then you come to me with white gloves
upon your hands."

"I am sure of it, Mr. Cavanagh—with white
gloves upon my hands."

The Chevalier laughed, a little coarsely, I
thought.

"It is the powder from her pretty face," he
said, and offered me a cigarette.

" You have yet to tell us what you think of old Andrea, the Dalmatian ? " exclaimed Mr. Cavanagh.

Of course, I was astonished.

" Then you know that he is arrested ? "

" My dear boy, I asked them to arrest him last night, and you cannot suppose that they would be such fools as to disobey me. But we are all fasting. Let us take off the white gloves and go and eat—in my room below. Strange, Ingersoll, that I should come to rooms in a hotel. Well, you see what old age is doing with me. Beware of it ! Don't grow old upon any account. It is the unpardonable sin."

I told him that I would be careful in the matter, and we went down to breakfast, but did not speak further either of Pauline or the old Dalmatian.

Many telegrams were brought into the room as we ate, and one dispatch, which unmistakably came from the police. The latter appeared to trouble Mr. Cavanagh not a little, and he handed it over to the Chevalier with an observation I failed to catch. When they had both written something upon it, the Chevalier left us hurriedly, and Mr. Cavanagh lighted a cigar and went over to the window.

" How do you like Bruges, Ingersoll ? "

" It depresses me, Mr. Cavanagh."

" Too many stories, or too many sabots ?

" Too much of yesterday, which is always

depressing, however much we admire it. All the
people who built those churches and painted
those pictures are dead. I wonder what our
generation will leave behind it ? "

" Good canvases for those who come after to
paint upon. Plenty of paper for a new generation
of authors, and not a little sawdust. Our merits
are written upon gold—the English sovereign
largely. I am glad you do not like Bruges ; it
depresses me also. Have you good eyes, by the
way, Ingersoll ? Could you see a cab down in
the street there ? "

This seemed to me something of a sneer, but
he did not mean it.

" Possibly I could," said I; " would it be a
cab with wheels or without."

" Oh, a real cab ; the blinds drawn down, and
a red-headed man on the box. They call him
Dave Mahoney, and he comes from Chicago,
Ingersoll. Will you watch here this afternoon
while I am out; and if you see our friend, will
you send this note to the Gendarmerie the very
same moment ? Ring that bell; they will
understand ; my servant will be ready."

I was greatly mystified, so much goes without
saying ; but I promised him to do exactly as he
wished. He himself now made ready to go out ;
but before he went, he returned to the subject of
the white gloves.

" The girl protested her innocence, I suppose,"
he exclaimed, raising the subject without any

preliminary observation whatever. Of course, I
told him that she did not.

"She persists in her confession," I said, "but
I have discovered the reason for her persistence.
She has a lover—one might have expected it. I
am sure she is lying to shield him."

I saw that it had not occurred to him before,
and for one instant he stood quite still debating it.

"No," he said at length, "our evidence con-
tradicts that. The men with her were two—
Andrea, the old rascal now in prison, and a
Greek priest, by name of Euclythenes. There
would be no lover there."

"Evidently, sir."

He stopped and looked at me in that queer
way of his.

"Good God, Ingersoll, are you glad that she
had no lover?"

"Yes, I am glad."

"Then I must make you sorry—quickly. I
must not spare you, Ingersoll."

"I hope you will not, Mr. Cavanagh. The
truth, after all, is what we want."

"I agree with you—the truth. Tell that to
the women who are mourning their children at
Antwerp this day, and they will say 'Yes, the
truth—and then its consequences.' "

It was a lesson to see the iron in his eyes when
he uttered this. A man of determination beyond
all words adamantine; I read in his glance a

righteousness of purpose, and a steadfast resolution
which no argument in all the world might shake.
He would deal with these people as a merciless
judge, I said. Pity had no place in his gospel.
He would destroy them root and branch, take up
the glove in whatever city they chose to cast it,
devote his life, his vast fortune, to this single
aim—his vengeance and the peace of the world.
Thus, his glance. But it turned from me, and
he was my kindly patron when next he spoke.

"But we are forgetting the cab," he said,
with a laugh ; " it is time for me to go, Ingersoll.
Here are the cigars ; I won't offer you the papers.
Remember, to the Gendarmerie before you count
ten—if the cab is there."

I promised him, and he went. It would have
been about two o'clock of a very sunny day, and
the street below was busy enough to make my
task no unpleasant one. Cabs passed incessantly upon their way to the Central Station ; but
not a cab shuttered and driven by a red-headed
man. Of this I did not complain. The cigars
were excellent ; the people in the street, quaint
Flemings, boisterous Frenchmen, Americans
going at a gallop, showed me many a pretty
comedy. There were honeymooning couples
from " across yonder," and these I liked best of
all. " She " had lost her bashfulness by this
time. " He," abject slave at her heels, did the
blushing for the pair; while she bargained with the
cabman, or announced to all the world her poor

opinion of Bruges and its people. And this was
the end of the love-dream, the awakening to
cold reality frozen upon the window-panes of
imagination ; the beginning of the long road
whose sign-posts are monotony, whose goal is
grandfatherdom.

Oh, I thought about it all, be sure, upon that
long afternoon—thought of the guilty woman in
the prison ; of the old man who had followed her
across Europe to protect her ; of the lies she had
told me, and the brazen demeanour with which
she met my accusation. Of her guilt there
could now be no doubt whatever. I had been a
child to suppose that the shot which had killed
Jehan Cavanagh's father had been fired either by
the old man Andrea, or the Greek priest who
stood by her side in the café. Had it been so,
she would at least have protested her innocence
to me. I had passed my word to treat her confession as a sacred thing, to protect her from its
consequences, and if need be, never to reveal the
name of her guilty confederates. What forbade
her then to be frank with me if not her guilt—
the plain truth as she stated it so defiantly, and
with such amazing courage ?

She was guilty ; there could not be a doubt
of it. That little schoolgirl with the big, staring
eyes, and the tongue which babbled of chocolate
and the red lips ripe for kisses ; she was a
criminal deserving of any fate that might over-
take her. Whatever fortune awaited her in

Russia, it could be of no concern to me. I had
but to forget that I had ever seen her, to obliter-
ate her memory from my mind ; perhaps to suffer
some shame that I had ever listened to her at all.
This I said with conviction and with meaning —
and saying it, it may be for the hundredth time,
I looked down into the street and perceived the
cab for which I had been waiting.

CHAPTER XVII

THE RED-HAIRED MAN

IT was there, sure enough, and very different
from the cab my imagination had been expecting
all the afternoon. For, firstly, it was a cab with
natural wood wheels and quite a showy horse in
its shafts. And then the blinds were not drawn
for the simple reason that the shutters were
down, while the red-haired man had but a few
scattered tufts of hair, and these were as grey as
they were sandy. Not going at a gallop, as I
had expected (foolishly, it would appear), the
fellow drove the horse at an ambling trot towards
the Central Station ; and although his face would
have convicted him in any court, he seemed no
more concerned than an Irishman driving a pig
to a fair. This I noticed as the carriage went by ;
but it had not gone a dozen yards before my
hand was upon the bell: nor thirty when a
servant answered my ring.

" For me, sir ? "

" You will take that to the Gendarmerie
immediately. Mr. Cavanagh left instructions ? "

" Yes, sir ; I understand."

The man wore the hotel uniform, but I do
not remember that I had seen him before. When

he was gone, some half an hour passed and found
me still watching at the window. That Mr.
Cavanagh himself would soon return to the hotel
I had no doubt; and half an hour latter he
appeared, dressed apparently for motoring, and
insistent upon my accompanying him. When I
told him of the letter, he dismissed the subject
as one already dealt with, and of no further
concern to him.

"I am here in answer to it, Ingersoll. Take
your travelling coat and a scarf. We are going
out, and we may be late."

"Then we go in the car?"

"It is at the door waiting for us."

I would put no further questions, and we went
out immediately. A big Renault, one of the
20-30's then just on the market, stood purring at
the steps of the hotel. I noticed, much to my
amazement, that it was driven by the same man
who had taken me from London to Cambridge.
Why we were going, or whither, Mr. Cavanagh
did not think fit to tell me. Not less anxious
than he had been at lunch, he drew the hood of
his long coat well over his head, and put on
goggles before entering the car; while the driver
handed me a pair that I might imitate him.
Without another word spoken, we began our
journey, making, as far as I could judge, for the
Ostend gate and the sea. And in ten minutes
the town of Bruges lay behind us, and with a
sudden right about we began to skirt it to the

northward, as though we would drive to Brussels and not toward Ostend at all.

" You find the Belgian *pavé* detestable, Ingersoll ? "

" Detestable, that isn't quite the word."

" But in our case secure. Did the innocent lady in the prison tell you how uncomfortable and dangerous it would be to travel over this road with explosives in the carriage ? "

"I don't remember that we discussed abstract questions."

" She found you highly volatile, no doubt. You must write an article on 'Women in the Social Revolution' when you get back. Show how easily they become the friends and the slavish advocates of the worst ruffians in Europe. Say that their natural qualities of truth and fidelity are debauched by this sham sentiment of freedom until they become the greatest liars and the most reckless criminals the world has ever known. I wouldn't spare them. They are more difficult than the men ; and God knows the men are difficult enough."

"I will write the article. You quite convinced me this morning, Mr. Cavanagh."

"I am glad of it. What we are now going to see will help you in another way—if we are quite in time, Ingersoll ; if nothing stands between us and many lives that are well worth saving—as life commonly is, by the way."

He had my interest in his net, and he knew

L

it. I could see him looking at me with half
closed eyes as he was wont to look when much
excited by that which he said.

" Then the Antwerp horror is going to be
repeated, Mr. Cavanagh ? "

" I think not, if we are in time. Pray to
God that we are in time, Ingersoll. Imagine
that your own flesh and blood are, well, say
in the afternoon express from Brussels. Tell
yourself that three or four human devils are lurking somewhere upon the line to prevent the train
reaching its destination. I'll just put it to you
that the woman you love may be arriving to-night
and you are thinking of all her home-coming
means to you. She does not come. There
are telegrams at the station, whispers, going
to and fro of officials. The truth leaks out.
Europe has been impressed again. A lesson
has been taught to kings and rulers. How ?
Through you—by something that is brought to
your home, something that will never move or
speak again. You are a lover, and Europe is
nothing to you. I'll put it no plainer. Would you
thank a man who hunted the ruffians down ; would
you cry 'Assassin' if he showed you their dead
bodies and not the others ? There's something
for a paper, by-and-by—when I am dead perhaps
—who knows ? But yours is the pen. I knew
it when I had read a hundred lines of your work
in the *Quarterly*. Yours is the pen, and you will
be my advocate. Good God, how the car crawls !

But it's my fault; we mustn't go faster. We are before our time as it is."

The inconsequent change of subject, as you will perceive, betrayed a man face to face with many conflicting emotions. I felt no call at the moment to respond to his indirect appeal; and it was very evident that he expected no response. We were now upon a great flat marshland, stretching away unbroken to an horizon of fleecy cloud. Bruges lay upon our right hand, its monstrous church spires dwindling as we left them still further behind us. So far as I observed it all, the colour tone of this monotonous picture was just that diminishing green which Claude has so finely expressed in his landscapes. Vastness the scene conveyed, and upon vastness an impression of spotless white farm-houses and stunted pollards by the waterside and countless mills; a fertile land snatched from the sea, but still paying tribute through its many canals and sluggish rivers. And across this seemingly measureless plain we went at a very crawl, knowing that many lives depended upon our discretion (for that was clear now to me), and waiting, as I imagined, until night should befriend our movements and speed be no longer a danger.

In this latter surmise I was not mistaken. We rested nearly two hours that afternoon at a beerhouse some fifteen kilomètres from Bruges. When the sun had set, and but a glimmer of twilight remained, we were on the road again, this time at the best speed of which our splendid car was capable. For half an hour we raced on towards Brussels; then stopped as suddenly, and, wheeling from the highway into a spacious farmyard, we descended. I perceived that the moment for action had come. This was the time, and this was the place.

"Leave your wraps, Ingersoll; we are going to walk."

"Far, sir?"

"A mile or less. Take this; you may want it."

He passed a revolver to me, and I saw that every chamber was loaded. Hastily thrusting it into the side pocket of my coat, I followed him through the deserted farmyard, and passing the house and the orchard behind it, the red signal lights of the Brussels railway came suddenly to my view; and I knew that our journey would take us, not upon the high road, but upon the glistening metals before me. So much he told me as he opened the orchard gate; but he could not conceal his anxiety from me.

"We shall walk at the foot of the embankment until I give you the word. Then do what you see me do. I trust you, Ingersoll."

"I hope so, sir."

There was good grass at the foot of the embankment, and we walked well. By here and there, where canals crossed the waste, we were compelled to climb up to the track above and crawl, hand and foot, across the parapets. A goods train passed us rumbling on towards Brussels, but neither driver nor fireman perceived us. When we made a halt at last, I was in the shadow of a signal-box, whose bright lights stood out in the darkness as the beacon of a harbour. I observed that a little river or canal dipped under the rails immediately beneath the signal-box, and was crossed by a plank bridge, the road leading to a farm-path beyond. But more I had not time to observe, for Mr. Cavanagh went suddenly upon his hands and knees, and I imitated him immediately. Thus we crawled up to the very signal-box.

" Stay here, Ingersoll ; if a man appears on the line, shoot him without challenge. You understand—he will be here to destroy the night express — shoot him wherever you see him."

He gave me no time to reply, but went on immediately, crouching past the box, into the shadows. And there was I alone, squatting upon the grass of the embankment, the night breeze singing in the wires above me ; the lights flashing in the darkness, a pistol in my hand, a whirr of sounds in my astonished ears. For I believed, or thought to believe, that I could never do what he had asked me to do. To shoot a man down in cold blood, whatever the circum-

stances, seemed to me so dreadful a thing that
my very fingers turned to ice upon the pistol.

Upon the other side, came the thought, no
less terrible, that the oncoming express might
be saved by this supreme sacrifice of my
principle. I could depict it as it would pass—
a stream of lights through the darkness, a comet
of the mists, thundering above me. Good God!
to what madman's trap or trick, to what insanity
of teaching or of creed. The suspense, above
all, was horrible. I watched the line as though
it would create figures for my undoing. Every
shadow had the shape of a man stooping to the
rails. The wires above droned a constant
warning. I thought to hear steps about me,
and at this my fingers closed upon the pistol
bolt and mechanically I worked the trigger.
Irony, in truth, if I must shoot in self-defence!

I had seen nothing more of Mr. Cavanagh
during these long moments; nor did I see him
again until the affair was over. As to that
which actually happened, I must speak first of
the appearance of three men in the field below,
at the gate of the little bridge which crossed the
canal or river. They loomed up suddenly, without any sound of footsteps, or a single word
spoken; and I saw them stand all together at
the bridge and consult apparently in whispers.
When they had come to a decision, one of them
began to crawl up the bank (but not upon my
side of the box), and having reached the top,

he disappeared instantly from my view. And now it came to me that these three were intent upon gaining command of the signals, and that it was for this very reason that Mr. Cavanagh had brought me to the place. I could well imagine that if they planned a mischief to the express, they desired as much grace as might be to permit of their escape; and when I remembered that the man had gone into the signal-box, and that Mr. Cavanagh was certainly there before him, then, I say, every nerve in my body began to tingle, and my breath came and went as though I had run a race.

What had happened; what did the continuing silence mean? I heard no cry; I could see the signalman quietly working his instruments. The express was already overdue, as the semaphore told me; the men by the bridge had not yet made an end of their close talk together; but, presently, one of them whistled softly and, being unanswered, whispered to his companion and deliberately took something from the inner pocket of his coat.

With this, he set out to cross the bridge and, as it appeared, to gain the track some hundred yards or so from the place where I stood. What made him halt at the outset I do not know; but halt he did and rested while a man might have counted ten. And, while he halted, I heard for the first time that droning hum upon the metals which told of an

approaching train, that weird, unmistakable
message of the lines which no ear, trained or
untrained, can quite ignore.

The express, I said, was approaching ; there
stood the man with something which his hands
concealed ; he took a stride across the bridge,
halted again, went on once more, and then
with a loud cry, the planks beneath snapping
suddenly, he fell headlong into the canal.

Now, as you will perceive, all this happened
as in a lurid instant of time, too brief to permit
of any clear impressions, too terrible to be
lightly recalled. That which astonishes me
chiefly is the vividness with which certain
details are still to be remembered. Perfectly
well do I recollect how the man went down,
his hands pressed close to his body, his head
thrown back as though he would keep the water
from his lips, his shoulder leaning toward the
further bank. If he rose to the surface, the
darkness hid him from my sight. I heard no
second cry from him—the fellow on the bank,
running wildly to and fro, did not appear to
make any reasonable effort to save him—there
was no sign from the third of the rogues, who
had entered the signal-box, no commotion
whatever to tell you that a man choked in the
water, and must already be past help.

For my own part, I did not move a step
from the place I had been appointed to guard.
As in a swift vision, I depicted the approaching

express, looking into its crowded carriages, heard once more those earnest words that Jehan Cavanagh had spoken to me. Whatever might happen to a madman down yonder, my duty lay there at my post; and I stood to it, trembling none the less like a man with an ague, and so woefully afraid that I could have shouted for very dread. And as I stood, I saw a man upon the line, running swiftly across from the marsh upon the further side, and I fired my pistol at him—without a challenge, without a question to myself whether it were just to fire or no.

I fired my pistol, I say, and the report of it had not died away when the express went thundering by me, its engine belching cinders aflame, its cab a blaze of light, baggage-wagons, sleeping-cars, dining-cars, saloons—a great fiery trail, with an instantaneous vision of faces by the windows, and lights above and the blue and the green and the gold of panelled ceilings. The silence which fell upon its passing endured for some ten seconds, perhaps. Then as though some expected signal had been given men came running out from every side—armed men turning this way and that, searching the very sleepers, spreading abroad and crying to one another as though some human hunt must begin. I heard the report of pistol shots far away across the fields; a shunting engine, with a saloon attached, approached us upon the down line bringing some twenty gendarmes to the scene.

Then Mr. Cavanagh himself appeared, walking at a rapid pace, the officer saluted him and they fell to earnest talk. But he had not forgotten me, for presently he beckoned me to go to him, and the first word spoken concerned my unlucky pistol shot.

"I must teach you to use the revolver, Ingersoll. If you had been a little cleverer, the greatest scoundrel in Europe to-day would not be still at large. Our old friend Dubarrac, of course."

"Was that Dubarrac who ran by me?"

"It certainly was, and as certainly you missed him. Well, we have done what we could, and these gentlemen must do the rest. We will now return to Bruges, at a little better speed than we came, Ingersoll. The Chevalier is otherwise occupied or we would take him."

"The Chevalier is here then?"

"In the signal-cabin. He has excellent fingers for a tough throat, and there will be another figure in the cells to-morrow. Did you see much of it, Ingersoll—did you follow what took place?"

I told him that I had seen the three men at the bridge and one of them go down.

"But the fellow who entered the cabin I knew would be your affair," said I.

"As you say; but Blondel caught him. We sawed the bridge this afternoon, because it was quite clear that they would not make their

attempt exactly at the box, but a little way
down the line. Of course, they might have
come your way, and then you would have had
a little more to do. I was prepared for that,
but we are rather short-handed to-night, for I
sent twenty men to Madrid only yesterday. In
plain truth, this was unexpected. Had we not
taken your old bearded scoundrel at Bruges,
the train would have gone to Jericho. They
thought the Grand Duke Ivan was in it—the
papers said that he would be. But, you see,
Ingersoll, people are not always where the
papers say they are nowadays."

He was plainly excited; nor did my interest
lag behind his own. And, for that matter, the
scene itself and the business in hand would
have excited any man. Far over the marsh we
could hear the cries of those who hunted out
the rogues. The steaming engine cast a great
blot of crimson light about the place where we
stood; there were soldiers with torches moving
up the line, the red lights of the signals above
us, the stolid face of the signalman whom we
had saved as by a miracle. And we ourselves
were going back—to what?

I did not attempt to answer the question,
but, entering the saloon with Mr. Cavanagh, I
sank back upon the cushions and asked myself
what my thoughts would have been if I had
shot the assassin, Dubarrac, and seen his body
lying stiff between the shining rails.

CHAPTER XVIII

THE special train travelled very rapidly, and we were in Bruges in thirty-five minutes. Mr. Cavanagh, who had left the city secretly, entered it again without any disguise. Whatever rogues it had harboured this morning, clearly it harboured none to-night. Our saloon pulled up at the chief platform, and we alighted without hesitation. I saw by the station clock that it was nearly nine, and I remembered, as he remembered, that we had not dined.

" Eat when you cease to think, Ingersoll," he said, " it is a golden rule. Never trust an after-dinner judgment, especially one concerning women. I have eaten little to-day, and now I remember that I am hungry. Let us go to the buffet ; the food here will not hurt us. And we can look in at the theatre afterwards.

I made no comment, and we entered the buffet and got a tolerable basin of soup, a cutlet, and an excellent bottle of white Bordeaux. Mr. Cavanagh's ability to rid himself of the aftermath of circumstances has always amazed me, and never more so than upon this occasion at Bruges.

172

Not a word would he speak of that which he had done or of its consequences. He might have been a traveller determined upon enjoyment, yet a little jaded with it all. If I learned anything of his talk, it was that he contemplated an early journey to Spain, and wished me to go with him.

"Perhaps you would enjoy yourself more, Ingersoll," he added, "if we could step over to yonder platform and take the night express to Vienna. There is one, I remember, which follows the Brussels fast at half-past nine. Could we go by it, I would show you why Vienna is the most delightful city in Europe, though your countrymen often find it the slowest. But I must be in Madrid directly; it is imperative, I fear."

I told him that I would willingly accompany him, whatever his destination. Never before had I been conscious of such a willingness to serve him or of such pride in his service. A psychologist might have told me that the pistol I had fired at his bidding was a mental assent to his claims upon my fidelity. Dimly, but surely, it came to me that he was a great man who, rightly or wrongly, believed that he had a monumental work to do in the cause of humanity and of man's liberty. His very courage won upon my devotion as nothing else could have done.

"I have always desired to see Spain, Mr. Cavanagh," was my next remark.

"I don't wonder, Ingersoll. We go there with the curiosity that takes men to the bedside of a dead bishop. Spain is of yesterday—the mitre, the cope, the stole are there, but the body of the Archpriest is buried. I could show you many things in Spain, if I had the leisure. Perhaps we can find the time when the Palace has done with us. Meanwhile, we must be very busy to-morrow, writing a full account of all that we have done in Bruges—not even forgetting your bewitching Pauline at the Palais de Justice. You must write the story of her crime as I shall dictate it to you, and then of this affair. But I will not speak of it to-night; why should I, when there is good wine in the glass ? "

He broke off with a rough gesture, and lighted a cigar. I could see through the window of the buffet, that the Vienna express was just due, and that the customary bustle of departure had begun. With ringing of bells and alarums of voices the gold-laced officials exhorted the people to advance or to keep back. Presently, a huge ten-wheeled locomotive steamed into the station ; a shimmer of crimson light glimmered upward fantastically, and the glow from the furnace shone upon the faces of the men.

When the signal for departure was made, the express did not leave at once, but drew up at the far end of the platform while a shunting engine backed a single and very dingy carriage to the rear baggage van. This decrepit vehicle—third-class

and with hard wooden seats—was dimly lighted
by an old-fashioned oil lamp, and had no glass
windows whatsoever. By the merest chance in
the world, I caught a glimpse of its passengers
—two police officers and my little schoolgirl
from the Palais de Justice. Had my own sister
been the prisoner of these men, I do not think
that the shock could have been sharper or the
scene more pathetic.

She was going to Russia, then, the child
whose sad eyes had made that dire appeal to me
this very morning, the child I had held for a
brief instant in my arms, telling her madly that
I loved her. She was going back to the monsters
at Baku—good God! to what! My blood raced
through my veins at the thought. Not for an
instant had the reality of it come home to me
until I saw her there, the prisoner of these men,
without one friend in all the world. And at this
thought all the scene went black before my eyes
—station and people, the flickering lights, the
room about me. She was going to be flogged—
perhaps worse, by the police of Baku—and this
morning she had babbled to me of love with my
chocolates in her hand!

Mr. Cavanagh touched me upon the shoulder,
and I looked up quickly. The train had left the
station, the silence of night had come down upon
the place. But I saw only the black eyes of the
man looking into my own, and heard but his
angry words.

"My God, Ingersoll," he cried in my ear,
"then you don't believe her guilty after all!"
I did not answer him. For an instant he
stood, irresolute, watching me. And then, with
the kindest gesture imaginable, he said :
"I will think of this, Ingersoll, I will remember it. Let us go now, for we have our work to
do."

CHAPTER XIX

UPON THE PLAZA DE TOROS

WE arrived at Madrid three days after the episode at Bruges, and went at once to an apartment in the Calle de Alcalá. I knew nothing of the business which carried Mr. Cavanagh into Spain and had no curiosity to inquire. This swift current of a changing life we were leading suited itself admirably to my mood. It mattered nothing to me whether we were in Spain or St. Petersburg, in Europe or America. I had learned to live as one following some great campaign— leading me I knew not whither, but certainly to great issues.

There was a Doctor James waiting for us in the Spanish capital, and he, I learned, had come from Cambridgeshire—doubtless with news of the unhappy lady I had discovered there. Whatever his tidings were they gave considerable satisfaction to my patron, who took an early opportunity of telling me that the Doctor was a worthy man who should not have been the mere country practitioner that he was.

"He is an odd creature, Ingersoll, and you must deal kindly with him. I think he knows

more about medicine than the average—but that
is little enough. He will tell you much of the
service he saw at a small town in India with an
impossible name. A chief, I understand, was
wounded in the hand on that occasion, but
James received such a shock that it killed his
poor wife. Be a little patient with him, for
he will amuse you——"

"A little patient, Mr. Cavanagh——"

"Yes, with his dead wife at any rate. He
brings me very good news from the Fen, and
I am grateful to him. Have you ever thought,
Ingersoll, what a splendid thing it is to go
through life bearing good news to your friends?
Remember it when you find all else stale, flat
and unprofitable. Carry the good tidings—
better still, seek them out that you may carry
them."

We were interrupted at this moment by the
return of Dr. James himself, a fat, florid man
with abundant sandy hair, a heavy jowl and an
enormous professional waistcoat. His hands, I
noticed, were thick and soft ; his nails white but
overgrown. He wore old-fashioned plaid trousers
and a shiny black frock coat. When he spoke,
his talk leaped up like a torrent, and even in his
periods of silence, his eloquence still appeared to
bubble.

"Your friend, Cavanagh ?—then my friend
he is to be sure. Let me look at you, young
man—why, the very living image of Maurice

Kirkpatrick, who was shot at Shaikawati. Never dare I tell my poor wife about that— the shock would have killed her. I'm glad to meet you, sir—we are to slay bulls together this afternoon—let us begin by knowing each other well."

He shook my hand for above a minute, while I turned to Mr. Cavanagh.

"I have never seen a bull-fight," said I.

To this, however, the doctor answered—

"Then brace yourself up, my boy, and see one now. When I was at Shaikawati, young Ned Forrester, the lancer, went into a dead faint because I asked him to hold the leg we amputated. Never saw such a thing—and a pretty leg too. He got the Victoria Cross afterwards for saving half of John Morland, of the Manchesters. Poor John, a big shot cut him clean in two—couldn't have been done better at Bart.'s; but you see Ned saved the wrong half, for we couldn't bring John's legs to life. Never dare I tell my poor wife that—the shock would have killed her."

"She must have been a nervous lady," I ventured to remark.

The idea drove him to a frenzy.

"Nervous, sir—when I was in action at Shaikawati she called fifteen times every day at the War Office and five times at night. There's devotion for you. They reported me wounded, and it killed her. Poor thing. I was in England three months afterwards, as sound as I am this day."

"Then you weren't wounded, Dr. James?"

He stared at me aghast.

"Not wounded, sir! Why, I had a ball through the lobulus quadratus and a sword cut which touched the inferior vena cava. Not wounded, sir!"

Mr. Cavanagh fortunately saved me from further reproach upon this very delicate matter, and we all went down to breakfast. Directly the meal was done and we had taken our coffee, carriages came to take us to the Plaza de Toros, and I set out to see my first bull-fight. This was something that, despite my English prejudices, I very much desired to see. No man can write justly of other nations until he knows the truth about them—and nothing is more difficult to be learned by a foreigner than the truth about the Spanish bull-fight. So I set out with great expectation, Mr. Cavanagh in the carriage with me and the loquacious doctor at his side.

Remember that it was a burning hot day of July, and although we had the hood of the carriage up to protect us from the sun, never have I known such torrid heat. As for the scene in the Calle de Alcalá itself, that defied all restrained description. A very saturnalia had already begun to be celebrated upon that commonly dignified thoroughfare. Every variety of conveyance that the memory might recall, from

the ancient calesas with wild drivers running at
their side to the most modern of automobiles
with stately hidalgos for their passengers, served
those who were going to the fight. And what a
shrieking, roaring, lusting mob it was! How
the bright colours, the yellow, the crimson, the
Moorish greens showed up against the background
of the stately white houses! For a truth, we
seemed to be caught up by some mighty human
stream, alive with the livid faces of those who had
forgotten all else but the blood-lust.

"A wonderful thing, Ingersoll," said Mr.
Cavanagh as we went, "that this can be after
nineteen hundred years of Christianity. But,
remember, the same desire lies at the heart of all
the Celts. If civilisation keeps it under for the
most part, it is by brute force and not by teaching. These Spaniards at least are honest. They
do not prate of the Millennium and then cut off
twenty thousand heads by way of illustration.
Judge them by the light of the facts—not with
your English eyes."

"Exactly what I would have said," chimed
in Dr. James, "in Shaikawati, they used to cut
off your head to prevent your catching the fever.
But they meant well, sir—they meant devilish
well. Look at that fellow down there beating
the girl with the whip. He means well, and will
go to Mass on Sunday. Who are we to judge
him? In England we should like to punch his
head—in Spain we remember than he carries a

knife and that we have no antiseptics at hand.
Let us be cosmopolitan and discreet."

I looked down at his words, and there, sure
enough, a doughty young Spaniard had just
finished lashing a little Spanish girl with a heavy
whip. No one interfered; no one remarked the
circumstance. This multicoloured crowd pressed
on headlong as though the very moments were
precious. Commingled in one panting democracy of lust were rich and poor, soldier and
civilian, priest and layman. Those who fell
were trodden upon and spurned. The dust rose
in blinding clouds ; the sun shone intolerably as
though to search out the mad passions of
men and to inflame them. In truth, it remained
a miracle that so many arrived at the amphitheatre at all, and when we three climbed at last
to the security of our own box, I seemed to have
escaped from a dreadful rout and to have left a
pursuing army at the gates.

This bull-ring at Madrid is a municipal affair,
and does not possess, they tell me, the splendour
of the amphitheatres of the south, especially
those of Seville and Granada. Knowing but the
one, I am unable to pronounce an opinion. The
ring which I visited appeared to be of great size,
and the seats and boxes round about, built up in
the manner of our circuses, would accommodate
some fourteen thousand people. We ourselves
had a little box near to that reserved for the
Royal party, and our Boletin de Sombra declared

it to be as much in the shade as the building permitted. For that matter we had a most excellent view of the whole ring, and I readily confess that the brilliancy of the scene both surprised and delighted me. These are not the days of the mantilla in Spain, and yet the old picturesque national dress was by no means lacking to the arena; and I beheld swarms of jaunty ruffians who seemed to have stepped out of the picture books of a hundred years ago. These were all crowded upon the lower benches, while above them in the boxes were the noblest women in Spain, dressed as Vienna or Paris had taught them to dress, and accompanied by those puny cavaliers in blue and silver, who are never tired of telling you that they are the salt of the earth. When I add that there were priests and even monks among the number of spectators, and that precisely at two o'clock the Royal box alone remained untenanted, you will have some idea of the picture as I beheld it upon that intolerable day in Madrid.

"Will the King be here?" Dr. James asked me as we sat down and unstrapped our glasses.

I told him that I had not the remotest idea and turned to Mr. Cavanagh for an opinion.

" Do they expect the King, Mr. Cavanagh? "

" They did expect him, Ingersoll, but he is not coming. The Marquis of Mercia is the President for the day."

"But I know that the King is in Madrid," persisted the doctor.

Then a smile crossed Mr. Cavanagh's face, and he merely shrugged his shoulders. For me a look was sufficient. I knew that he himself had prevented the King coming.

"Keep your eyes on the Royal box when the Marquis enters," he whispered to me presently, "you will see a girl dressed all in white with a great pink feather in her straw hat. Somewhere below, a man will make a signal to her. Tell me if you see them, Ingersoll—but it won't be just yet."

The mob below was all expectancy by this time, chatting, perspiring, laughing, and even shouting. Over in the sun the thieves and wastrels of Madrid sang filthy songs, or exchanged raucous witticisms with their comrades who were at play in the sandy ring. Presently a trumpet sounded from the Campos Elisees outside, and the Marquis of Mercia, accompanied by a suite of gaily-dressed officers and smiling women, entered the box, and instantly made a signal to the alguaciles below to clear the ring. If you have seen the police of London trying to keep the peace in Piccadilly Circus upon a night of public rioting, or the park-keepers chasing roughs from the frozen Serpentine when the parks are to be closed, this business which the Spaniards call the *despejo* will be readily understood. What shouting, oaths, and horse-play attended the *mêlée*, it would be waste of time to chronicle. I remember only that the ring at length was cleared and that mounted police instantly heralded the Procession, which, surely, was one of the gayest things a man may ever live to see. And first a scene of dazzling colour as the picadors on their sorry Rosinantes came ambling into the ring and showed their tawdry silken jackets to the multitude. Lances, with pennants streaming, are lifted as they ride; their legs are swathed in leather and iron as though they were to play upon an American football field; their nags would, perhaps, fetch three pounds apiece, and even that would be an extravagant price. But you do not look at the horses when there is so much else to see; and the chulos, who contribute not a little to the glory of the spectacle, demand their share of your attention. These fellows have gay cloaks and the silk stockings our grandfathers used to admire when Figaro took them to the Opera; they will fling their cloaks in the face of the bull just now when our friends, the picadors, are hard pressed. And upon their heels tread the banderilleros with their wicked darts, to be had by the bull for the asking when the right time comes. Last of all is that very flower of Spain, the matador—the killer; my lord of the people's creed, who stalks proudly at the head of a team of mules and will be a hero or a forgotten martyr when half an hour is gone.

The mules trotted out of the arena to the jingling of many bells, and the President in the Royal box immediately threw down a key into the hat of one of the aiguaciles. Then a trumpet sounded loudly, and that mighty audience settled down as to a banquet long awaited. Far away across the amphitheatre a gate had been opened in the wooden wall and a dark aperture revealed. The players in this tragic and cruel game ranged themselves about the ring as fielders upon a cricket pitch—the picadors nearest to the barrier and the oncoming bull, the chulos at the back awaiting their turn. Then, for the briefest instant, a hush fell, and upon that the splendid horns and the noble head of a Jamara bull appeared above the sand; and the superb creature, defiant, perplexed, and half blinded by the glare, stood awaiting his aggressors.

We should have called him a small bull in England, I suppose ; but the power of neck and limbs none could deny. By what means they forced him into the arena I could not say, but out he came presently, trotting for a few steps and then halting again as though to spy out the scene. Fierce cries from the benches, the rattling of sticks and the cat-calls of the rabble were needed to awake him to any overt act ; but when he did awake it was instantaneously as though a lance had already pricked him. In truth, he charged so swift at the nearest picador that both the assault and the escape were done with almost before I realised what was happening.

Just a wild rush, the flash of a lance in the sunlight, a horse adroitly wheeled about upon a tight rein, a crash of good horns against the barrier, and there stood my lord the bull, pawing the sand restlessly, and there rode the picador, bowing to the multitude. Henceforth I kept my eyes so closely upon the scene that nothing could escape me. The bull, enraged by the prick of the steel, charged with amazing speed at a second cavalier who had halted upon the sand immediately below our box. I saw the blade flash as before, and then, in a twinkling, man and bull and horse rolled on the ground together —and such a roar of delight arose as must have been heard at the other side of the city.

The man was down, but the wretched horse lay between him and the terrible horns. It was unendurable, I bear witness, to watch that which followed when the maddened bull thrust deep into the soft body of the screaming animal. Again and again the horns pierced the gaping flank, and at every blow the quivering flesh was ripped anew. Those who have heard the screams of a horse in agony agree that there is no more pathetic cry under the sun; but to these Spaniards it appeared to be an ecstatic harmony. They stood up in their excitement—women, ay, and children craned their necks to lose nothing of the bloody spectacle. All the revolting horror which I experienced was for them a sentiment to be derided. Had they not paid their money for just such an exhibition ?

Chulos now occupied themselves with the dying horse, while the bull was after one of them head down, nostrils distended, the sand flying from his hoofs, his eyes crimson with fury. Headlong for the wooden barrier the fellow went, but it seemed impossible that he would gain it. The half of a false step, one instant of uncertainty would have written his epitaph in letters of blood. So close, indeed, did the bull press him that the stroke, which should have tossed him, touched his very clothes as he leaped the barrier. And this was plainly to the disappointment of the mob—their chilly applause said unmistakably, " Would that he had gored you."

" Well," said I to Dr. James, " there's a good ' left-wing ' lost, at any rate. That fellow ran like a hare. If the bull had centred a second earlier, he would have scored a goal. I wonder if our football professionals would like this for a change. We are getting a little tired of drawn games, and the referee no longer wears armour. If they popped him in the ring here, he would have to do something for his money. And think of the flagman's job ! "

" My dear friend, at least there would be the decorations—look at those fellows with the darts. I do believe they intend to make the bull a present of them."

I turned my eyes to the arena again and there, sure enough, were the banderilleros ready with their wicked darts. The bull now stood almost beneath the President's box; his flanks heaved; the foam dripped from his protruding tongue; his head was poised in an attitude of singular majesty and grace. For his part, I doubt not that he would have been well content to return to the plains of the Jamara and leave these savages to go as they came; but his death was foreordained; nothing could save him; no down-turned thumb here asked the pity of a tired Cæsar—the Spaniard remained insatiable in his blood-lust. And so the majestic beast permitted the nimble ruffians to approach him. Brave to the point of wonder, quick as the lightning, they carried themselves with the assurance of a tight-rope walker, while step by step they drew towards their quarry, who watched them as a lion may watch a poaching jackal. Here time stood to an instant the arbiter of life and death. Let them delay but a second, bungle by a thumb's breadth, and their fall is sure. So they come up with every nerve at a tension. The bull, doubting and per-plexed, at length lowers his head to charge. And in that swift moment the deed is done. One upon either side as though the very distance were measured to a nicety, the darts are planted in the terrible neck. The banderillos flutter as the bull bellows and charges in his agony. But my gentlemen of the cloaks have stepped nimbly

aside, and the pursuit is elsewhere—the picture
that of a raging beast tearing, foaming, stamping
to shake the steel from his flesh and rid himself
of this intolerable burden.

And now we are to have the last act in
this sorry comedy of the abattoir. The matador,
the tawdry butcher in the gay clothes, the man
whom Spain worships above any of her heroes,
he is to kill the bull for us that the arena may
be cleared and the play recommenced. To-day,
the first of these monstrous gladiators is a fellow
by name Gregorio de Prado, aforetime a common
herdsman on the hills about Granada, now a
belarded image of price and insolence and jaunty
courage, smothered in spangles like a circus rider.
The fellow's weapon is a sword, and nothing but
a sword ; but he approaches the bull too leisurely
for the taste of my gentlemen upon the benches,
and cat-calls are heard and the rattling of sticks.
Let Gregorio beware, for he is plainly out of
favour. This I saw with some hope for the bull
—a vain hope, as I was perfectly well aware.

The man, I say, was annoyed by the mob's
impatience, and resented it. His steps became
halting—he cast a swift look of disdain toward
the crowded benches—then advanced once more
until he stood within a yard of the wretched
bull, who had now scarce strength enough to
charge. At this fateful moment the outcry
became deafening ; orange skins, water bottles,
even stones, were thrown down upon the sand as

though to mark the extremities of contempt—the
chiavata was rattled ceaselessly. Meanwhile the
bull stood motionless—had he charged there
would have been one matador the less in Spain
that night.

I have learned since I witnessed this debasing
spectacle, that it is a matador's business to read
the character of his bull—whether he be fierce or
cunning, a rogue at the game or an honest actor
who will come, neck down, to the sword's point.
Gregorio, angered by the rabble's contempt, did
not pursue his studies by the light of old experience, but in answer to the mob's imperious will.
He should have waited yet awhile—allowed the
bull to charge him—for this was no blind fool of
a beast, but a wily customer, dodging and twist-
ing like a Rugby forward, and coming anywhere
but to the place you looked for him to be. And
thus he foiled the angry Gregorio, bringing the
man to the attack while he should still have been
defender, and luring him at last to the fatal
thrust which missed by a hair's-breadth that
vulnerable flesh above the shoulder blade, where
alone the death stroke may be placed.

It was all over and done with before a man
could have counted five. I saw the blade gleam
in the sunlight—the dramatic attitude of the
matador, his body bent slightly backward, making one line from the angle to the crown of his
head; his left arm lifted as a fencer's; his right
leg drawn back. Before him stood the bull

with bent head and neck twisted slightly to one side—and thus for a brief instant they contended. But the keen blade had struck the bone of the shoulder, and turning with a loud bellow, the brute caught Gregorio upon his horn and instantly transfixed him.

And what of the people when this befell? Were words of pity spoken, of regret or shame? Nothing of the kind. They began to howl as wild beasts about a carcase. Every time the bull thrust his horn through the quivering body, at every blow of his savage head, while he trampled the battered shape and literally tore it to pieces, there were ruffians to applaud him, fine figures of men to hiss the dead, even those who cried, "Viva Toro!" Not for one moment did this outcry abate while the body of the dead matador still lay upon the sand. The blood-lust had been gratified, and that which followed after was a very pæan of gratitude. I saw children with smiles upon their faces, harridans mouthing as though demented, bony fingers trembling with delight. I heard a great buzz of sound arise as they carried Gregorio away, and the jingling mules again trotted across the arena. And then, and then only, I came back to my senses and heard Dr. James speaking to me.

"Is that enough, Mr. Ingersoll?"

"Quite enough, doctor."

"Then had we not better tell our friend so?"

I looked at Mr. Cavanagh and the expression
on his face amazed me. Not yet had he lifted
his eyes from the place where Gregorio fell.
The nerves of his hands were twitching and his
face was ghastly white. When I touched him
upon the shoulder, he started as a man from
sleep.

"Well, Ingersoll?"

"Shall we not go, Mr. Cavanagh?"

"Would you be better for going, Ingersoll?"

I do not know what came to me, but I
answered him frankly, "We should both be
better for going."

He stood up at once—I think he reeled
slightly as we left the box—but it was quite
evident to me that I had told him nothing but
the truth.

For the blood-lust had fallen upon him also,
and my words had made him ashamed.

N

CHAPTER XX

A CLOSER acquaintance with Dr. Luther James convinced me that he was a very remarkable person, who had been born out of his generation. Fifty years ago he would have joined admirably in the common diversions of that plausible mediocrity, the mid-Victorian paterfamilias. I think that his drugs were half a century old and his ideas of surgery as primitive. Why Mr. Cavanagh brought him into Spain at all I could not say, unless it were for the safety of the patient he had left behind him at the Fen. And here at Madrid, if you please, I must find myself alone with him and dine in his company at the Restaurant Viviana, of what he was pleased to call " French fallals."

" What I want in life, Mr. Ingersoll, is very little," he said when we set out, " give me a good round of roast beef, a bit of crackly pork to follow, some Stilton cheese, and a pear, and I'll complain to no man. Of course, it would be all the better for just a drop of the sparkling and a pair of black eyes on the opposite side of the board—but that is between you and me and the bed-post. I should never have said it in my poor wife's time.

194

Why, she wouldn't let me see any patient under forty-three, and didn't much care about 'em under sixty. And just to think she's gone, and I might propose to any of these merry señoritas and nobody go and tell her about it. Eh, Ingersoll, it's the people who go and tell 'em about it who do the mischief in this world, isn't it?"

I admitted that it was; but being anxious to know why Mr. Cavanagh had not joined us in the excursion, I tried to find out what he knew about it. This was a vain quest. It became quite plain to me that he knew absolutely nothing concerning my patron's intentions.

" He's gone to see the King, I believe," was the extent of his information. " You know he's very rich, Mr. Ingersoll. I pity him in his misfortune—though I do believe the lady will recover. At any rate I've done what I could for her, and you can't expect a doctor to do more. Is this the Café, do you think? Dear me, what a number of lovely women to be sure—and they told me Madrid was empty!"

" So it is," said I, " except for an odd million or so. Just the way London is empty in August. These people, I am told, drove in from the hills to see the bull-fight. It's a local Festa, or something—a day out of the ordinary, and so, I suppose, we are in luck. But, of course, the Court's not here."

" Their misfortune, Mr. Ingersoll "—and at

this he laughed so loudly that half the people in
the restaurant turned their heads. " We would
have dined with 'em and told 'em our best stories.
Will you order the chop-chop, or shall I ? Perhaps you'd better do it while I look at the women.
God bless me, what should I have done if my
poor wife had been here ? "

" She'd have blindfolded you with a serviette.
Shall we take some Bisque soup and just a plain
dish afterwards ? · The prices here would break
Vanderbilt, if this card is to be believed."

"Ah, but don't let them sink us—my boy,
Cavanagh's paying. He gave me twenty, and
they're here in my pocket."

" Then let us be reckless—what do you say to
a *sole à la Victoria*, a sweetbread, lamb cutlets and
a duck ? The wine had better be Valdepaenias—
it's the only Spanish wine I know how to ask for.
And all the champagne is sugar-candy. What
do you say, Doctor ? "

" I beg your pardon—a very fine woman to
be sure she is—did you mention the wine ?—ha,
ha, these places make me feel I'm twenty again.
I shall be kissing my hand to her if this goes
on."

" Then you'll certainly be run through the
middle. My dear fellow, you must remember we
are in Spain——"

" In purgatory, if you please. I am always in
purgatory when I see a pretty woman and have
not the honour of her aquaintance."

He laughed uproariously, and upon my word,
I began to be ashamed of him. There is a type
of Englishman who, with harmless intent, invari-
ably plays the fool abroad to the great discredit
of the nation. This worthy man would never
have so behaved at the Savoy—I failed to see
why¸ he should do so at the Café Viviana in
Madrid.

"I don't care a farthing for the Medical
Council," he exclaimed presently, when he had
drunk a very goblet of the rich red Valdepaenias.
"When you are in Spain, do as Spain does."

"But Spain does not stare at pretty women
she does not happen to know."

"Not stare at 'em sir—why, old Colonel
Hartlook, my neighbour at Waterbeach, stared so
hard at a pretty Spaniard in Malaga, that she
left him fifteen thousand pounds. You see, he
was as short-sighted as a mule, and while the old
girl was five-and-fifty, he took her to be twenty-
three. Couldn't back out, Mr. Ingersoll, and
had to play beau sabreur through a hot summer
with a woman almost old enough to be his grand-
mother. Fortunately she died of senile decay,
and he walked off with her money. Don't tell
me not to stare ; I shall throw the Colonel at
you if you do."

Really, the old fool was incurable. He talked
incessantly ; the pitch of his voice rising with
each glass he drained. Presently we had half
the Café looking at us, and what was my astonish-

ment to see the girl in the straw hat and the
great pink feather—the very girl I had been
asked by Mr. Cavanagh to watch during the
bull-fight. In the same moment that I saw her
and remembered, the doctor saw her also, and
began to exclaim upon her beauty.

"Now, that's what I call a thoroughbred," he
said, with a thwack of his heavy fist upon the
table. " Look at the carriage of her—a bit on
the black side, Mr. Ingersoll, and a devil of a
temper, I'll wager. But what's temper matter
when you're leaving the country to-morrow
morning ? That girl has two thousand hidalgos
to her story. You can see it in the way she
squares her elbow. I wonder if there would be
any chance of our getting an introduction."

" What ! " said I, " and three officers of
Hussars with her ! There are shorter cuts to
suicide, doctor."

He admitted it reluctantly.

" The officer of the Hussars is a very unpleasant person—in foreign countries, that is to
say. One of them offered to run me through the
middle in Berlin, merely for telling a lady that
my poor wife was dead. She happened to be
his wife—but that was my misfortune. Well,
well, the world's a funny place, and I should
never trust a girl with eyes like that. Do you
know, I think I've seen her somewhere, and I
can't remember where. Would it have been in
Paris, I wonder ? "

" You saw her this afternoon," said I, "in the
Royal box at the slaughter. She must have
come on here without changing her dress. No
doubt she's staying up in the hills, where all
decent people are at this time of year. Ride
about a hundred miles to-morrow, and you may
discover her address. I should strongly advise
you, meanwhile, to look anywhere but in her
direction. Our friends the Hussars are evidently
resenting your gratuitous admiration."

He turned very pale at this, for I knew him
to be a shocking coward at heart.

" I say, do you think we'd better be leaving ? "

" Well, if you've finished your coffee and have
that note ready."

He got up with astonishing alacrity and
bundled me out of the restaurant—almost as
though the blue Hussars were already upon his
heels. Not until we had entered a cab and were
upon our way to the Summer Garden did he
recover his equanimity.

" A near thing that, Ingersoll," he said,
dropping the prefix for the first time. " Cavanagh
wouldn't be liking us to fight any duels, or that
sort of nonsense."

" Would you be liking it yourself, doctor ? "

" It's in the blood, sir. My father, when he
was doctor to the Embassy at Paris, fought five
Frenchmen and carried three bullets to the day
of his death. We used to hear 'em rattle every

time he went downstairs. The little affair I had
at Shaikawati seems nothing after that, but I
have the mark of it on my back to this day."

"On your back!" cried I, and observing the
slip he flushed like a girl.

"The coward struck me while I was turning
away—this is the Garden, isn't it? I am told
you can see half the pretty women in Spain for
a couple of pesetas. I feel just about two-and-
twenty at this moment."

"And look about five-and-sixty," I added to
myself.

The Summer Gardens offered the usual inane
entertainment which is hashed up in all Continental cities for the benefit of the travelling Englishman and the equally curious son of Chicago.
We listened to some cheap French vulgarity,
bawled by a ruffian with a voice like a bassoon ;
a juggler did feats as old and as simple as Queen
Anne ; a tripping maiden of fifty-three summers,
or thereabouts, told us of love in a lilting strain,
which rattled along like a motor-car. For my
part, not only did the thing become intolerable,
but I had an impulse to return to our apartments which nothing could explain or control.
I felt that I must return—must, for some reason
or other, see Mr. Cavanagh immediately. And
to this impulse I was glad enough to surrender.

"You sit it out," said I to the sandy-haired
Don Juan, who had just told me that his poor
wife would have never survived the evening.

"If you want me to arrange any preliminaries, I shall be round in the Calle de Alcalá. Perhaps you had better buy a guitar in the morning—and a brace of good pistols. But don't consider my feelings, I beg of you."

He said that he would not, and having called my attention to another ancient monument who, he declared, was the very image of his dead wife, and had already smiled twice at him, I left him in the place and returned on foot to our rooms. It would then have been about ten o'clock, and all Madrid was out of doors. The fight, I imagined, was the universal theme of talk, and I pushed my way through excited, laughing throngs to the Calle de Alcalá and the apartments which Mr. Cavanagh had engaged there. Not for a moment did I expect that he would be in when I arrived. The *arrière-pensée* of this visit to Madrid remained a secret which I had not been invited to share. On the whole I was content that it should be so, and I determined to go straight to my room and to bed without any further reflections upon the matter.

Let it be said that the farcical idea of hypnotic suggestion no longer troubled me. I had forgotten all about it directly I quitted the café. Less satisfactory was the reflection that I had failed to remember Mr. Cavanagh's instructions of the afternoon, and had become so immersed in the pitiful drama of the arena that I had forgotten all else. The pretty woman he had wished me to watch, the signal she was to make, the old man who would answer her, they might have never existed so far as I was concerned. And with this, I felt sure Mr. Jehan Cavanagh would charge me. Had he not made so much of the fidelity of his servants! The thought put me to some shame. I determined that I would confess the whole circumstance, hiding nothing, for who could conceal anything from such a man?

Now, this was in my head as I went up the staircase and rang the bell, which brought the sleek valet Edward to the door. In a whisper, very familiar to me, he told me that Mr. Cavanagh had returned and, he believed, was sleeping in his arm-chair.

"But you can creep through without waking him, sir," he went on, "and I don't suppose he'd mind if you did, for he doesn't like sleeping in arm-chairs."

I nodded my head and pushed open the door of our sitting-room very quietly. The bed-rooms, I should tell you, were upon either side of the sitting-room, and had no doors of their own to the main corridor. So, to gain my own room, I must risk waking Mr. Cavanagh, and this I was not at all anxious to do. Very cautiously, therefore, and with a light foot upon the thick carpet, I opened the heavy door and peered in. You shall judge of my astonishment when I beheld, not only Mr. Cavanagh, but one of those very

blue Hussars I had seen not a couple of hours
ago at the restaurant.   The fellow stood within
three yards of my patron's chair—a single reading lamp lighted the great apartment ; there
was not a sound to be heard.

I had entered the room so quietly that the
intruder, intent upon his own task, had no ear
for me.   This, perhaps, is not so very astounding
after all.   When our thoughts are concentrated
upon a single purpose, the senses, which are not
employed upon that affair, play strange tricks
with us.   This soldier, I perceived, needed only
his eyes, and not for one moment did I doubt
his business.   He had come there to kill Jehan
Cavanagh, and had I entered the room two
seconds later he would have effected his purpose.
This much the nervous hand closed about the
butt-end of a revolver—the furtive step, the
halting gait betrayed.   The man stood self-
confessed, an assassin.

You will imagine with what swiftness I
realised the meaning of this strange scene and
the most tragic irresolution which overtook
me as I stood there.   What, in God's name,
should I do ?   A step would have been fatal
to my friend's salvation ; a single cry would
have been his undoing and perhaps my own.   I
thought at one moment of leaping upon the
assassin's back and trusting all to that wild
chance—then, in a flash, I said to myself, " You
must turn out the light ; your hand can reach it ;

you must not move—the other plan will never
do." And, mind you, while all this was being
debated, the unknown soldier crept step by step
toward Mr. Cavanagh's chair; I saw that he
would shoot my patron through the very heart;
and in a moment of overwhelming despair, I
risked all, stepped to the table, snatched up a
heavy marble paper-weight which lay there, and
flung it at the man. He fell senseless on the
hearthrug, and in the same instant Mr. Cavanagh
awoke and uttered my name.

"Ingersoll! Good God! What is
this?"

"I do not know, Mr. Cavanagh. That man
has a pistol, and I——"

But the words failed me. All the horror
and the truth of it came rushing upon me
overwhelmingly, and believing that I had killed
the man, I found myself sobbing like a child.
And there stood my patron, still regarding me
amazed, and there lay the soldier, his face buried
in the black rug on the hearth and the pistol
still clasped in his nervous hand.

"My poor lad! I am very sorry—and I
understand."

He bent over the prone figure and turned it
about. Making a great effort to recover my
composure, I stood up again and tried to tell him
all. But his quick mind needed no telling. He
understood the circumstance as well as I did.

"There has been great negligence," he said

quietly. " I feared to come to Spain with so
many of my best agents away, but the journey
was necessary. This will never occur again,
Ingersoll, and it will teach me two lessons, the
first of which is wakefulness. Now let us see if
there be any intelligent men left in Spain. Please
to ring the bell twice, Ingersoll. It will be good
for you to be doing something." I rang the bell
as he directed, and the answer to it positively
amazed me. The whole room seemed instantly
to be filled with men—officers of police coming
in like wolves to a carcase. With the chief of
these Mr. Cavanagh exchanged the briefest of
words. I did not understand them, but I
watched while they seized the recumbent figure,
and shaking the man until he opened his eyes,
dragged him brutally from the room. When
they were gone Mr. Cavanagh rang the bell for
Edward, his valet, and told him to bring the
decanters.

" Why did you return so early, Ingersoll ? "
he asked me. " I thought you were going to the
Summer Garden ? "

" We did go, but something compelled me
to return. I fear you would laugh at such an
idea."

He mused an instant, lighting a cigar while
he did so.

" It would be a very foolish man who would
laugh at an impulse," he said presently. " So
you left the worthy doctor and felt compelled to

come here ? The man was in the room when you entered ? "

"Yes; he was standing just by the table. That's the mystery : how did he get in with all those men about ? "

" He got in because they had orders to admit him. Think of it, Ingersoll : I knew he was coming and yet I dozed. Good God ! upon what a thread our fate hangs ! Is there not a moment in every life when this fatal instant of sleep overtakes ? The man was late by half an hour, and I fooled myself into the belief that he had been warned and would not come. But I am not sorry that it has happened. You saved my life, Ingersoll."

" I should be ashamed to make any such claim. I did no more than the first stranger would have done."

" I shall not permit you to say so. Look me in the face, Ingersoll—let me read your eyes— the eyes of the friend who has twice saved me to-day."

" Twice ! "

" You know from what—at the butchery. My God, Ingersoll, if you have been chosen for this to save me from myself after all—to lift me above this—to teach a man to know himself. Did you not speak of impulse ? What impulse is born of itself in this shadow play we call life ? I like to hear of impulse. Let me hear of it every day—the impulse which first called you to me from Cambridge, the impulse which brought you here to-night. Yes, I would hear much of impulse."

He had become strangely excited, pacing to and fro and halting before me when he spoke. When he pressed my hand as he did I believe he had some great story of his own life to tell me, but before he could begin there came a knock upon the door and three police officers entered together. Then a gesture of annoyance crossed his face, and he bade me " Good-night " in a manner that was strangely abrupt.

" Be early to-morrow," he said, " for we go to Barcelona."

And I left him upon that.

CHAPTER XXI

TO BARCELONA AND THE SEA

I HAVE never known Jehan Cavanagh in better
spirits than those which attended our journey to
Barcelona. It is true that we began the day
sadly, but thereafter his good humour was un-
flagging, and I am sure that the worthy doctor
wished he had never been born, so unceasingly
was he chaffed.

I say that we began the day sadly. This is
to tell you that we drove, on our way to the
station, to the old prison by the Puente de
Toledo, and being immediately admitted by the
governor, we discovered, in one of the chilliest
cells that ancient dungeon boasts, the young
soldier who had attempted Mr. Cavanagh's life
yesterday. The nonchalance of this man, his
jaunty air, his impudent boasts that the whole
thing " tired him," could not hide from me the
real dread of death which had overtaken him.
I saw that he was afraid to die, that the tragedy
of his creed now overwhelmed him by its attendant
penalties, and that his own youth called him
pathetically back to the pleasures and friends
he had quitted so madly. When we had left
the prison, I learned that his name was Juan de

Villegas, and that both he and his sister were enrolled in that band of fanatics at Barcelona which numbers the most militant and the most reckless of the Anarchists of Europe.

" I have interceded for the man, and especially for his sister," Mr. Cavanagh told us as we drove away, " but you may imagine what intercession is worth in such a country as this. No mercy will be shown them, I fear. The garotte is already prepared for them both."

I made no answer to this, for a curious circumstance had recurred suddenly to my mind. Dr. James, however, could hardly believe his ears.

" The dark girl with the pink feather in her hat ?—but, Cavanagh, I was on the point of being introduced to her."

" My dear doctor, thank heaven for your prudence. Had you done so, you might wear gyves upon your wrists this morning."

He went on to tell us that fact, which is so very difficult to realise in our own England, that the highest society in Germany, in France, in Italy, and nearly every Continental country is not free from these morbid creatures of decadence, who would recognise no law and by death establish chaos.

" The age fosters the idea which asks, ' Why should other men compel me ? ' " he said. " ' Why should I submit to restrictions once necessary to society as a whole, but now become the

o

instruments of despotism?' The teaching is
too utterly false to justify any comment upon it,
but it is there, and its disciples are becoming
more numerous every day. How to combat it,
the governments have yet to teach us. We
know that like cures like, but this is a maxim
your man in authority will not hear. Let us
suppose, Ingersoll, that I attended the great
Anarchist meeting at Barcelona to-night and
were to toss a bomb among the company, should
I not be practising the revolutionary precept?
Would you call it murder or retribution? I
could show you how to do so with no risk whatever to those who were the ministers of this
brute justice. Would the governments punish
the man or call him a benefactor? You cannot
tell me—the question is that awkward one which
all governments must answer sooner or later.
Look at our contented friend, the doctor. Here
he is, treating the subject as though it were a
thousand miles from his own house. Is he quite
sure that we are not marked men as we ride
to-day? Does he feel quite safe in this carriage?
Credulous and happy state. I wish that I could
share it."

Luther James did not like this at all.

"Do you mean to say that we might be
marked men, Cavanagh?"

"My dear doctor, no one who once looked
into your eyes could ever forget them. You
tried to procure an introduction to the Señorita

Inez de Villegas. How if her friends name you for a spy and stab you to the heart at Barcelona? Could I protect you? God knows, I should be as helpless as a child. And yet here you are humming a tune as though we were both in Trinity Street at Cambridge looking for strawberry jam in a grocer's shop."

"My God, Cavanagh, you make me go hot and cold! This is worse than India. Does the train stop anywhere between here and Barcelona?"

"About two hundred times. You might be assassinated as many."

"I shall speak to the guard——"

"The guard? Is he not the notorious Doacono who led the mob at Barcelona last Easter? If you speak to him, you are a dead man. Calm yourself and read a paper—it doesn't matter that it's in Spanish. You can always get something out of the newspaper if it's no more than the capital names. Light a cigar, man, and look cheerful."

He might as well have asked him to light a beacon on Mont Blanc, so far as I could see. But I confess that Luther James' imbecility made but a poor appeal to me this morning. Knowing the earnestness of Mr. Cavanagh's convictions, his faith in himself and in his mission, this flippant mood said one of two things; either that he would conceal from us how much it had cost him to send Villegas and his sister to the scaffold, or that he had learned to steel himself against all human emotions, and had begun to gratify that blood-lust which I had detected in his attitude at the bull fight. This latter supposition was so horrible that I put it away instantly. It would have made a monster of a man whom I had begun to believe heroic among men, a figure of the world's story, a lonely general fighting in the name of God the legions of murder and of chaos. And to this there was added those secret thoughts of my own which no resolution had extirpated. What of my little schoolgirl? Had I not read of her being at Barcelona in the very house occupied by the Villegas? Their name recalled her own to me. I repeated it bitterly, reflecting upon that which she must have suffered since they carried her from Bruges. Who would dare to say that her white shoulders had not been bared already to the whip?

Of course I said nothing of all this to Mr. Cavanagh. Whatever were the hopes and fears I took with me from Bruges, I had determined that none should be my confidant. Let our exile carry us whithersoever it would, by no freak of possibility could I arrive upon any scene where I might help Pauline Mamavieff or redeem those promises spoken in an instant of boyish chivalry.

Indeed, the very words now made me ashamed, for I was as a man trying to hide some great secret from himself, seeking to justify it by profound argument, covering a treasure in the cloth of self-deceit and declaring that it no longer existed. Had I confessed all I would have said that Pauline's image was before me, waking and sleeping, that my belief in her innocence remained unshaken, perhaps—who knows?—that I would have made any sacrifice to save her.

Let it be sufficient to say of this journey that we arrived in Barcelona very late at night, and went at once upon Mr. Cavanagh's yacht, *Sea Wolf*. Magnificent ship that this was, I saw little of her that night beyond the fine saloon wherein we took supper, and the equally comfortable cabin wherein I was quartered. Luther James, frightened out of his wits, but truculently heroic directly we were safe on board, drank almost a bottle of Scotch whisky to keep up his courage, and then went to bed. Mr. Cavanagh himself, telling me that he had something to say to me, but must first glance at his correspondence, went into his own saloon and left me upon deck to watch the weighing of the anchor and all that orderly excitement which attends a fine ship's departure. We sailed, I think, exactly at midnight, and were but a couple of miles from the shore when that great event befell of which all Europe has talked, an event which must remain for me the most stupendous spectacle my eyes have ever looked upon.

I remember that I was at the taffrail when
the great moment of it came. Barcelona stood
for a spreading fan of dazzling white lights
shining at rare intervals upon the hills but
clustered together at the water's edge. There
was no moon that night, and the sea had hardly
a ripple to mar our wake of foam. Upon the
yacht's decks I remarked the celerity with which
the seamen had settled down to the routine of
their common duties, going and coming with the
leisurely assurance of those who had been afloat
not for half-an-hour, but for a week. A light at
the companion, the glow from the binnacle, the
pretty red and green of our starboard and port
lamps, these added that touch of romance
which is ever associated with a ship's deck at
night.

As for me, I say that I stood by the taffrail,
watching the wake of foam behind us, and
wondering to what new scenes, what fresh
emprise, this strange voyage would carry me.
Whither now, and upon what task of mercy or
revenge ? Never had I so rightly appreciated
Jehan Cavanagh's power or that mastery of men
and of kingdoms he had achieved. Hither,
thither, as the judge of men he went. He had
but to speak, and all obeyed him. His word was
law above that of courts and parliaments. He
came as the saviour of those who abandoned
faith in our common humanity; he went as
one who would receive neither thanks nor

honours. Well might I ask whither and why? The mystery of it fascinated me beyond all experience. My vanity delighted in the thought that I was this man's lieutenant, his trusted servant, his friend. An exaltation of spirit such as I had never known led me to desire new scenes and new perils that I might go with him and prove my devotion.

Now, these were my thoughts when the great event befell. The fearful tragedy in the Rotunda at Barcelona is now the world's history; but I wish to tell you of it as I saw it; out there at sea upon the deck of the yacht *Sea Wolf*. To me it came firstly as a cloud burst, that is to say, the sudden appearance above the water of a mighty crimson cloud, lurid beyond belief and capped by a flame which seemed to cleave the very heavens. Not a sound attended this. Though the whole city was revealed to me in that awful moment, the spires and domes and dominating houses, the hills beyond and all the city's environment, an age passed before the thunder of the report came rolling over the water, attended by its rush of hot airs, its moaning, horrible wind which might have been the death wail. The sea, placid an instant previous, now began to be violently agitated, to fall dead calm again when the rush of air had passed. And then darkness fell, utter, impenetrable, and upon this a crash of sounds terrible beyond words, the echo of shrieks and

cries of agony, the rending of great buildings,
the fearful appeal of those who must die that
chaos might come.

Be assured that I knew nothing of the story
of it as I stood there at the taffrail. Naturally,
as you may suppose, I thought that there had been
an earthquake, and that the leaping tongues of
flame, now to be discerned in many places, were
the unavoidable aftermath of such an act of God
as I had witnessed. In truth it is very difficult
to say what a man's thoughts have been in such
instants of life as this. So far as I remember,
no one upon the yacht's decks showed any
excitement above the ordinary, but that is a
seaman's way, whatever the peril. I recollect
that an old sailor rolled aft and stood by my
side, remarking pleasantly that "there's something queer ashore." The captain of the yacht,
whom I came to know subsequently as Jack
Greenwood, walked to the port side of the bridge
and waited there as though listening. But the
number of our revolutions was not less, nor did
we alter our course a single point. And there
behind us lay that inferno, flames leaping high
above the stricken city, the shrieks of the victims
loud to be heard, the church bells ringing—panic,
I felt sure, everywhere.

"What do you make of it?" I asked the
man who had joined me.

He took a roll of tobacco from a paper and
answered leisurely :

" Why, I make nothing at all, sir—unless the
King of Spain be giving a party."

"Do you think it's an earthquake ? "

" No, I don't, and that's plain, sir. Like as
not, we'd have been pooped if that were an
'arthquake. Skipper wouldn't hold his course
as he's doin', don't fear it, if he'd hev said
'arthquakes. It's a blow up at the arsenal, in
my opinion, and precious lucky you and me
may count ourselves as we 'adn't cleaned ourselves and gone ashore—but here's the guv'nor
comin', and he'll know. They don't have no
ixplosions nowhere, and 'im nothin' to say
about it."

He touched his hat and drew back, detecting
Mr. Cavanagh's quick step upon the companion.
A moment later my patron crossed the deck and
came to my side.

" Well, Ingersoll," he said, in a tone inex-
pressibly sad, " so we have been unable to prevent
it after all ? "

I looked at him in wonder.

" What is it, Mr. Cavanagh ?   What has happened ? "

He took me by the arm and drew me toward
the taffrail.

" There are the friends of your little friend at
Bruges ; they are blowing each other up, Ingersoll, that the Millennium may come.   Do you
remember our jest in the train, that like cures
like, and that authority might some day throw a

bomb amongst those who live by bombs? As God is in heaven, the Spaniards appear to have taken us at our word. I shall know more when we arrive at Trieste, but the conclusion seems unavoidable. There was to be a great meeting of the friends of chaos in a building they call the Rotunda—it appears to be now in ashes and the flames spreading. If the police are not responsible, then we must set it down to the friends of the friends. I warned the authorities, and the affair is theirs. Let them deal with it —I can take no more upon my shoulders. Indeed, Ingersoll, if you knew how very tired I am, if you could understand what this means to me sometimes——"

"It is done nevertheless of your own free will."

He turned upon me almost angrily.

"What has free will to do with you or me. If I see a woman down in the gutter and a man holding a knife to her throat, is there free will for me while my honour remains? If I am at work in my laboratory and I discover the germ of some dread disease, have I, as a man, free will, or shall I keep the gift from humanity? Ingersoll, they killed my father at Baku, and I am doing that which his spirit commands me to do. Not for one hour, while life remains to me, will I rest from my labours to turn aside from my purpose. That is my unalterable determination—I owe it to humanity and to myself to do no less."

"But humanity did not send you to the Plaza de Toros yesterday?"

I was half afraid that my temerity would anger him, but, to my surprise, he heard me very patiently.

"There is that danger always—for every man," he said; "the lust which delights in suffering, even in its lighter phases. Your slave driver had it; your great employer nowadays is not always free from it. Indifference to human suffering—that is a terrible thing, Ingersoll. Think what our imaginations could do for us if we permitted them licence to-night. Burning houses, wrecked streets, the dead mutilated beyond recognition—panic indescribable in the city, the shrieks of women, the oaths of men—could we not imagine all this if we permitted ourselves to do so. That's what I am fighting against to-night. A general has no place upon the field when the battle is won; but who would turn away from such a sight as that? My God! the whole city is on fire. What a spectacle, Ingersoll; what a story for Europe to-morrow!"

I perceived that the dread scene fascinated him as he feared. In vain to protest that he had conquered all his desires. He stood there at the taffrail as a figure carved of stone, the lurid glow of crimson light playing upon his massive head, his cape thrown open, his neck bared to the throat. The same lust of spectacle to which he had succumbed at Madrid here conquered him.

He knew that many were dying in yonder city,
and his own purpose of vengeance spoke loudly to
him. Plainly it were idle to argue with him at
such a moment, and I stood there watching the
spectacle as he did, and amazed that the sea
could so magnify it.

Verily might Barcelona have been doomed.
And yet, as the newspapers have told us, the area
burned was inconsiderable, though two great fac-
tories were laid in ashes. When the flames at
length died down and the northern sky began to
lose that glamour of golden iridescence which
was the most beautiful thing I have ever looked
upon, Mr. Cavanagh appeared to remember his
own teaching, and he led me abruptly from the
deck to the saloon.

"Ingersoll," he said, almost as one reproach-
ing me, "why did you allow me to stop there."

"I don't know, Mr. Cavanagh. I was thinking of another——"

"You have been thinking of her night and
day since we left Bruges, Ingersoll. Am I blind
and a child ? You have been telling yourself that
she is innocent, unjustly persecuted, a victim to
my implacable hatred. Sometimes you have
been upon the verge of quitting my service. A
fidelity you cannot explain keeps you with me.
You think to help her by serving me. Have I not
seen it from the beginning ? Should I not have
been amongst the most foolish if this possibility
had not occurred to me when I sent you to

Belgium? Come, Ingersoll, I will tell you what
you never imagined. I will show you how just
a man I am. If this child be innocent, who
could prove her innocence to me as the man who
loves her could prove it? Will he, if love of her
be anything to him, rest night or day until he is
able to say, ' She is not guilty; there is another
—I have his name.' At Baku I did these people
many services. Her own mother owed more to
me than she will ever know. What is my reward?
The red bands put a cap on her head and a pistol
in her hand. She shoots my poor father, because
she is vain and a woman, and they have taught
her to call herself a martyr for Holy Russia.
And now you, her advocate, have not a word to
utter in her favour. She is carried away to the
whip and the torture, and you say, ' Let her go.'
Ingersoll, is the reproach yours or mine? Am I
the judge or you—— ? "

He halted, facing me as he walked, and
bringing such a flush of hot blood to my cheeks
and such a sense of shame upon me that I could
not utter a single word. No reproach I have
ever heard stung with the bitterness of his
reproach. God! that I had been blind to it
all, blind to his just purpose, a coward in my
friendship, indifferent, idle, abandoning that very
child at the first word spoken, ready to go my
own way, to my own pleasures, while the ultimate
ignominy was put upon her. This was the fearful truth as it presented itself to me that night.

I had abandoned a helpless child when my
friendship might have saved her. Oh, the shame
of it, the cowardice of it! And now it was too
late, and they had taken her back to Russia, and
I should never see her more. Let it be told
without reserve that I broke down utterly as
those sharp thoughts overwhelmed me and hid
from him the tears which coursed down my
cheeks.

"My dear lad," he said, touching me on the
shoulder with a gesture full of kindly sympathy,
" you did not understand, and I have been harsh.
We will speak of this at Trieste. There may
yet be time. I pray that if Pauline be innocent,
your lips shall tell me so."

But I could make no answer to this, any
more than I could to the other, and I left him
at last to toss in my bunk until morning came,
and to tell myself that Pauline lay in a Russian
prison and that my cowardice had sent her
there.

CHAPTER XXII

AT THE PALAZZO DA PONTE

IT would have been in the first week of August that we passed the Lido and came to an anchor off the Riva dei Schiavoni at Venice. By common consent our voyage had been so ordered that we caught our first glimpse of the city of a hundred isles at sunrise; and assuredly there is no panorama of sea or sky in all the world to surpass that first vision of Venice as she rises, " a new Cybele," from the deep.

Glamoured in grey mists, presently to become golden; a mirror all blue and silver at her vain feet; crowned by jewels of the sun's creation; spires and domes and the citadels of palaces towering up in their majesty—a blend of colour and of shape unsurpassable, who has not worshipped her at such an hour, who has withheld homage from such a shrine ?

The very seamen on our deck could exclaim in wonder when Venice stood revealed to them. Silence was no less a tribute than eloquence to the spell she cast upon us. We had steamed slowly from Trieste, a clear moon showing us the silver waters of the sleeping Adriatic; and now at daylight the city came suddenly to our

view. One by one we recognised the familiar
sea marks—the Dogana, and the Salute, the
island of the Guidecca, San Giorgio Maggiore,
and beyond these the Grand Canal, and all that
wonderland of suggested mystery which makes
Venice what she is.

I had visited Venice many times, but never
at such an hour as this, when her people were
sleeping, and her wonderful bells silent. Approaching her from the Maestre by the railway
there is, after all, no other spell but that of a
growing curiosity. The lagoon is then but a
sheet of stagnant water decked out by sorry
posts; Venice herself has no shape to show you
as you peer from the window of a railway carriage. But viewed from the sea after a voyage
by moonlight, what an entrancing vision bursts
upon your wondering senses as you leave the
Adriatic and the mists are gathered up and the
hundred isles revealed! All Europe has nothing
like it to show, it remains the one new experience with which travel rewards you in this
twentieth century of tired eyes and *blasé* indifference.

But I am not writing to tell you of Venice
or a traveller's opinion of her. In truth, when
my first sensations of delight had given place to
the more solid satisfaction of remembering that
we had several days to spend ashore, I fell back
again to the old speculations, and chiefly to the
business which brought Jehan Cavanagh to Italy

in August and the urgency which compelled
him to be roasted in Venice when he might well
have been sailing northern seas. Assuredly the
voyage had been no mere pleasure trip for me.
I had worked like a slave since the day we
quitted Barcelona, writing volumes at Mr.
Cavanagh's dictation and finding fresh correspondence awaiting me in almost every port of
call. Let me say at once that these were commercial documents, and had nothing whatever
to do with Mr. Cavanagh's private affairs. Despite
his wealth, here he was hungering still for
money; pursuing still those ends which are
achieved by figures in a bank-book; as anxious
to be afoot with the market as any broker in
Wall Street. His genius for finance amazed
me if it did not please me. I perceived that he
also was seeking to forget.

"The most pitiful life is that which has but
one side to it," he would say almost in apology.
"I make money, Ingersoll, just as other men
collect porcelain of the Ming dynasty. And
why not? Is it not just as beautiful to look
upon, the fine, crisp bill which rustles to your
hand—is it not as beautiful as a tea-pot made in
China two hundred years ago and about as
valuable for the brewing of tea as a vase with
a hole in it? There is a great deal of humbug
in the world about money, my dear fellow. Never
believe the man who tells you that he would not
like to make a fortune. He is a liar, for such a

P

being does not exist. What he means to say
is that he does not like the trouble of making
money. There are a great many tired people
about, Ingersoll. I think it is the commonest
complaint of them all."

" But, Mr. Cavanagh," said I, "is not the
very act of making money a pitiful perform-
ance?"

" Do not believe it, Ingersoll. The highest
qualities of character, patience and endeavour
are required to make a great fortune honestly.
I say ' honestly,' for any rogue can steal a
diamond, any fool can float a fraudulent company. But the man who amasses a great fortune by fair means has done more for the good
of mankind than the greatest of kings."

This was a doctrine I would not dispute, and
I fell to my work again, as anxious as he to
forget the days we had lived through at Bruges
and at Madrid. All that was done with now. I
would walk the steamer's deck at night—what a
superb yacht she was!—and tell myself that my
future lay in the hollow of the night. I was
without hope, without resource. To this despair,
heroic impulses succeeded. Why should I not
land at Venice, journey to Baku, and save Pauline
Mamavieff even at this, the eleventh, hour?
There were hours when I resolved to do so,
other hours when I said, " She is guilty, I dare
not save her." And so to Venice and the supreme
doubt.

We took a very early breakfast that morning,
Luther James, the laziest man I have ever met
in all my life, condescending to join us. Certainly he cared little about any city at sunrise.
He was all for talk of fever and dysentery.

" I should like to have a bottle full of these
germs in my laboratory," he remarked, as I
remember, at breakfast ; " we should certainly
find the bacillus of typhoid abundant, and are
probably swallowing it at this moment. I don't
want to discourage you, Cavanagh, but a medical
man has a duty to perform. Now, my own
opinion is that we should stop on board the
yacht and take no risks. What's Venice, after
all ?—some mouldy old buildings about a ditch.
They won't bury me in St. Mark's if I die, and
I can't speak enough Italian to get into heaven
from these parts. Besides, there are doctors
ashore, and long practice has taught me that
human life is in peril wherever there are doctors.
So I shall stop aboard."

" Then you have forgotten what I said to
you at Barcelona ? My dear James, reflect
upon the ease with which a man could put off
in a small boat, climb to these decks—but I will
not push it further. The evening mail takes me
to Milan. If you care——"

I looked up quickly at these words, and heard
little of the doctor's excited protests. Were we
to return to England, then ? The mere possibility brought upon me a dejection of spirits I

could not master. What would my resolutions
be worth when I found myself again in London?
This, to be sure, was not lost upon Mr. Cavanagh.
He was ever a man who loved to play a mystery
in a jester's cap ; and now, when he had finished
with the doctor, it was of a mystery that he
spoke to me.

" You will take a gondola as soon as may be,
Ingersoll, and go to the address upon this
letter. They will give you further instructions
at the house, and you will act upon them. If I
am not here upon your return, Captain Greenwood will be at your service. Lose no time,
and remember that the responsibility will ultimately be your own. I am entrusting great
interests to your keeping, and you must do your
best for me."

This he said and much more, of which I understood the meaning but vaguely. Apparently
he himself was about to quit the yacht, and
would leave me money for a further voyage. The
instant hope that this might carry me to the
Black Sea fell to pieces, however, when he added
that the *Sea Wolf* would call at Gibraltar for
letters, and perhaps at Lisbon as well. This
could not possibly mean that we were going east-
ward, and I came at last to the belief that some
commercial interest was at stake, and that I had
been chosen for lack of any other ambassador.
As excuse was out of the question, I accepted the
position with what grace I could, and waiting

until the exquisite bells chimed the hour of eight
o'clock, I bade " Good-bye " to them both, and
set off in a gondola.

So here was a new and bewildering develop-
ment. Alone in Venice, not a notion of the
affair which kept me there, a return to England
by sea before me, a letter in my hand addressed
to a certain Madame Mornier at the Palazzo da
Ponte, wherever that might be. Luckily, the
latter difficulty was no difficulty at all to my gon-
dolier, who nodded pleasantly at the direction and
instantly took me under his fatherly protection.

" Inglesh—si, si—my vader—also Inglesh.
Mi spik him well—certamente, Signore—you ave
the fortune—all many swindler in Venetzia—ci
saremo in dieci minuti—not long as nothing—
eccoli ! "

He was very delighted with himself, and driving the gondola with fierce thrusts, he turned
aside from the Grand Canal, and threading innu-
merable waterways quite unknown to me, pulled
up at last before a very ancient mansion not far,
as I learned subsequently, from the Church of
San Zacaria. Here, pitying my ignorance of
Venice, he exchanged the usual greetings with a
concierge upon the first floor, and an instant
later I had stepped out of the sunlight into one of
those beautiful old halls which are the just boast
of the palaces of Venice.

It was dark within the house, though a beam
of clear white light filtered through an open door-

way at the further side of the hall. This, I perceived, led to a little garden, a mere court with a fountain at its centre and some rare crimson flowers growing about it. The great staircase of marble, rising up on either hand, had once been resplendent in gold and marble, but was now faded and worn. I just distinguished the outline of vast canvases upon the wall, but of any human thing I could not discover a trace. This astonished me not a little, and I was altogether in a dilemma when the sound of a voice from the garden brought the blood rushing to my face and set my heart dancing.

For it was the voice of Pauline Mamavieff, and without a word spoken to anyone, I went out into the garden and understood at last why Mr. Cavanagh had sent me here, and what was the meaning of his letter.

CHAPTER XXIII

PAULINE IS AFRAID

SHE carried a great bunch of crimson roses in her hand, and stood by the fountain romping with an ill-shaped poodle which tried to snatch the flowers from her fingers. To this brute, and not to any human being, her words had been addressed ; and so intent was she upon her occupation that I was beside her and had caught her hand before she detected my footstep upon the path. Her dress was of a light shade of blue, but Italian and odd to my English eyes. They had left her beautiful hair loose upon her shoulders, and, strange fate, she wore a bonnet, also of light blue, and not unlike those which a fad of the theatre has made known to us in London. Indeed, she was my little schoolgirl, after all.

" Pauline," I cried, " have you forgotten me, then ? "

She trembled at my touch, and the flowers fell from her nervous fingers. A face which had known the flush of happy colour a moment before became pale as the marble of the fountain. She did not resist me, did not respond to my ardent question ; but standing mute she turned upon me

those unforgettable eyes, and then I knew she
doubted me.

"It is the English friend who brought me
chocolates," she said at last, and asked: "Why
do you come again, sir? Why are you here
in Venice?"

"To take you to England, Pauline, that is
why I come.'

"Mr. Cavanagh sends you, sir——"

"Who else would send me? We are going to
him to tell him the truth—the truth at last. I
have pledged my word that it shall be so. Pauline,
you must help me——"

"You—help you!" she cried, and I shrank at
the tone of her contempt. "But you left me at
Bruges. Oh, how you talked of saving me, and,
sir, you did not speak to me at the station. I saw
you there; I had no friend; you did not speak to
me——"

Her face blazed at the memory, and she drew
back from me in a just accusation I could not
answer. How true it all was! All my talk at
Bruges had ended in a tame submission to those
who judged her. I had seen her carried to
Russia, and not lifted a finger to save her. The
assurance of her guilt, the flat denial of her story
had satisfied me. What was the good of arguing
that my efforts must have been futile whatever
they were? So much was the truth, but the
truth of it would have helped me but little that
morning.

"Do not judge me for a word," I stammered, seeking to hold her near me. "Remember how little I knew of your story until I went to Bruges, Pauline, you did not tell me the truth about Baku—you did not give me the chance to help you. What could I say to Mr. Cavanagh—that you were self-convicted, but that I believed you innocent? I told him so; he answered that your story was a lie. Then came the affair upon the railway——"

She heard me with quick ears.

"What affair?"

"An attempt by your friends to destroy the Vienna express. It did not succeed—we prevented it. I was out there with Mr. Cavanagh, and when we returned to Bruges I saw you in the carriage, but too late to speak. Pauline, was all that my fault? Are you not a little to blame?"

She did not answer me immediately, but her hand within my own trembled, and I could detect the hot blood pulsing in her veins. If we had come thus swiftly to an intimacy in speech passing all expectation, the garden and the solitude answered for it. How remote it was, of what antiquity it spoke! Many a lover here had clasped a mistress in his arms; many a soft sigh had echoed in the spreading branches above. And the bells of Venice had chimed for them as they chimed to-day for us.

I say that she did not answer immediately,

and, in truth, my words had set her thinking.
When she did reply, it was to accuse me again,
but in a manner I had not looked for.

" You think that I have strange friends ? "

" I think that which I am told——"

" There are many foolish people who do
that——"

" Why do you speak in this way ? "

" Because you say an unjust thing.   No
friends of mine were in Bruges while Mr. Cavanagh was there—none but old Andrea, and he is
in prison."

" But, Pauline, you have travelled amongst
these people—you have visited them in Rome
and Madrid and Naples ? "

She laughed mockingly.

" They are governed by children and obey me,"
she said quietly, and there was such cynicism in
her response that I had not a word to answer.

" I shall never understand you, Pauline—not
until I have known you for many years.   But we
are going to England now, and that will be a beginning.   Tell me—for I must not forget why I
came here—who is Madame Mornier, and where
is she now ? "

" She is a very old woman, so old that she
must have been born before Venice rose out of the
sea.   Why do you speak of a letter ?   She could
not read it ; she is nearly blind."

" Then you must read it to her and bring me
her answer."

She did not demur to this, though I perceived that my news had greatly troubled her. Taking the letter in her hand, and reading the direction very earnestly, she presently uttered an exclamation I could not understand, and, upon that, ran swiftly to the house. And now a full quarter of an hour must have passed before anyone came out to me again. There was not a sound in the garden save the murmur of the leaves above me. I heard the gondoliers' cries on the canal, and their voices came over as from a distant world to a palace prison. Then, as though in irony, a lacquey appeared upon the steps, and I saw that he carried a letter in his hand.

"Sir," he said in English, "I am to bring mademoiselle to the yacht at six o'clock. My mistress regrets that she is not well enough to see you."

"And mademoiselle herself?" I asked him.

"Is with Madame Mornier."

It was too amazing. The letter which he carried was not for me. No excuse could in decency keep me in the garden. And so I left him—as perplexed a man as any in Venice that day.

CHAPTER XXIV

WE sailed for England on the following morning
at dawn. I have little to write of our voyage,
nor am I very willing to dwell upon the difficult
position in which it placed me. Those who have
followed me so far will readily comprehend my
strange situation, made responsible as I was for
the safe custody of one who had been charged
with the gravest of crimes, set to probe the truth
of her story, a free agent to act as I would toward her, and yet withal answerable to the man
I had learned both to fear and to love.

I say that we were the passengers of the
yacht, that little schoolgirl and I. Each morning when I awoke, often with the sun, my first
thoughts were of the moment when she would
come running out of her cabin to meet me, her
hair loose upon her white shoulders, her cheeks
aflame with the good sea colour, her eyes dancing with the joy of life, but averted from my
own. And what a game of hide-and-seek it was
—all her amazing evasions, her demagogue's
nonsense but half learned, her prattle of truth
and justice and liberty got from madmen's books
—and upon this her fine air of womanhood pro-

236

voking the impulse which bade me take her in my arms and dare all the world to accuse her.

Now, did Jehan Cavanagh desire this or did he not? Pauline herself astounded me, one night when we were off St. Vincent, by telling me as boldly that he did.

" He is afraid of my friends," she said mockingly. " You are to become my jailor, Mr. Ingersoll, and then he will be satisfied. Even at Baku he would have been afraid of me. But if you protect me——"

I caught her hand in mine and pressed the question home :

" We could leave the yacht at Lisbon," said I; " who's to forbid us ? We could lose ourselves in the world, Pauline ; live where none so much as remember our names. Who's to prevent that ? In England there may be anything before us, but from Lisbon we could go to America, and I could work for you, teach you how to live, make you my wife, little Pauline."

She stopped me with a gesture that was almost callous.

" I would go with you," she said, " but I shall never have the right to be your wife, Mr. Bruce."

Such was the reply which brought me to reality. Sometimes I thought that the moral sense, as we understand it in the West, was lost to her altogether. Her ethics were the ethics of the children of the East. Quivering with a

young girl's passionate life, I did not doubt that
she would have followed me to the end of the
world had I but said "Come." Nor would I
claim any virtue of my hesitation. The crime
of which she stood accused ever spoke to me
with a voice I must respect. For the time
being, I had become the protector, and must
answer for her in honour's name to Jehan
Cavanagh. The victory cost me much—I am
afraid to tell how much.

Let it be said that her moments of anger
towards me—and there were such moments—
did not find me without defence. I had held
her in my arms almost brutally, and tried, as it
were, to wring confession from her. "You are
not guilty," I had said; "I will make you tell
the truth."

Her fear upon this, the white face flinching,
the trembling limbs, defied persistence. And,
remember, this tragedy of the quest must be
played every day. There was no respite from it.
From the moment when she came running from
her cabin at breakfast until my long "Good-
night," she and I were alone in the great saloon
or merry companions of the upper deck. Captain Greenwood, if he knew her story, guarded
his knowledge of it with a tact I had not looked
for in a seaman. He joined us at the table—he
smoked a pipe with me when she had gone to
bed at night—but her name he never mentioned
in my presence.

And so the days of that sunny passage
slipped by, and one morning when she came out
of her cabin I showed her the white cliffs of
England and tried to be as sentimental as the
occasion demanded. That she was not impressed
disappointed me. There had been heavy rain
overnight, and the morning mists drifted up over
the land most gloomily. The misfortune convinced her that our national love of melancholy
had not been exaggerated. I am sure she expected to find all Englishmen dressed in black.

"They come to Baku, and the air grows
cold," she said, speaking of my countrymen.
"Even when they kiss you, they seem to be saying their prayers. If you put an Englishman in
the sunlight he shivers. He says 'Oh, damna-
tion,' because my people love the sun. I have
seen him in Paris looking so sad and so tired
that I wished to die. You are just like the
others, Mr. Bruce, but I make you laugh
sometimes. And when you kiss me, you do
not say your prayers."

"Is there so much in the world, Pauline,
to set us laughing?"

"There is everything," she cried with a
quick laugh, "all that we see, all that we do—
every day, all day—is it not sham, unreal, false?
Just at this minute, when you tell me that my
eyes are blue as the sea—you think that I am
vain and shall be pleased because you say it.
When you go on land, you will tell Mr. Cavanagh,

' She is an obstinate little devil and will say
nothing.' I know and I laugh—I laugh even in
prison when your friends come to threaten me.
So much laughter is locked up here "—and she
pressed both hands to her breast—" that I must
be a very old woman before I have used it all.
But I shall be—what do you say?—extravagant
in England, Mr. Bruce."

" All the same, you are pleased to go there
with me?"

The laughter left her face, and she looked
straight into my eyes :

" Yes, with you," she said, " but with you
alone."

" Don't be afraid; there is no one else going
ashore."

" That is not true, Mr. Bruce ; Feodor is
going."

" And who may Feodor be?"

Now this question came naturally enough to
my lips, for I had no notion who the man might
be. But I perceived in a moment that she did
not believe me. Doubt and the contempt of
doubt were to be read in her wondering eyes. I
am sure that she suspected me of lying to
her.

" Feodor is Mr. Cavanagh's servant. It is
impossible that you do not know him."

" That does not make it less true. I have
never seen the man in my life. Cannot you tell
me what he is like?"

This, however, she refused to do. My protests had failed to convince her. She would not tell me one half her thoughts about it. But I could not hide it from myself that a certain element of distrust had intruded and must be reckoned with. Fortunately, ere the matter could be pushed further, they rang the bell for breakfast, and Captain Greenwood joining us at the table, I had no opportunity of resuming the subject.

"I have come down to tell you that we shall be in the Thames when you breakfast tomorrow," the Captain said.

This was the first time he had told me that the Thames was our destination.

"You will drop anchor at Gravesend, Captain Greenwood?"

"Not quite so far down, Mr. Ingersoll. I am to put you off at Port Victoria. We go on to the Tyne for engine overhauling. This yacht has been at sea for three years, and yachts grow old very quickly."

"And like women," said I, "when they grow old they grow obstinate. You will be glad of a time ashore."

"Oh, as to that, it's well enough for some; but I was born to live in a blue bowl, and I'm not happy out of it. What's wrong with the shore is that it rarely makes you feel glad you're alive. The sea does that every day; fair weather or foul, noon or midnight, I'm glad to be alive

Q

when I'm on the sea. And that's odd enough
for a man whose father went down in the
Victoria. Let the habit of loving the sea
grow upon you, and you're done for. But of
course, the young lady won't agree with that."

Pauline, who had listened with interest,
replied to him at once :

"But I should agree with it, Captain Greenwood. I have lived five years by the seashore,
and I understand you. Just to look away to the
blue sky, to be asking always what is ' over there '
beyond the clouds—to have all the glittering
stars for your own—that is the seaman's life.
We do not live in the cities because our eyes are
blinded, but it's no good telling Mr. Bruce so.
He has been talking of London ever since we
sailed from Lisbon. All Englishmen do that;
wherever they are, they talk of London. What
a happy person I must be since I am sailing to
London."

We laughed at her together, and so the talk
ran on. When breakfast was over we began to
think of St. Katherine's Point, and after that of
the white cliffs and the sand ramparts, of the
towns I knew and the stories I could tell. They
were commonplace enough, God knows. Who
that has come out of the East could suffer the
legends of Littlehampton or the Decameron of
Deal? But I was glad to forget in talk the
ordeal which must await me on shore. Whither
did our voyaging carry us and why? Would

London reveal its secrets? Would London answer the countless questions which had tortured me since I left Venice? The hour alone would tell me—no ship that ever was built would have sailed fast enough for my thoughts that night.

We were off Dover, I remember, at eight o'clock, and a great full moon helped us to make the Thames. Pauline had fallen very silent and rarely spoke to me. It was in her head that we should be separated at an early moment, and that this man of mystery, Feodor, would be the agent of her misfortunes. I had spoken to her very plainly, and could do no more. Here, as in the prison at Bruges, she had no word of self-defence to utter, remaining mute though her silence might destroy her life and my own.

"You will not speak, because you love the man you are shielding," I said to her.

She had never denied it; she did not deny it now.

"It is true, Mr. Ingersoll. I am shielding a man and he has done me a great injury."

"Pauline! Good God! but your eyes deny the story. You have another motive. It is not because you love."

"That is true," she said very quietly; "it is not because I love."

"Nor because you have loved?"

She evaded it, speaking of the things of the
night, the distant shore, the lights of the towns,
the flashing lanterns above, the sands ; of anything but that of which I would so gladly have
spoken. When she said " Good-night " to me
her manner became almost restrained.

" You have done much for me, Mr. Ingersoll,"
she said. " If it is anything to you, I shall never
forget it."

" I have done nothing, Pauline. You have
forbidden me to do anything."

" Time will justify me, and it is not a little
thing to have a friend. Let a child wish you a
woman's ' Good-bye.' "

And with this she left me, and for a full hour
I walked the quarter-deck thinking upon it all,
and chiefly of that admission that the man she
was shielding had done her an injury. Common
parlance would have put but one meaning upon
her words, but this I could not accept. Nevertheless, I stood astonished to admit how much
the mere repetition of her phrase could torture
me. If she had been the man's mistress—but,
good God! what an affront to the truth of those
unforgettable eyes, all the little tricks and ways
of her innocence and the sure knowledge in my
heart that as her life had been so would I that
my wife should live.

Thus to my cabin, but not to sleep. For, lo
and behold, who should be there when I entered
it but the very Algerian (as I would call him)

who had ridden with us to the Fen when first Mr. Cavanagh carried me down there. And it came to me upon the instant that he was the man she had named Feodor, and that he had been on the ship with us since we sailed from Venice.

CHAPTER XXV

FEODOR

THIS, mind you, might have been a false supposition. There were other possibilities. The man might have boarded the yacht at Gib or Lisbon —he might have put off from Dover in the night. Against this was Pauline's story that she had long been aware of his presence aboard. In either case it was immaterial, for there he stood by my cabin door, bowing from the very hips, but upon his swarthy face such a black look as would have hanged him out of hand in any decent court.

"Bon soir, M'sieu."

His French had, as aforetime, an odd accent I could not locate. Whence he came, of what nation he was, I knew no more than the dead. But the exclamation which started from my lips neither prudence nor good manners could hold back.

"And where the deuce have you come from?"

Again he answered me in his mongrel French.

"From my master—to take the young lady to Cambridgeshire."

"Do you bring a letter?"

"No letter, sir—my master is not well—he does not write."

It was wonderful to see the black eyes flashing and turning while he answered me. This fellow should not have walked abroad without a fez or a scimitar. I thought that the baggy breeches of the East would have suited him to perfection.

"When did you come on board?"

"From Plymouth, sir—in the launch."

"Is Mr. Cavanagh at his house?"

"He has been there five days—a week."

"Why did you not come to me before?"

He shot a glance at me which I could almost feel.

"It is necessary to be cautious; the girl has many friends in England. My master has many enemies. If I had been imprudent——"

He broke off abruptly with a wave of the hand, as one who should say, "But you can imagine all that." For the rest, I perceived that it mattered nothing whether he lied about his coming off or told me the truth. Plainly, if he had been aboard at Venice, he might none the less have received despatches from Plymouth or even from Dover. I remembered that I had seen a pilot's boat upon our port quarter as we passed the new Admiralty pier.

"Has Mr. Cavanagh sent any instructions for me?"

"That you are to await his letter in London."

" At any address ? "

" At any hotel to which you may choose to go, sir."

" He will find me at Lady Elgood's house in Montagu Square——"

" Your only message, sir ? "

" No other ; or if there should be, I will send it myself."

He bent his head in a salute which was quaintly Oriental, and went shuffling down the corridor for all the world like a Pasha who is crossing the courtyard of a mosque. I had feared this man from the outset, and you may imagine with what apprehension I now heard that he was to be Pauline's cicerone when she quitted the ship. Upon the other side I must put Jehan Cavanagh's known love of such dramatic eccentricities as this, nor would I believe his decision to be without a purpose. He would take Pauline to the House of the Fen that he might hear her story for himself. My presence in the house must be an embarrassment, not a help, at such a time. And undoubtedly he trusted this fellow out of the East, for his knowledge of men remained remarkable, and I have never known it to fail him.

Thus it befell that I was, at ten o'clock next morning, alone with Captain Greenwood upon the yacht, as lost for a plan of my own as though they had set me ashore at Goa and told me that I had become the Jam of Bangalore. In answer

to my questions, the captain told me in a word
that Pauline had left the ship at half-past seven
o'clock that morning, and had forbidden anyone
to awake me.

"She went with the Algerian?" I asked him.
He admitted that it was so, and added, to my
satisfaction, that the valet Edward had also been
of the party.

"But Feodor's no Algerian," he ran on; "the
fellow comes from Tiflis, and is a wild man out
of the woods. Mr. Cavanagh shipped him at
Cattaro after he cut up three-quarters of the
population with a two-handed sword. We bought
him of the prison authorities, and read him the
Lives of the Saints. His forefathers must have
looted the Ark on Ararat, but he's a beautiful
man if you wish to paint the town, and no dog's
half so faithful. Be sure Miss Pauline's safe
enough with him, sir."

His words showed very plainly that he understood my own interest in the matter, and I could
not but be grateful for such assurance. For my
own part, I had determined to go to London, and
there await the summons from Mr. Cavanagh of
which the swarthy Feodor had spoken. That
this was not a desirable proceeding, the month
being August and the weather intolerably hot,
goes without saying; but London, after all, is
the city of action, and out of London, the restless
man is in purgatory. Taking this for my gospel,
I left Port Victoria by an early train, and was at

the door of my Aunt Mary's house in Montagu
Square exactly at two o'clock.

It is an old house in a dingy old square, and
dull enough on a common day. My good aunt's
gaieties were sporadic and upon occasion gregari-
ous. Solemn vicars frown upon would-be merry
curates at her tea-tables. There is a very old
doctor, who dispenses *aqua pura*, and a very old
butler, who nearly dies of apoplexy every time
he draws a cork. Usually upon my arrival it is
necessary to wake this antiquity from sleep by
much hammering upon a mahogany door and a
great pulling of a jangling bell that was a very
triumph of the maker's art in the early days of
good Queen Victoria. Judge, then, of my amazement when, upon entering the square that afternoon, my cab could hardly pass for the carriages
in waiting, and I found no fewer than twenty-five
nursemaids and as many errand boys about her
ladyship's door.

"By all that's nuptial," said I, "it's little
Una's wedding day!"

There could be no doubt about it. The days
and weeks had slipped by so quickly, so much
had happened for me since Una met Harry
Relton at the Trinity Ball, that I had almost
forgotten her very existence until the rank of
carriages and the rubicund faces of the smiling
coachmen recalled me to her story. And here
was I, not only without the wedding garment,
but wearing a suit of yachting flannels which

would have put Trinity Street to shame. In
truth, the cabby himself would have done better
at the ceremony than I.

"My best wishes for the lady, sir," said he,
"and may she have as good a husband as you'd
have made her."

"Which means to say that you would like to
drink her health."

"Being a teetotaller of lifelong standing, I'll
try the liquor at Madame Tussaud's round the
corner, sir. Thank you kindly, but I can't wish
you matrimony, sir. I've buried two of 'em."

I pushed my way into the house through the
gaping nursemaids, and found a great press of
mild-mannered people upon the stairs.

The five vicars were already in a corner, dis-
cussing the national disaster which must attend
any tampering with the ornaments rubric. The
five curates appeared to be agitated chiefly about
champagne and sponge cakes, which they chased
from table to table with a hunter's eye for quarry.
Old Doctor Tubbs, holding a satin shoe in his
hand, drew patterns with it upon the frock coat
of a rival practitioner while he derided the theory
which gave a bacillus to the bald. My aunt herself was here, there, and everywhere, almost
crying for joy of the day. When we had come
face to face, she stopped as though she had been
shot.

"Bruce—my Bruce! What in heaven's
name——!"

"A glass of champagne, Aunt, and a ham sandwich to save my life. Shall I die of hunger 'upon your doorstep?"

She clutched my hand with warm fingers and drew me through the throng. There by the chimney—though heaven knows a fire would have been sudden death upon such a day—stood little Una in her wedding dress and my old friend Harry Relton, the very picture of an Englishman who was not born to wear a frock coat but had it thrust upon him. When the pair of them saw me, they cried out together, but Harry's was a view halloa.

"Of all the sweet, affectionate cousins," says Una, holding up her face to be kissed, but glancing at Harry as who should say, "Never mind, you will have plenty by and by," "of all the dear kind boys, never to write or send a single word, and then to come to my wedding in the clothes he cleans his motor in."

"My dear Una, nothing of the kind. Excellent flannels, I assure you, bought in an English tailor's at Monte Carlo. The pockets are made big to hold the losses. Now, really, did you for one moment suppose that I knew of this insanity?"

Harry chimed in, throwing her a glance to say, "He's a beast, but we don't mind."

"I wired you to the address you gave in London, and the wire came back. You'd been sent to the 'dogs' home,' or something. Lady

Elgood had your letter from Trieste, but her
telegram didn't fetch you. My dear chap, what
have you been up to, and who is the lady ? "

"I knew there would be a girl," says Una,
"he's so deceitful. Perhaps he's married himself."

"Look here," said I, "when I am married I
shan't hunt down my friends with telegrams to
tell 'em of my misfortune. I shall sneak off like
a thief in the night, and it will be a moonless
night. Did you get my present, Una ? "

It was beautiful to see the look in her eyes
when I said this. She clasped her little hands
together with frantic ecstasy, and struck an attitude which the sentimental would have called
divine.

"Oh, I know it's something beautiful. Has
it come, Bruce ? "

"Well, I don't think so, for I haven't bought
it yet."

"The most horrid man in London and the
dirtiest. Thank heaven we go away at three
o'clock."

Their thanks appeared to be mutual, for they
looked at each other once more in a way that put
me to some shame, and then began to talk loudly
about the weather.

Immediately afterwards Una discovered that
she must go upstairs and change, and Harry took
me aside into an embrasure of the window and
began to talk to me very earnestly.

"There have been fifty stories, and I believe all of them," he began. "The last said that you were at Venice with a Turkish girl. Of course that must have been true. Then old Blaker, of Jesus, says that you have taken up with the American madman, Jehan Cavanagh. Now, that's not right, is it, Bruce?"

"Decidedly not. Jehan Cavanagh is not an American and he is not mad."

"But he must be. He appears to have left his business and gone to the devil just because they shot his father at Baku. Blaker tells the story. He actually declares that you are his secretary."

"He is evidently well informed. I must ask him where he got his information."

"Then he's on the right nail. But, my dear chap, is Cavanagh sane or mad?"

"That's a question I ask of half the men I meet. Are they sane or mad? generally implying a second question—do they consider others are sane or mad? It's too long a story now, Harry. I'll tell it when you come back."

"That won't be for a month. We're going down to Pangbourne to-night—love in a cottage, eh? and then on to my uncle's place in Somerset. Una wants me to take up the Bar seriously. I suppose she's right."

"It depends what the Bar has to say. Did you hear, by the way, how Blaker came to know of my affairs?"

" Why, of course, that old fool, Luther James,
who use to practise at Trumpington, he told him.
He's Cavanagh's doctor, and a bad time he has of
it. The wife's gone mad, and tried to murder
the child. An awful business, but of course you
know all about it. They say Cavanagh is a raving
madman since the thing happened."

But at this point a stir among the bridesmaids, the hilarious distribution of the harmless
but necessary cereal, and the violent agitation of
the old doctor with the shoe recalled Harry to the
circumstances of his own misfortune, and with a
" By Jove! I believe it's time to go," he wrung
my hand and slipped away. Thereupon followed
all that ancient comedy of departure which, a
relic of mediæval barbarisms, is still considered
necessary to the respectability of weddings. Up
and down stairs went the giggling bridesmaids;
all the servants came up from the kitchen and
stood in a decorous row near the front door ; the
men tried to look as unconcerned as possible, but
their hands were full of rice ; my Aunt Mary
alternately cried and laughed, and it was always
difficult to say whether tears or laughter stood
for sorrow or for joy. When Una appeared the
air became white about her. She made a dive
for the carriage, Harry upon her skirts ; the
coachman whipped up his horses, the old shoe
flew through the air, we had a glimpse of smiling
faces at the window, and then the carriage swept
round the corner on its way to Paddington, and

one bachelor had been taken from a selfish world.

"Are you stopping here, Bruce?" asked my aunt, as we went upstairs again.

"For a few days, if you will permit me," said I.

"My dear boy, you couldn't do a kinder thing. Let me look at you, Bruce. You are not well, sir. I believe you are in love."

"Then old Tubbs shall administer an antidote. What are you going to do to-night, Aunt Mary? Not dance, I hope?"

"I couldn't, dear; I haven't the heart. Stop with me, Bruce, and help me to forget that I am an old maid. I am sure you have a great deal to tell me."

"So much, my dear Aunt, that one half of it will never be told at all. Now, let me go upstairs and change. I feel like a gas-stoker who has walked by mistake into Buckingham Palace."

"But you'll dine here, Bruce, and then we'll talk?"

"Perhaps," said I, and so we left it.

CHAPTER XXVI

My aunt naturally had little love for Montagu
Square when Una had gone, and we left London
together next day to spend a few weeks at Eastbourne. To this course I consented after a
solemn assurance that Fownes, the ancient
butler, would forward my letters every day, and
would not neglect to expedite the telegrams.
Eastbourne is not an exciting watering-place, but
for a lover of tennis it has many charms. And
I welcomed the kindly company of the sweet
woman who had now become my counsellor.

Frankly, I told my Aunt Mary much. There
are precious women in whom it is possible to
confide; sympathetic, clever women in whose
judgment we do well to trust. Mary Elgood
was one of these. Her husband had died, at the
early age of forty-one, of a fever in Persia. The
honours he had earned in the Civil Service
heralded his death. I know that my Aunt Mary
mourned him with a gentle, unselfish love which
betrayed little to the world; and I had always
been her favourite. Here at Eastbourne we
drove and walked together every day, and played
piquet sedately o' nights. The life I had lived

R   257

during the past three months seemed so remote
that I could almost believe it to be wholly unreal.
My aunt herself was but half convinced.

"There are many queer people in the world,
my dear Bruce," she said to me one afternoon
when we sat together, up on the grass by Beachy
Head. "Isn't it the fashion nowadays to interest
yourself in crime? If you will think about it all,
you will find that Mr. Cavanagh has done little
more than that, but he has done it with a millionaire's opportunities. What those may be only
millionaires could tell us. I can quite understand that the police would be very glad to listen
to one with so much money and so much influence. But all the rest is nonsense. These
great social troubles are not to be put down by
any one man's genius. Does your friend hope to
do what the Tzar of Russia could not do? Does
he think that he can put back the hands of time?
Of course, we should be very sorry for him. But
how did his father come to lose his life? Why,
by going into a wild man's country to make
money, when he had more than he knew what to
do with already. I would have nothing to do
with people like that, Bruce. I would avoid an
association which seems able to influence your
own life so greatly."

"Aunt," said I, "if it were not for Pauline,
I would leave Jehan Cavanagh to-morrow. You
have told me what I have been telling myself
since I came back from Venice. It's the personal

magnetism of Jehan Cavanagh himself which
cheats me into accepting his theories of justice
and of law.   When I am away from him I can
see how false they are.   He has a great wrong to
avenge, and he is trying to avenge it brutally.
Upon the other hand, he is a man whom other
men must love.   If I could save him from himself, it would be the happiest day of my life."
    "You will never do that, Bruce; the day's
gone by for that.   As for the child, do you forget
that we are in England?   In your case, I would
go down to this house of his——"
    "My house, Aunt—he took it in my name."
    "To deceive those who were spying upon
him, I suppose.   But it doesn't alter the case.
I would go down to the Fen and fetch her
away.   You heard what Harry said—there has
been a great trouble there—the mad woman tried
to kill her child.   This will not make it easier
for Pauline Mamavieff, be sure of it.   I detest
panics, Bruce, but I am really very sorry for
that child, and if I were you, I would lose no
time."
    "It had not occurred to me," said I at last.
"You think she may be in danger, do you not?"
    "Oh, that's too much to say.   But I think
her situation is an undesirable one, and since
you mean to make her your wife——"
    "My wife—now, Aunt!"
    "My dear boy, it's been as plain as the light-
house down there ever since you came back to

me. Have I no eyes, then? Bruce, who used
not to have a single care in all the world!
Bruce, who made me laugh all day! Bruce the
philosopher, and Bruce the misogynist! Can he
deceive me? My dear boy, you are in love with
Pauline Mamavieff. You love her because of her
misfortunes; you love her because she will not
tell you the truth; you love her because there is
between you the common sympathy of a cause
you do not understand—a just cause and very
honourable. Let Mr. Cavanagh preach to me
as much as he likes. He will never alter my
opinion about that. And really, Bruce, I don't
think he wishes to alter it. The child's courage
convinced him also. You can see it in every
act. Her journey to Vienna was a sham. He
sent her there to prove you. When he left the
pair of you on the yacht together, he believed
that you would either tire of her or compel her
to marry you. You have been faithful to his interests, and if you leave him alone, he will be
faithful to yours."

"Then you did not really mean that I should
go to Cambridgeshire?"

She became grave in an instant.

"I did mean it," she said; "all that we have
been talking about takes no consideration of
what has happened since. Go down to-night,
Bruce. Bring Pauline to me. I'll have the
truth out of her. There never was a child who
could keep the truth from me, and I've yet to

meet one. If you like, I'll come to Cambridge and wait for you there. If that is not wise—and your Argus-eyed friend would certainly get to know of it—then you must leave me alone for a day or two and go yourself. A clever head will make an excuse, and really, my dear Bruce, a man in love needs no excuse."

Well, we discussed this again and again, watching the blue sea far below us and the white and brown sails and all that restful, calm day of summer. A man is ever constrained and foolish when speaking of his love, but few could have been that with my Aunt Mary, and certainly she is one of the wisest women I have ever met. In the end she persuaded me, altogether against my own judgment, and that very evening I left by the last train for London, and was in Cambridge by twelve o'clock of the following morning. Here, however, my courage failed me. How could I go on to the house unasked, and what excuse could I make? A telegram to the House of the Fen might be unwelcome to Mr. Cavanagh, and work him a considerable mischief. My advent unannounced must speak distrust as loudly as distrust could be spoken. Driven from a plain "Yes" to as emphatic a "No" I lunched at the Bull Hotel, and went afterwards to walk in the Backs. It was much, at any rate, to be but a few miles from the house which sheltered Pauline.

Needless to say, Cambridge is a dreary place

enough at the beginning of September. Even
the long vacation men have gone down by that
time. Half the shopkeepers are away at Yarmouth, the other half frolic commercially upon
the Cam or loll at their doors and pray for the
nomadic American. In the courts of Jesus I
discovered that even Homer nodded, and that
our porter was away. It seemed impossible to
believe that in six weeks' time these rooms
would awake to the far from ghostly presence of
the " fresher " and the don, that there would be
tubs on the river again, bells tinkling in the
steeples, all the pomp and circumstance of learning as Cambridge alone can foster them. And
but three months ago I had the right to say *quorum pars sum.* How melancholy a thing is the
passing of our youth. What shadows we embrace
in the hours of youth's supremacy !

My walk helped me not at all—it merely tired
me. I could come to no resolution, either to
abandon my intention or to pursue it. The pros-
pect of a melancholy dinner table, added to a
solitary evening in a deserted hotel, should have
done something to stimulate my faculties, but, in
truth, I rather welcomed this innovation. A
couple of American ladies with a Baedeker and
a King Charles terrier, a very old parson who
must have been " up " fifty years ago, showed no
desire for my acquaintance. I sipped my coffee
alone in the lounge afterwards, and for a full
hour remained undisturbed. Then a new figure

entered, and I turned to stare after it with interest.

The man was short, and wore a tourist's suit. His hat had clearly come from Paris, his hair was black and crisp, and his pince-nez obtrusive. Smoking a cigarette from a long amber tube, he went with some deliberation to the cloak room, then shuffled back across the lounge straight to my table.

"Permit me, Mr. Ingersoll——"

"The Chevalier, by all that's wonderful!" cried I.

But he raised his hand warningly, and I saw that I had made a mistake.

CHAPTER XXVII

"WHEN I determined to come to Cambridge," he said, " I did not expect to meet anyone who would know Maurice Fournier."

"And certainly when I set out it was not in my mind that you would walk in here," said I, for I understood immediately that he did not wish to be known, at any rate by his own name.

" Is all well at your house ? " he asked, still speaking in a loud voice.

" I am going there to see," was my reply ; "that is to say, I am debating the intention of going. To-morrow morning will find me at a decision."

" Pardon me, you are out of fashion, Mr. Ingersoll—our forefathers decided to-morrow morning ; we decide to-night. Well, I am driving to a little village near here in an hour's time. Perhaps you will go some way with me."

I said that I would do so. Despite his warning, I could not take my eyes from him. A more wonderful disguise it would have been impossible to imagine. And, of course, he was upon his way to the Fen.

" They tell me," said I, " that one of our

264

friends is ill—the man we met in Paris. Do you
know if it is true?"

"It is quite true; we will speak of it upon
the way. Let us drink kummel and go. That
is the only liquor for a man who works—kummel.
But it is a very good liquor to do without."

He touched a gong upon the table and a
waiter appeared.

"Have you told them that you are not returning?" he asked me pointedly.

I did not deny it, but, taking the hint, I told
the waiter :

"I find that I shall not be staying in Cambridge to-night——"

"Or to-morrow night," added the Chevalier
pleasantly.

The waiter left us, and Blondel rolled himself
a cigarette with juice-stained fingers, adroitly,
and with the air of a connoisseur. When we
were served he bade me go and pack my bag.
Ten minutes later I sat by his side in an old-
fashioned gig, and we set out rapidly upon the
Huntingdon Road. When the outskirts of Cambridge were passed and the dark of the high road
enshrouded us, my companion condescended to
make another observation.

"I am glad to have you with me, Ingersoll,
although you came without orders."

"That's true," said I, "and it goes without
saying that there is something the matter at
the Fen."

" There is everything the matter—our friend is discovered."

" By whom ? "

" By those who will make good use of their discovery. He has been imprudent—it is what I have foreseen. A man who goes into action with the lights of his own house before him is already a candidate for the ambulance waggon. Our friend has had a great shock—it has bred imprudence."

" Who are the men ? " I asked laconically.

" To begin with, our old friend Dubarrac——"

" The man who escaped me at Antwerp and then at Bruges ? "

" No other ; see what comes of a mistake. If you had shot him——"

" Well, I did my best. Is he in England ? "

" He is somewhere in the woods about our friend's house. Cavanagh himself no longer counts. He is mourning a son——"

" You don't mean to tell me that the child is dead ? "

" He was alive when last I heard, but the doctors had little to say for him. That's where we have broken down. These people are very quick. They appeared to know in four-and-twenty hours that their old enemy was laid low."

" How did you come to hear of it ? "

" I sent a telegram to Victoria Street—it was not answered—the first telegram of mine that

Jehan has not answered since I entered his
service. Then the man Feodor summoned
me——"

"Have you informed the local police?"

"The what!"

"The police at Cambridge."

He took his cigarette from his mouth and
uttered an odd sardonic laugh. His reply found
a phrase in his own idiom.

"Mr. Ingersoll, there is still some sense left
to my head. Shall I telegraph for the abbess of
the ladies' convent? She would be as useful."

"Then you think that it is well with Mr.
Cavanagh?"

He touched the horse with his whip, and
answered me more leisurely.

"If we find him alive—well, then I shall
hope. Your presence gives me courage. You
are not a *bon tireur* exactly, my friend, but you
have the English—what shall I say?—bull-dog,
and that is worth something to us. I shall give
you a pistol—it will tell me where you are.
Come, now, this is the inn, we will descend
here, Mr. Ingersoll."

The talk had so engrossed me that I had lost
all count of the road. We appeared to have
turned from the highway to a narrow lane, which
brought us out at a shabby inn, a mere thatched
cottage with a bright light shining from its
solitary window, and many barns and stables
about. Nor were we unexpected, for a man came

running out directly he heard the sound of our
wheels and another watched him from the
doorway. To my astonishment, the Chevalier
addressed them in French.

" Well, there is news ? "

The man who held the bridle answered.

" We have carried out your Excellency's
wishes."

" It is good. And your master ? "

" Is at the observatory, Excellency."

The Chevalier tossed the reins aside.

" We shall go at once," he said. " Let the
horse be stabled here until I send for him."

But to me he said :

" You must be very careful, Ingersoll, you
must be very wise."

I could but hazard what he meant, and I
made no answer. When the horse had been
taken to the stable, the man who stood in the
doorway came out, and I recognised him for my
Algerian, Feodor of the ship.

His greeting was no less astonishing than his
appearance, for he merely shot a glance at me
from his glowering eyes and told me that of
which I was well aware.

" Mr. Cavanagh will not be pleased," he
said.

" So much I understand. Is Mademoiselle
at the house ? "

" She is at the house," he said, and in
such a tone and with so much satisfaction of

his answer that I could have struck him
where he stood.

The Chevalier was ready to set off by this
time, and we went on without further parley.
The man, Feodor, swung a lantern in his hand,
but appeared to carry no weapon. The Chevalier
had put on a long, close-fitting waterproof coat,
with a hood almost covering his face. In this
order we left the inn, and, going down the lane
some hundred yards, we passed through a gate,
but not before I had seen the light disappear
from the window behind us and the inn's very
existence, as it were, blotted out.

We were now in a close-set thicket, treading
a narrow path which many a beater had trod and
would tread when November brought the guns to
the Fen. The night, I should tell you, was
intensely dark, the path cumbered by brambles
and treacherous roots. There is always something mysterious and not wholly natural in a
wood at midnight, and this wood I found no
exception to a common rule. I could already
people it with uncanny figures of the shadows.
Creeping things upon the ground, the gliding
stoat, the unseen habitants of clump and bush,
the dim mysterious sounds from afar, these played
upon nerves already wrought to a high pitch by
all that had gone before. Such alarms, however,
were entirely premature. Whatever we had to
do was not to be done here, and to my surprise
the Chevalier began to talk to me as freely

as he had done in the gig upon the high
road.

"I am glad to have you, Ingersoll," he repeated, "your presence may help us very much.
Take this pistol, and do not hesitate to use it.
We are dealing with those who will stand upon
no ceremony, with men who are determined to
kill Jehan Cavanagh whatever the consequences.
Remember that we come at a time when he is
not able to help himself."

"Are you telling me that he is ill?"

"I am telling you that he watches by the
bed of a child he loves. We must be strong for
him, Ingersoll; we must show him that we have
not forgotten our duty. When he is imprudent,
we shall be prudent."

"Prudence, then, brings us here to-night?"

"Prudence, yes. I will make it as clear to
you as I can. Our friend has acquired the habit
of taking his recreation in the observatory. We
shall find him there when we arrive. That is not
so very bad by itself, but there is a mile to be
walked each way, and the road is lonely. One
of us must go upon that path with a lantern to-
night, Ingersoll, as Jehan was foolish enough to
do yesterday. The man will be—what do you
say?—a risky fellow, but the others will follow
upon his heels. Now, who will volunteer for a
thing like that?"

"I will carry the lantern, Chevalier. It is
right that I should do so. Feodor will be more

useful with you. I may be able to defend myself,
but he is as strong as a bull."

" I was going to say so, but I left it to you.
Your decision finds me contented. You will
carry the lantern as I shall direct—*attendez*, the
very thing."

He stopped suddenly in a clearing of the
thicket, and espying a hazel—for there was a
glimmer of autumn night here—he stooped and
cut a whip off it with a dexterity I should not
have looked for in a man of such habit and
manner. Taking the unlighted lantern from
Feodor's hand, he next spliced the swinging
handle to the switch, and then—and not until
then—explained himself.

" They will shoot at the light, Ingersoll ; but
they will fire behind it as the habit is when we
are not *de bons tireurs*. Carry the lantern over
your shoulder, behind you—so—and your chances
are many. I shall be upon your heels ; there
will be others not far off. Should you unfortunately meet your man face to face, you will know
what to do. Now, see that your pistol is loaded,
and from this time not a word."

He drew me aside behind the outer hedge,
and there, striking a light, he held it while we
examined our pistols. I judged that we were
now upon the very borders of the home park,
and in this idea was not mistaken. Crossing a
dyke by the customary ligger, we found ourselves
on the open grass lands, and across these, at a

distance perhaps of three hundred yards, we
espied the great outer ring of trees which stand
sentinels to the House of the Fen. These we
approached cautiously, following a low hedge
which crept about a paddock, and thence into
the undergrowth beneath the yews. From this
spot there was a view of the house itself, which
recalled instantly to my mind the moving events
of the past few months, and, greater than these,
the fact that Pauline Mamavieff was a prisoner
at the Fen.

There were lights in the house, I should tell
you, and a brighter light shining from the dome
of the observatory. The great lantern, however,
was not visible, nor could I observe anything
which might have led me to believe that the
house had been alarmed. These woods through
which we walked, the crisp grass beneath our
feet, the shivering leaves above, spoke of anything but tragedy. It seemed impossible to
believe that men had crossed to England from
the dens of the Continent to be the judges of
their judge in this remote country. But I knew
Prosper de Blondel too well to doubt the truth of
it. The very mystery began to stimulate nerves
long racked by anxiety and indecision. It was
something to believe that the bushes hid the
human devils from our sight, that every step
might bring us upon them, and that what we did
was to be done in the name of Jehan Cavanagh.

A hundred yards from the observatory, perhaps, we stepped aside from the path into the shelter of a copse, and there lighted the lantern. This was no stableman's antiquity, but a brass hand lantern such as is used in a motor carriage, though, be it said, it had a paraffin lamp and a red and green glass at either side. Whence the Chevalier had got it, I knew not, but his perspicuity and the swiftness of his thoughts amazed me. A common lantern would have betrayed the man who carried it. This, depending from the switch, would betray nothing.

"Keep your light low to the ground and walk quickly," he whispered to me; "it is Jehan's habit—to walk quickly. Imitate him, and they will think he is returning to the house. Now, I will show you the path, but I count upon you, Ingersoll, I count much upon you."

There was great warmth in his words, and I understood, it may be for the first time since I had known him, that all that he did for Jehan Cavanagh was done because he also had come to love this master of men and to serve him for affection's sake. For my part, a consuming anxiety to be up and away warred upon my prudence, and might have done me a mischief. It was intolerable to be creeping through those bushes toward the light, and to say that Mr. Cavanagh might already be face to face with those who had sworn to destroy him. None the less, the Chevalier restrained me.

"We must not be seen," he said, still whis-

s

pering. "From bush to bush, Ingersoll, and
then straight away from the observatory ladder.
Do you understand me? Is it clear to you?"
I nodded my head, and, turning to be sure
that the man Feodor was still upon our heels, I
said that I understood everything and was ready
to go. And now began a very game of hide-and-
seek, which I could but find hazardous to the
last degree. From bush to bush we crept, crawl-
ing upon our hands and knees, afraid to snap a
twig or rustle a leaf, three figures crouching in
the darkness. Any turn might bring us face to
face with the new denizens of the woods. A
false step would undo all. But we persevered
and were successful, coming out at last into the
aureole of the observatory's lights, and there
halting swiftly.

"Now," said the Chevalier, "there is the
path. Go on, and God-speed."

I swung the switch from my shoulder, allowing the lantern almost to trail to the ground,
and, with my pistol in my right hand, I marched
boldly to the path and set off upon a road I knew
for the lake and the gates of the house. A desire
to run almost overmastered me, but I checked it
at the outset. Such a backward trend as my
thoughts took reminded me how that, once
before, premonition had sent me to Jehan
Cavanagh's assistance, as premonition sent me
yesterday from Eastbourne into the very heart
of this unimagined emprise. Without me, I

reflected, Prosper de Blondel might have been
hard put to it to do all that we were now able to
do. This could be but a coincidence, and yet in
the darkness I let it stand for more than coincidence. The distant lights of the house, the sure
knowledge that I should find Pauline therein,
gave me courage. I went with firm strides, trying to look neither to the right hand nor to the
left.

How dark it was ! How the bracken cracked
and rustled beneath my feet, the fronds unavailing to deaden the sound of my footsteps. All the
sweetness and quiet mystery of the night told me
plainly that the Chevalier had been befooled, that
he had conjured up men of his brain to people
these silent depths. Indeed, a reflection could
bring no other argument. A few steps farther, and
I stopped again to ask myself whether these few
months had made a coward of me beyond redemption. My God, how I trembled while I stood
there ! Not fear as we understand it, but a
sudden realisation of all that I might lose if the
instant brought the worst upon me. Life with
all its promises as the " twenties " understand
them : Pauline and my dream of a young girl's
love ; sight, sense, consciousness of existence
gone in an instant, engulphed by the darkness.
Myself but as the earth beneath my feet ; black-
ness everywhere, and the terror of death as
night alone can paint it. These phantoms
of thought overtook me, for I heard a cry

in the wood, and that cry came from a woman's throat.

At first I said that it was a cry afar off, or not a woman's cry at all, but that of an animal stricken suddenly, caught by fox or stoat; or even a dog baying at the moon. The attempt to believe this, however, failed utterly when the note was repeated, as it were, from the path before me, but at no great distance. Now I knew it to be the sound of a human voice, and, although a great silence fell after, I went on rapidly running when I could without danger to the light I carried. From this imprudence a low whistle restrained me—I do not know to this day whether it were one of my friends who whistled or another —but I understood it to be a signal for me to halt, and I stood a little while trying to learn if Blondel and the Algerian were still upon the path. The attempt was unavailing. Listening intently, nevertheless, I heard something which I had not expected to hear, the patter of a hound's paws upon the grass, and a low snarl of the brute as he drew toward me. I have never been one to fear a dog, and I was not afraid this night. Let him come or go, it could matter nothing.

And so I went upon my way again, my nerves at a tension, the light still swinging behind me. If I had the idea that there were men upon the dog's heels, the situation and that which I knew of it justified the opinion. But not so much as the shadow of a man did the woods reveal. In

vain I peered to the right and the left, stood listening in the clearings, straining eyes and ears in
that vain quest.   The dog followed me—I could
hear his sinuous movements through the brake—
but of men not a trace.   The assurance gave me
new courage.   I went on swiftly again, and,
coming out into a clearing, I saw the woman.

She was standing by the trunk of a huge tree,
a hand stretched out to it for support, a long
black cloak wrapped about her, her fair hair
tousled about her face and shoulders.   Believing that I recognised her, but not quite sure of
it, I crossed the sward and lifted my lantern,
and in the same instant the dog sprang at me,
and with a startled cry I let the lantern fall
from my hand, and stumbled to the woman's
feet.

CHAPTER XXVIII

THE dog had caught me by the shoulder, but his fangs hardly touched my flesh. The lady—for as I fell I perceived that she was Mr. Cavanagh's mad wife—ceased to cry, and stood rigid before me. I heard a loud outcry from the wood upon the left hand, and then a pistol shot. All this, mind you, as in the flash of a picture upon a screen, for the dog and I were upon the ground rolling over and over as though the brute had become a man and the man a brute.

I have heard many tales of an animal's strength; have often dreamed the horrid dream which puts white fangs to the throat and warms the cheek with a beast's foul breath. Here, upon the sward of the Fen, I was to live through the dream with its horror unabated, to experience awake that which sleep had made so terrible. Nor can I explain to you what instinct sent my hands to the dog's throat and let me catch him in a grip that seemed to strain my muscles to the breaking point. This, however, is what it came to be. I half turned as I stumbled, and, falling upon my back, I caught the hound by the throat and so held him, while he, in his

278

agony and strong beyond belief, dragged me hither, thither across the grass, his breath whistling through his dripping jaws, his eyes shining red as coals of fire. More wonderful to be told was the glare of light upon us both, and yet no miracle, for the paraffin had been spilled upon the ground, and the undergrowth was burning.

So now you will depict the scene: the tall trees suddenly lighted by the glare of the conflagration, the monstrous Russian boar-hound worming in my hands, the mad woman standing as a figure of stone by the tree, in the near wood the cries of men and the crack of pistol shots. Above all these sounds there arose, for a long instant, a wailing cry which I knew to be that of a dying man; but even this moved me but to a kind of savage anger as the dog writhed above me and my very nails were thrust into his heaving throat. The lust of the fight had seized upon me now. Driven to brutality by the horror of the brute, I twined my feet through the cordlike roots and knotted myself to the ground with the ferocity of a savage. The fœtid breath, the foam dripping upon my face, could not deter me. My muscles were straining like tightened cords, the blood flushed to my face and head, making me sick and giddy; but it was my life or the brute's, and no living man could have dragged me from my hold.

I say that I had a certain ferocious satisfaction of this encounter, and I do not think this is any wilful exaggeration. There is a point of conflict beyond which the desire of life is supreme, and a man becomes indifferent to all else, thinks nought of the consequences, makes light of any wound that does not disable him, and will continue his efforts above any necessity of the moment. Such would have been my own case that night but for the intervention of an agency more potent than the blood-lust. I doubt not at all that the hound's strength would ultimately have prevailed, that he would have twisted himself from my grip, thrown me back upon the turf, and snapped his fangs upon my gaping throat. That this did not happen must be set down neither to my friends nor to their agents. The spreading fire amid the undergrowth came upon us as we wrestled, the hound had dragged me toward it, and now must suffer by it. A supreme effort upon my part, the sudden consciousness that the flames were upon us, the woman's resounding shriek—this brought me to my feet, my hold released suddenly, the thread of my intention broken. Giddy and faint, I staggered up to see the hound dead at the Algerian's feet, to hear the calm voice of Prosper de Blondel asking me if I were hurt, and to discover the mad woman's deep-set eyes turned shrewdly upon my face. The question I answered by another, making light of my own bruises, and asking what had happened to Mr. Cavanagh.

" He has returned to the house, Ingersoll—

he expected to find you there. Ion, his son, is worse."

"Then I will go at once. What of the others, Chevalier?"

"That is a question I would much like to answer, but there is one over there who will not trouble us again."

He hesitated to tell me more, for the poor woman, who had listened to us with apparent unconcern, now burst into a flood of tears, at which the Algerian crossed over to her side and addressed her as though she had been a child. How greatly had I misjudged this ill-looking fellow!

"How did that lady come to be here at such a time?" I asked the Chevalier aside.

He answered with a shrug of his shoulders:

"Cavanagh insists upon her liberty. What can we do? You see that she understood us when we spoke of the child. She may have been going to the observatory with the news. Leave her with Feodor; she has no better friend."

I could not demur, and we went on toward the house together. Some of the gamekeepers and farm servants had now come out of their cottages, and were running across the sward to cope with the fire in the brake. The place seemed to be alive with men.

"Your ambuscade was a rumour, then?" I put it to the Chevalier.

He would not admit it.

" There is a man in the woods who will give you the lie. I do not wish to speak of it. From this time, Ingersoll, we are besieged in our own house. So much comes of imprudence. And I will tell you more : if you brought a regiment of soldiers here you could not alter what is and must be."

" At least," said I, " we must hear what Mr. Cavanagh has to say."

" See him, and then decide. He is waiting for you, Ingersoll."

CHAPTER XXIX

IN THE LIBRARY

THE House of the Fen was wide awake when we entered, and the sleek valet, Edward, met us at the foot of the great staircase. I caught a glimpse of a nurse's white apron on the landing above; while a Frenchman, whom I remembered to have seen in Antwerp, greeted the Chevalier effusively and immediately engaged him in earnest talk. My own road, however, lay to Mr. Cavanagh's private library, and thither I went immediately.

"Your rooms are all prepared, sir," Edward whispered to me at the door, "but we expected you yesterday."

"Then you knew that I had been to Eastbourne, Edward?"

"I cannot say, sir—I was told to get the rooms ready. Mr. Cavanagh has been very ill. You will be surprised to see how much he has changed."

"And what of Mademoiselle?"

He avoided the question, turning his eyes away from me.

"Mr. Cavanagh will speak about the young lady, sir."

283

And so he held the door open for me, and I entered the library.

It was a spacious room, the bookshelves of satinwood and the furniture in keeping. To my surprise it was now lighted with extraordinary brilliancy, all the lamps, concealed by the frieze above, being ablaze to the point of discomfort. Jehan Cavanagh is not ordinarily a man who loves much light—and I could not but remark the circumstance. Elsewhere, little things attracted notice—a screen drawn before the bow windows, a conspicuous gong upon the chimney-piece, and a decanter of brandy, with a single glass, upon the writing table. These I did not fail to observe as I entered—but Mr. Cavanagh's changed appearance remained the greater wonder, as the valet promised me I should find it.

He was dressed in a smoking suit of crimson serge, the coat open to show a soft-fronted shirt —but no waistcoat beneath it. The brightness of the light, it may be, heightened the natural pallor of his face ; but there were meaning black rings beneath his sunken eyes and the hollows of his cheeks were eloquent of distress. All the attitude of the man pointed to this—the unkempt hair, the restless movements of the lips, the quick pacing to and fro, the cigarette, in the long amber tube, smoked almost with ferocity, as though the task were a burden. Upon the table by which he walked there lay but a single paper—the doctor's latest bulletin concerning the child Ion. He read it and re-read it constantly as though to confirm despair or discover a source of hope.

I had entered quietly, but not so quietly that he did not look up at my step and nod to me. The act was very familiar. He was not a man to waste his words, and this was his old manner of greeting. Had I gone by it alone, nothing might have been changed since I left him at Venice—nothing but the man himself, worn out by illness and anxiety. This impression, however, speedily gave place to another.

"Why did you come here, Ingersoll?"—he asked me, in a tone which plainly said—"you had no orders to come."

"I came," said I, as quickly, "because something compelled me to come."

He looked at me very shrewdly.

"Your own interests or mine, Ingersoll?"

"My own, sir—I came because Pauline Mamavieff is here."

"An heroic mood—Leander in a gig and an assassin's castle at the end of the journey. Is that your view of me, Ingersoll?"

"It would not have been—but it may become so."

"Seriously?"

"Seriously—I have not forgotten what has happened, Mr. Cavanagh."

He stood a little while to reflect upon my words. Then he fell to pacing the room again.

" They have told you that my child is ill ? "

" Yes, indeed——"

" There is nothing so sad as the illness of a
little child, Ingersoll—there is nothing on God's
earth half so terrible. Reflect upon it, our own
impotence, the gulf between our desire and our
achievement—the necessity of being watchers, we,
who command what we will, to be compelled to
stand helpless and to know that this soul is passing beyond our ken, the soul of the child we
have loved. Even sacrifice is denied to us.
What is anything that we can give in this scale
which Nature holds ? She mocks us — our
human offering is spurned. We cry into space,
' my life, and not that of the child.' We are not
heard. The memory is her armament. You go
to the child's room and there is some trifle of
yesterday speaking more eloquently than tears.
Lock it away, that ever afterwards it may keep
your grief alive—that is the common sentiment.
Ingersoll, the world is wrong when it derides
such emotions as are common to humanity. I'll
put the rich at the bedside of the poor man's
sick child and make kings of them both. Come,
the child, this little lad of mine, is dying, and
his mother has killed him. What shall I do,
Ingersoll? Where does my road lead me now ? "

He sat as he spoke, and buried his face in
his hands, but he could not hide the tears from
me. What to say to him, what word of consolation to speak, my troubled will could not decide.

For how impotent are words in such hours as
these !

"Has the doctor told you that he is dying ? "

"He does not tell me—it is not his business
to tell me. But I know it. And, Ingersoll, this
is a woman's work—a child, if you will have it
so. She brought this upon me—your little
angel of the red-caps, that her vanity might be
gratified, that they might say to her, ' She is
Mamavieff's daughter and has avenged him.'
That's a thing a woman would like to hear—
brings all the men about her. They're born ad-
vertisers, the women, when the mood takes them.
That's what your chaos is living on—wheels of
anarchy to a goal of pride—the sensation in the
newspapers, the trial, the glamour even of death.
Women can have no other motive, for their
brains are not big enough. You never yet heard
a woman state a political theory with a grain of
common sense behind it, and you'll wait a long
time for the achievement. But, Ingersoll, we
must punish vanity of this kind—it is our duty
to do so—we must punish it, even if we call the
law to our assistance."

"Do you mean, Mr. Cavanagh, that you will
send Pauline back to Russia ? "

"I mean it, Ingersoll, if my friends do not
anticipate me. Let her go back to those who
have the first right to judge her. I was a fool to
listen to other counsels. I have used my influ-

ence wrongly. Your own judgment will uphold
me eventually. It would be madness to believe
that you can again become her advocate. All
that is past and done with. She must go back
to Russia, and take the consequences of that
which she has done. For the rest, the others, I
swear to God that if money and brains can
do it, I will exterminate them like rats. There
shall no longer be any talk of truce, Ingersoll.
I will go from city to city and continent to continent. My fortune shall be spent to the last
penny in doing by these people as they have
done by me. They are cowards, and as cowards
I will meet them. Why, think of it—there is
not a city already wherein my name does not
bring them to their knees. I have seen strong
men tremble before me—merely because I know
them. That is the work of a few months, Ingersoll. What shall the work of years be? Let
your gift of prophecy answer that."

He stood before me the very picture of madness grown logical; the great figure of a man
with staring eyeballs and veins drawn as whip-
cord, and moist lips and clenched hands. Just
as I had feared at Madrid, so it had come about.
This tragedy at the Fen, this fearful blow
which threatened the life of his child had snapped
the last thread of his tolerance, and bidden him
strike without mercy. And who should save him
from that? What wit of friend or enemy could
destroy the devil which possessed him?

"Mr. Cavanagh," I said, at last, "it is not my master who says these things."

"But, Ingersoll, I am not ill. Why do you believe it? You know that I am not ill."

"The man who speaks to me," said I, "is not Jehan Cavanagh, but another. The friend I have known could never become the assassin!"

"Good God! Ingersoll—what a charge. Assassin—of those whose life's work is assassination!"

"Society has not made you their judge. The laws are not yet proved impotent——"

"Law—that for your law! The cowardly refuge of the mentally destitute. Law has destroyed men, Ingersoll—ask yourself what the nations were before law became the cant of every poltroon who had not the courage to think or to act for himself."

"Mr. Cavanagh," said I, very quietly, "you are preaching the doctrines which have made men anarchists."

The truth of it, I think, astounded him. He stood quite still, smoking furiously. Then he went to the table and helped himself to brandy.

"Well," he exclaimed, at last, "there's little time left for argument, and to-night is no opportunity. I'll give the girl three days, Ingersoll— three days to tell me the truth; and, hark you, save her from Feodor, for he's a raving madman

T

where my interests are concerned. Three days, you understand—and then no more argument. Do not come to me again until you have news to tell. I am very displeased with you, Ingersoll, very displeased."

I made no answer—for deep in my mind lay the conviction that I had said something to which he must listen. When I left the room he turned his face to the wall, and I heard him utter his child's name amid his sobs.

CHAPTER XXX

THE BOAT AT THE GARDEN GATE

It was very late when I quitted the library, and I was not surprised to hear the valet tell me that the Chevalier had gone to bed. In my own room, with the door barred (I knew not why I barred it), and the windows toward the Italian garden thrown wide open, I tried to get at grips with the amazing situation in which 1 found myself, and to ask what were the truths of it. Some little consolation, perhaps, lay in the memory that Pauline's room could not be very far from my own, that she was sleeping in the house, and that I at least might account myself the sentinel upon her slumbers.

Be sure that I had little thoughts of sleep that night. The mad words I heard in the library drummed in my ears like an echo from chaos itself. Three days of grace, the merciless war afterwards, the child avenged! What could a man make of that? Whither would reason direct him? No child could have been more helpless than I. And yet Pauline must be saved, and Jehan Cavanagh must be saved, because of the affection in which I had held him.

There would be patience lost if I narrated the

many ideas which came to me. At one time
I was for going to the lad Ion's room to get if I
could a true account of him. Then I was all for
finding Pauline at the risk of discovery, and
taking her from the house, whatever the consequences. Mr. Cavanagh's threat anent the
man Feodor filled me with a dread unutterable.
Here was a true savage who would deal savage
justice, let the victim be man or woman. I perceived that if the boy died, the consequences to
others, and chiefly to Pauline, might be disas-
trous. Nor was the danger less for the men
without. They must be reckoned with, our very
salvation might depend upon the bargain we
could make with them.

Upon the other side little could be put. I
did not believe that the Chevalier would help
me, nor had I any faith in accidental intervention. It is well enough to talk of law and the
police, but there are circumstances in the new
story of Revolution which deride the one and are
more potent than the other. My imagination
could not but smile at the thought that the
bumpkins of the Cambridgeshire force might be
called upon to pit their wits against the shrewdest brains of the Continental red-caps. Farce
could go no further, even the imminence of the
peril would not permit me to delude myself like
that.

And so I was back upon myself again, sleep-
less, vigilant, and yet without decision. When

the dawn broke, I recalled that day of summer when I had looked from these windows for the first time and watched the Algerian—I still called him that—riding back from the woods upon an errand beyond my comprehension. To-day, however, the brown park-lands could show me nothing. The mists rolled up to lay bare that vast acreage of grass and woodland, but to reveal no human being upon it. And I found it almost impossible to believe the Chevalier's tale that we were besieged in our own house, that Russia and Italy and Spain had sent the agents of Revolution to us, and that these men were now encamped in the woods. A great golden sun shone upon a very desert of meadow and of marsh. The gardens were ablaze in the full glory of autumn's unstinted colouring. The lake shone as a mirror of dulled silver.

This scene, with all its suggestion of peace and remoteness from men, held me at the window for a full hour. At the end of that time, the drawbridge below was swung over the lake and a man rode out toward the woods. I did not recognise him, and others who followed at short intervals were also unknown to me. But their going inspired me with a sudden curiosity which I could not master, and I determined to follow them, anxious, perhaps, to assure myself that the Chevalier's tale was folly, and that I could prove it to be so.

This, I remember, would have been at seven

o'clock of the morning, certainly no later. In
the hall below I came upon the women-servants
of the house as engrossed in their morning scrub-
bing as any maids of a conventional suburb.
One of them, with a quicker tongue than the
others, told me that Master Ion was still very
ill, and that Mr. Cavanagh was with him. She
had scarcely spoken when a stir at the door
announced the doctor's morning visit. I had
not yet met him, and we merely bowed as we
passed, but his appearance was my opportunity,
and the bridge was still across the lake when I
came out. So I answered no man's questions,
but lighter at heart because of the sweetness of
the morning, and carrying but a good stick in
my hand, I set off towards the Observatory for
the scene of last night's encounter, as determined
to disbelieve the whole significance of it as ever
I was about anything in all my life.

A foolish resolution, you will say—I know
to-day that it was so. I know that I came very
near to death that morning. But one takes
many risks in the " twenties," and laughs
at the shadows which are such grim realities
to others. Out here in the woods, a warm
sun upon my face, the sweetness of the air all
about me—what cared I for threat or counter-
threat, the Chevalier's tale or Jehan Cavanagh's
resolutions? I had saved Pauline by twenty
ways when I came to the Observatory, I had
laughed at the simplicity of the whole thing

when I reached the wood which we had set
aflame last night. Yet here I might well have
paused, for the carcase of the boar-hound still
lay at the foot of a scorched birch, and the
ground about was burned as black as tinder.

It had been no matter for jest then, that fire
in the thicket, and we were lucky to have the
woods still standing. Deep across the ashes I
could trace the nailed boots of the keepers and a
smaller imprint which an observer would have
found more significant. Beyond these, at the
heart of the thicket which had been saved, there
lay two empty cartridges and some scraps of
paper. I picked them up, and saw that they
were scraps of a Russian newspaper, though the
print had been almost obliterated by the heavy
dews. These were significant discoveries, and
they sobered me not a little. Standing with ear
intent, I listened for any sound in the woods.
A tit in a holly tree, a lark whirling at the zenith
above answered me. What, then, set my heart
beating? I cannot tell you; there are moments
when we know that strange eyes are upon us and
that strange steps follow after. That was such a
moment for me, and, not at all ashamed, I ran
from the wood as though it were haunted, and
skirting about the western wing of the house,
I came out upon the open parklands just where
the boat-house marks the river's course. A
luckier road was never taken.

I had not visited this northern side of the

house before, and some curiosity to inspect it led
me towards the river and the boat-house. Here
it became apparent that they had built a little
flower garden upon the apex of the island, and
this stood out above the lake at the western end
and was enclosed by a high wall pierced for a
wicket gate. So much I espied before I came
up to the boat-house, and I imagined that in
ordinary times this ferry allowed the people of
the house to pass freely to the park without
using the drawbridge at all. What astonished
me chiefly, however, was the fact that the wicket
gate itself stood open, even at such an hour of
the day, while the outer doors of the boat-house
were unlocked and swaying to the wind.

Now, this was a remarkable thing, and could
not but set me speculating. Had I seen a boat
at the steps over by the garden there would have
been nothing disquieting in the fact. But that
the gate should be open and the boat apparently
upon my side struck me as the oddest tribute to
the Chevalier's vigilance which perversity could
imagine. On the other hand, the boat might
have been lifted out of the lake altogether, to
prove which I walked boldly up to the house and
looked in. Then I understood in a moment;
and, dropping softly upon the grass, I asked for
all the help my wits could give me.

There was a boat in the house, and a man
lay fast asleep in it. I thought that I had seen
him before, but could not be sure of it. That he

was a foreigner, a Russian by the look of him, and apparently there for no amiable purpose, were conclusions as inevitable as they were hazardous. In a vivid picture I seemed to understand the meaning of the man's presence, and its testimony to some great coup which either had failed or was about to begin. There could be no difficulty whatever, I argued, in three or even four men passing from the park to the garden while the boat lay moored in the house and the wicket gate was open. This implied an oversight so prodigiously foolish that I forebore even to think of it. Minute by minute the conviction that I must entrap this man, or that all would be lost both within the house and without, obsessed my mind more surely. Ways and means I had none. The magnitude of the stake overpowered me—I could but remember that Jehan Cavanagh's very life was at stake—or, was it his life or that of the child ?

I must get possession of the boat, cost what it might. Peering once more into the shed, I discovered 'that the man still slept, but that he had turned in his sleep. If he were armed, his arms were not visible. I should not have called him a strong man, or one of any considerable physique—and for that matter his face was not without its kindly qualities. Prompted as much by his appearance as by my own want of invention, it came to me that I might leap into the boat suddenly, and, having previously cast loose

the painter, might be out and across the lake
before the fellow could do me a mischief. That
the outcry would bring men to the garden of the
house I had no doubt whatever. It remained to
be seen whether I could or could not master the
sleeper until this aid came to me.

Viewed calmly in these after moments, I
believe the plan to have been foolish beyond
words. But men do not reckon in this way
when the need is great and the moments are
few. To be plain, the idea had hardly come to
me when I would have put it to the proof.
Opening the doors of the shed with the lightest
fingers I could command, I crept along the board
toward the painter, and finding it hitched with
the common knot which even the landsman
knows, I cast it off with a flick and made to step
into the boat. In the same instant the sleeping
man awoke and sat up to stare at me.

So there we were—he half awake and blink-
ing, the painter still in my hand and my whole
plan gone at the very beginning of it. In truth
our mutual curiosity came near to undoing the
pair of us. There I stood at the bow of the boat,
my arm stretched out toward the gates to which
the painter had been hitched, my balance in-
secure, my intentions laughing at me. On his
part, there may have been the idea that I had
not come alone, and that my destruction would
but delay him. I saw him clap his hand to his
jacket pocket and withdraw it as quickly. His

frightened eyes, turned hither and thither as those of a scared animal, presently took in the fact that the outer gates (those toward the lake) were not locked, and, uttering a loud cry, he seized a paddle boat-hook and thrust the boat out toward the river.

It was all done in a flash, the glance of the affrighted eyes, the quick thrust, the bursting of the gates, the passing of the boat. No waterman's dexterity could have surpassed that of this apparent landsman, with his meek face and his humble eyes, and his mad desire to escape. Had I been thrice as quick-footed as I am, my nimbleness could not have arrested him; but this is to be said, that I sprang at the boat as it passed me, and, missing it, fell headlong in its wake. Five seconds later the man himself was struggling for his life in the water of the lake, and I understood with what injustice I had accused the Chevalier.

They had scuttled the boat, there could not be a doubt of it. Finding it difficult, perhaps, to house the craft upon their own side—that is, to house it safely—they had scuttled her where she lay and covered their handiwork by a pretty trap. Not until the boat was shifted did the truth appear, but it had hardly passed the gates when it filled to the very gunwales and went down instantly in seven feet of clear but rush-grown water. The Russian, unable to swim, lifted both his hands above his head and uttered as pathetic a cry as ever fell upon my ears. I thought he would be gone before I could get to him; but I

had him at the second attempt, and, shouting to
him to throw his head back, I set out, without a
thought about it, to swim to the garden gate and
to the assistance I should find there.

Let it be said that in ordinary circumstances
this would have been no remarkable feat. The
river, or lake—for it is called indifferently by
either name—is here but forty yards across.
The water, warmed already by the morning sun,
was tepid and refreshing; the rushes alone were
troublesome. By myself I could have managed
it well enough, but the Russian had no cleverness
now, whatever he might have shown two minutes
ago. His weight seemed almost insupportable;
his white face—for I believe he had fainted—
haunted me with a suggestion of death I was
powerless to combat. And upon this came the
question, Why save the man? what do you owe
to him? Had he not come there to bring what
evil he could upon the house?—it might be to
kill the child for whose life so many waged the
good fight. These thoughts flashed through my
mind, but were powerless to check me. I said
that I would save him, let the consequences be
what they might; and, holding him to me as
though the lake had delivered up some precious
possession, and not an unknown madman from
the East, I pressed on toward the steps.

And here, to my surpassing wonder, the Lady
of the Woods herself awaited me, and, staggering
up to the garden, I found myself face to face
with Madame Cavanagh.

CHAPTER XXXI

ROBINIOF

You will remember the circumstances under which I had seen this poor lady—but twice before in all my life; once upon the morning of my first coming to the Fen, and again when the Chevalier led me through the woods. Here in the sunlight of an autumn day I could appraise her beauty for the first time; remark the superb clearness of her skin and eyes, and tell myself that her almost flaxen hair was the most wonderful I had ever seen upon the head of a woman.

These were instantaneous thoughts, as you will have imagined. She had come to the water's edge, drawn thither by the outcry—I stood before her, my hair lank and dripping, the cap gone from my head, a sorry burden at my feet. How to tell her what had happened—she whose reason would help no narration—how to keep the shock of it from her, I knew no more than the dead. And yet the thing must be done quickly, and the house alarmed.

"Madame," I said—"this poor fellow has met with an accident. If you could help us——"

And there the words failed me. She, how-

ever, rocking to and fro as one in great distress,
presently fell upon her knees by the strange
man's side, and uttering wild words in a tongue
I had no knowledge of, she began to chafe the
man's hands with a tenderness and affection a
mother might have bestowed upon her son.

"It is Robiniof," she exclaimed presently,
pausing in her task and looking up at me with
eyes filled with tears—"my servant, Robiniof—
please send them to me."

And then as though my hesitation angered
her, she exclaimed, almost angrily—

"Go at once—there is a doctor still in the
house."

Now, the tone of this amazed me beyond all
experience. I had been told that this poor
woman was not only bereft of her reason, but
dangerously bereft, so that she had threatened
the life of her only son. And here she was,
giving her orders as calmly as any lady of the
house could have done. Such a blow upon a
supposition I had never known before—and be
sure the words were scarcely spoken before I
hastened to obey her.

"I will send them at once," said I; and
pocketing an affronted vanity, as young men
must often do, I ran into the house, to find
myself face to face with the servant, Feodor.
Twenty words told him the story—five more
summoned Dr. Hanson, who had just left the
child's room. The latter went to the garden,

with a doctor's deliberation—but Feodor ran there as though he had heard a fairy tale; and there were others upon his heels, their curiosity as apparent as his.

There is no great merit in dragging a man out of a pool, whatever the world may choose to say of it. Alone in my room, I remembered that some women would have spoken a word to me personally upon such an affair; but this passed in the greater question, " Who is Robiniof, and why does his coming move this poor lady so strangely? " I was still busy with this when the Chevalier himself entered my room without warning—as faultlessly dressed as ever and as imperturbably calm. All that had happened yesterday seemed already blotted from the mind of this unsurpassable schemer. He sat in my chair and watched me dress with the *sang-froid* of a farceur who has just taken refuge in a café.

" You English are always in the water of some kind," he said, with ironic affability, " but I think you prefer the hot water. Why did you go to the Observatory this morning, my friend? Why were you so very foolish? "

" Folly brings something home, at any rate, Chevalier."

" It is true, and I am perplexed. This poor lady, who has recognised no one for many months, remembers the face of her old servant Robiniof. What are we to say to that? "

" Is it possible that the man, who is in rags,

and does not speak a word of English, has made
his way from Baku to this country with nothing
to guide him but a name?"

"You do not understand the East, Ingersoll,
or it would be unnecessary to ask that. These
people possess a patience which is very wonderful. I will bet with you that the poor fellow has
been months upon the road, starving, hunted,
perhaps, but always resolved to find us out. Until this house became known to our unpleasant
friends over yonder, he set himself an impossible
task. But when a Russian in London knows
something, all the Russians know it. You see
what comes of the primitive emotions—I told
you at Cambridge how much the master had
changed."

"Shall we say for the better?"

He shrugged his shoulders.

"It is not my business. I have been trapping
men for twenty years, and if I live for another
twenty, I shall go on trapping them. That
is a habit which grows upon one like drug drinking. A faithful agent, I serve my employer while
he deserves to be served. For Jehan Cavanagh
I have an affection which nothing will alter.
But, my friend, I am artist first!"

The candour of this delighted me. I perceived that this redoubtable Chevalier had already
laid down his burden so far as the House of
the Fen was concerned.

"Are you returning to France, Chevalier?"

"Much depends upon what happens to-day. Cavanagh has not the qualities necessary to his own ideas. When he came to me, I said that I would make him the most dreaded man in Europe. I could have done so. Two things, my friend, will exterminate anarchy in Europe—men and money. But they must be men, and there must be no sick children."

"Ha, your human nature crying, ' God give me the child! ' while you would make the children fatherless. It's what I said, Chevalier, the world must work out its own salvation. There is no heaven-sent prophet who is going to save humanity from the accumulated consequences of tyranny and misrule. We must fight these people as a society, not as individuals. I have known it from the beginning, even while a love of argument led me to flout my own ideas."

He shook off the ashes of his cigarette, and leaned back a little wearily.

"All this may be true," he said, "but it has nothing to do with me. I am the servant of the master. If Jehan Cavanagh wants me, he has but to lift a finger and I am there. That will depend upon the child. Your talk is for books, and the clubs, mine for the bureau de police and the cell. I have no life beyond that—but I am artist always."

"And this artist, finding no canvas at the Fen, is about to return to Belgium. Meanwhile, what of us here—what of Pauline Mamavieff? "

u

"She will go back to her friends—Cavanagh is weak; he will buy his own security by her liberty."

"I wish to God I could think so."

"But it will be so—and when she is with them, she will marry the man she has been shielding."

"The man who was her accomplice, or shall we say the assassin ? "

He made a gesture of indifference.

"I will not argue it, my friend. Cavanagh has done with her, but I have not. There are some pictures the artist must return to. This is one of them. I shall make it my business. If she goes to America, I shall go there—to Spain, I shall follow her. One day her journey will end at Baku. That much at least I owe to society, Ingersoll."

"Say rather to your own vanity, Chevalier—and tell me this, why am I forbidden to see her ? "

"Then you are forbidden ? "

"So much has been implied. If you are of the contrary opinion——"

"My friend, as far as I am concerned, you may see her this very minute."

"Was that the message you came here to bring me ? "

He admitted it without a blush.

"It was the message," he said.

And so I understood, and followed him quickly to Pauline's rooms.

CHAPTER XXXII

THE House of the Fen is built about a quadrangle, as I have said, an older house shielding a modern habitation. They had lodged Pauline in what are known as the Chesterfield Rooms, a suite overlooking the ramparts and the lake upon the western side, and so situated that one can pass by a turret staircase to the garden of the island. The rooms are old and heavily panelled in oak, which time and not a furniture polisher has stained. Their ceilings are gilded and groined, and worthy of the place they hold in the esteem of guide-book makers; there is a good light from wide casements, and the fireplaces would serve a dining hall. In such an apartment I found my little Pauline again, in such I first guessed the true story of her captivity.

And first it should be said that she had been expecting me. She was too young, her wit was too bright to ape the common attitude which is so often ashamed of a little honest emotion. I found her standing by the open window; her greeting was the very greeting I had heard at Bruges—it seemed so very long ago.

" Where are my chocolates ? " she asked me,

307

and I swear no child ever asked the question
as naturally.

"They are in the shop in London, Pauline,"
said I, taking both her hands and drawing her
nearer, "the shop to which we are going together
as soon as it can be. Don't look so sad because
I say it."

She made a pretty grimace, freeing her hands
and arching the prettiest neck in Cambridgeshire
that day. A box of Russian cigarettes lay on the
table near by, and she took one and passed the
box to me.

"But I wish to be sad," she said incon-
sequently, and ceased to smile immediately.
"This is a sad house, Mr. Bruce ; you know how
sad it is."

I lighted my cigarette and then answered
her. This pretty indifference did not encourage
either eloquence or demonstration. She talked
to me here as she had talked in the prison
at Bruges. And I must fall in with her
mood, though I could hardly forbear to take
her in my arms and kiss her lips to new
confession.

"There is little good news, if you mean that,"
said I, "and the lad is no better. Have they
spoken to you of Ion, Pauline ? "

"They speak to me of nothing but Russia
and my people. The chevalier, your friend, is
here all day. 'Tell me how to destroy your
people,' he says, 'and I will be kind to you.'

That man, and the other, Mr. Bruce, they are
my jailors—"

"Pauline," cried I, "why did you let them
bring you back to England at all?"

Now, the question came naturally, for it had
always been a puzzle to me. Opportunities she
must have enjoyed without number to com-
municate with her people and escape from the
yacht *Sea Wolf* had that been her earnest intention. Whatever could be done by the aid of the
police in Europe could not be done here in
England. A word from me would give her liberty,
a line to the nearest police office would open these
doors to her. If I had not written it, set the fact
down to my fear of her extradition. The crime
she had committed must send her back to Baku.
I knew her to be innocent of it, I prayed to God
that she was innocent, but the record stood, and
would have overtaken her wherever she fled.
This led me to a great wonder that she had
suffered captivity both in Venice and upon the
yacht when a few resolute men—and her party
possesses those in abundance—could readily have
contrived her escape.

"Why did I come to England? Oh, there
might have been many reasons, Mr. Bruce."

"But tell me one of them, Pauline?"

She turned her face from me, but not so
quickly that I did not detect the blood mantling her cheeks. How blind I had been! As
in a very revelation, I realised the truth. She

had come to England because I was there. Say
that the thought was vanity—I knew it none the
less to be the truth.

"Pauline," I cried, and catching her in a close
embrace, I covered her burning face with kisses,
"Pauline, you shall tell me the truth, you shall
tell me what I must know—now—this instant.
Pauline, tell me! I love you! Will you not
speak?"

She shivered in my embrace, and her eyes
closed. I thought for a moment that she had
fainted, but anon she stirred in my arms and,
lifting her face, she kissed me very gently.

"Mr. Bruce," she cried—and now a woman
was speaking—"we are playing at being children.
And we are grown so old—the world has been so
unkind to us."

"But it is going to be much kinder, Pauline."

"Why do you say it? Are we not two poor
birds caught in the net which destiny has spread
for us? I come from the East where the people
cry 'Kismet!' That is fate, your fate and mine,
to have known each other when the night had
come. I say it, and I know. We shall remember—perhaps it will help us to remember.
But there is nothing else than memory—our
flowers are but ashes, and they are blown away
like poor dead things."

She laughed, but there was a catch in her
voice I could not mistake. Here, as in Bruges,
she could quicken my heart or still it almost

with a single word spoken. The child in her had kissed my cheek, but the woman thrust me from her.

"Pauline," said I, "this is all old talk. Why will you not listen to me? There is so much to say, God knows how much——"

"Am I not listening patiently, Mr. Bruce? Come and sit by me here, if you wish it." Her voice was very sweet and gentle.

She flung herself upon the window-seat and made room for me beside her. The day was almost at its zenith, and great bands of quivering light spangled the still air and set it quivering with dancing beams. Below in the garden the sound of voices betrayed the fact that Madame Cavanagh still walked there. I remembered that Pauline must have known her at Baku, and that set me thinking.

"Do you remember Mr. Cavanagh's house in Russia?" I asked her suddenly.

She stared at me in amazement.

"I used to pass it every day, Mr. Bruce. How should I forget it."

"Then you remember Madame Cavanagh?"

"Of course I do. She was a Circassian; my father knew her well before they sent him to die at Saghalien. Why do you ask me, Mr. Bruce?"

"Because she is down there in the garden— with an old servant of hers, Robiniof—I wonder if you know his name?"

I put it to her without emphasis, but such a

startled look came into her eyes as I had never seen there before.

"Robiniof!" she cried. "Oh, but Robiniof cannot be in this country!"

"You are wrong. I fetched him out of the lake this morning. He has come all the way from the Crimea to see Madame."

"Then—then—Mr. Bruce, I do not know what will happen."

"Pauline," said I, "this man has some of your secrets."

She would not face it out. Her hand, held close in mine, trembled while I spoke, the colour came to and went from her pretty face, now giving southern roses to her cheeks, now leaving them ashy pale. Presently she started up and, standing upon the seat, gazed out over the stone balustrading to the garden below.

"It is Robiniof," she said, and sat down again, her heart palpitating so that for a moment I thought she would swoon. By and by, however, she became a little calmer and began to laugh as though some droll thought had overtaken her.

"Robiniof was much attached to Madame Cavanagh, was he not, Pauline?"

"So was everyone in Baku. We loved her, Mr. Bruce."

"And when the accident happened?"

Her eyes opened wide at this.

"What accident would that be?"

"The death of Mr. Cavanagh's father."

"I remember it," she exclaimed, fallen in an instant to sadness, "that is why I am to be sent back to Russia."

"How would you like to hear that your own friends are to take you back, the men who have been watching this house for some days past?"

"I do not wish to hear it at all."

"Not to hear it? Come, I won't believe that. Aren't they your own people? With whom would you go if not with them?"

"They are my own people," she said slowly, "but Mr. Cavanagh will never send me away with them. Feodor would not permit it."

"Feodor! What in heaven's name has he to do with it? A dirty dog of an Asiatic——"

She laughed loudly.

"Am I not an Asiatic too? Oh, Mr. Bruce, what compliments you pay me!"

"Pauline," said I, "you are the most inscrutable mystery that ever puzzled honest brains. I tell you that Mr. Cavanagh has determined to give you your liberty and you laugh at me. I say that he will send you to your own people, and you——"

But she permitted me to say no more. A look of dread unspeakable had crossed her face.

"My own people say that I betrayed them when I came to England," she cried. "If I went back to them, they would kill me, Mr. Bruce."

It was plain to be seen that she meant every

CHAPTER XXXIII

I HAD intended to go straight to the Chevalier and tell him this astonishing news, but the valet Edward could not discover him in the house nor had the others any tidings of him. In truth, the fact that we were besieged had now come to the knowledge even of the meaner servants, and left them almost paralysed by fear. Chiefly, I think their master's new habits of seclusion affected them. In his absence men told ghostly tales. They warned me that it was no longer safe to walk in the park even by daylight. If I doubted their judgment, at least I could not doubt the honesty of their apprehensions.

And, to be sure, I had no courage to venture again into Mr. Cavanagh's presence. This was not so much lack of courage as the shrewder belief that he was powerless to help me in his present condition. The man who wars with the outcasts of many nations must never sleep. Jehan Cavanagh had been sleeping since they told him that the child was ill. And now it appeared that others must repay, and chiefly my little Pauline.

I have spent many days of doubt and per-

plexity in my life, but never such a day of trouble
as that. The very beauty of it tortured me. Here
was the sunshine pouring down upon the park ;
the lake a sheet of silver ; the woods murmuring
to the sweetest of breezes. In the house all
seemed to sleep ; the woodlands might have been
deserted since the Conquest. And yet truth
would have it that madmen from the East
now peopled them—that brake and glen hid wild
figures who were the outposts of chaos, and
that in England and not at Baku the last scenes
of this amazing drama must be played. So
much I could admit reluctantly, while for a
shadow of consolation there stood the truth, that
the wheels of anarchy had turned in our own
country before, and that this was not the first
time a man had been hard put to to escape them.

It was a poor reflection enough, and yet
neither the hours nor the circumstance gave
me a better. I dined in my own room at eight
o'clock, and still wanted news of the Chevalier.
At ten the valet Edward told me that " Monsieur " had gone to London, and that he did not
know when he would return.

" And Master Ion, Edward—has the doctor
been again ? "

" He is coming at ten o'clock, sir."

" Then there is no news that is good ? "

" None whatever, sir. My master is very ill."

" Do you think he would like to see me,
Edward ? "

" He will see no one, sir, until he knows the best or the worst."

This was plain enough, and, indeed, I had already discovered that this whispering valet did not lack outspokenness when the need arose. His honest intimation helped my own conviction that it would be unwise to try and see Mr. Cavanagh, at least to-night; and that whatever my anxieties they must rest until to-morrow. I was disappointed, to be sure, that Prosper de Blondel had quitted the house ; nor could I hold him altogether blameless for doing so. Possibly he had taken what precautions he could ; a suspicion which was emphasised when the great searchlight by the Observatory suddenly flashed across the park and showed up all the grasslands in a wonder picture of beauty unsurpassable. And now had I something to amuse my eyes. It was good to sit there by the window and smoke my pipe and fall to speculating upon the secrets which the thicket guarded so closely.

How still they were! How ridiculous our fears appeared to be while one watched the searching beams; now skimming the dewy grass ; now making silver of the trees ; now shooting as it were into the very heart of the brake and spying out its mysteries. This toy which Jehan Cavanagh had put up at the Fen, had it been built against such a night as this ? Did the master foresee that he, who would make war upon the outcasts of humanity, might stand some

day against the world, ashamed to call upon that
law which he had derided, stricken by the God
who would judge both accuser and accused ? Indeed, I thought of this to-night. How strong he
had been, how masterful in his own brief hour ;
and now this night of silence, the stricken cry at
the child's bedside, the threat against to-morrow.
The latter I found to be as fearful a thing as all
that tragedy had shown me. Let the child die,
and Jehan Cavanagh must become an assassin.
I could foresee no alternative.

I say that the light played about all the secret
places of the park, and this vigilance endured
until midnight. Upon my part, I would as
soon have thought of going to bed as of setting
out there and then for London. The freshet of
fears that ebbed and flowed in my heart—now
bitter regret that I had brought Pauline to England, anon a remembrance of the affection in
which I had held the Master of the House ; black
memories of the hours at Antwerp and at Madrid ;
a thought of my first meeting with Pauline in the
cell at Bruges—these came and went as the
beams of light themselves, robbing me of hope or
inspiring me to action. At one time I said that
I would meet Jehan Cavanagh in the morning and
claim Pauline's liberty by right of my love of her.
There were wilder resolutions to take her from
the house at daybreak, and, risking all, both the
dangers of the park and the remoter perils in
London, to go straight to Lady Elgood's house

and there let the world judge us. As the night
went on and the silence deepened I began to believe that I myself was also a prisoner, that I
should never escape the thraldom of this house,
that I must die the servant of a madman and his
dreams. This latter ultimately claimed my mind
to the exclusion of all others. I clung to it almost fondly until the great lantern suddenly fell
dark and the silver beams were upon the grasslands no more.

Did those at the Observatory sleep then? it
seemed so. I waited long at my window, smoked
many pipes before the lantern shone out again ;
and then I noticed that all the light was focussed
toward the northern side of the house, almost
upon that very boathouse in which I had discovered the servant Robiniof. This, however, might
have meant little. Those who manipulate search-
lights are given to resting thus, the beams
focussed for many minutes upon a distant object.
I could make nothing of the manœuvre, and I
should have disregarded it altogether but for a
sudden turning of the light which, sweeping
about the park again, showed me, as clearly as
ever I saw anything in all my life, the figure of
a man clinging to the narrow ledge above the
lake upon our side, and engaged, as I must imagine, in passing round the western angle toward
Pauline's rooms.

I would tell you that the walls rise almost
sheer from the water as they approach the garden

of the island, and that there the merest ledge,
barely wide enough for a man's foot, creeps about
the western wing. If I had not dreamed the
story, the intruder, whoever he was, went hand
and foot upon this ledge with an agility and a
quickness which amazed me. Naturally the
search-light showed me the crouching figure but
for the fraction of a second, but that was enough ;
and all the suggestions of the hour crowding
upon me, the fear of the hidden men and deeper
thoughts I would have been ashamed to confess,
I said that an assassin had crossed the river to
kill Ion Cavanagh, and that nothing but a miracle could save him. An instant later I was out
upon the landing, stumbling wildly I knew not
whither, while a voice whispering in my ear cried,
" Fool! you are hunting a phantom. Go back
and laugh at it."

Every man and every woman knows with
what hesitation we alarm a sleeping house at
night. There is something almost sacred about
sleep ; we pass with muted tread and a hush
upon our lips. Even in moments of fear we are
loth to cry aloud, so that the "whispers" of
melodrama have, in truth, something human
about them. Once beyond the door of my own
room, all these perplexities began to assail me
anew. Had I imagined the thing ? Had
there really been a man upon the ledge above the
lake or had want of sleep created him for my
willing eyes ? The silence answered affirma-

tively. I crept down to the great staircase, and could not hear so much as a sleeper breathing. No one stirred; if there were watchers, I could not detect their presence. And I began to shiver with the cold. What a fool to venture at all, said inclination. I had a kindly ear for that, and would have turned back at a nod.

If I did not do so, let curiosity answer for me. To be honest, there was something almost uncanny about the silence. Unless I must think the Chevalier and his servants traitors or imbeciles, the utter absence of visible sentinels could not be without its meaning. Where were the men I had seen yesterday who watched by the child's room? I asked myself this, and crept a little way up the stairs toward the western wing. Then I listened again. A sound I could not define had alarmed me. I waited an instant and heard it repeated. There were people talking in low tones, and one of them a woman. Common sense would have said that Madame Cavanagh or one of the nurses spoke; but this was no time for debate, and I avoided it, and climbed another flight. Here the sound of whispering became more distinct. I crept a little way along the corridor, and the sounds ceased suddenly. In the same instant the place was flooded by the clear white light from the great lamp in the ceiling above, and I looked up and found myself, not greatly to my surprise, in the presence of Jehan Cavanagh himself.

v

He wore a long dressing gown of some white cloth, and had a loose girdle about his waist. Upon his face there was a look I had never seen there before—of anxiety newly awakened, even of fear. And yet his whole air was majestic and kindly, and, so far as my own acts were concerned, he had no reproof to utter.

"Ingersoll," he cried, "please to come with me."

I made no answer, and he turned and began to walk quickly down the corridor, toward the door of Pauline's room. It was impossible in that brief space even to guess at his intention or to throw any light upon this strange encounter. Indeed, I followed him with an apprehension I pray that I may never know again.

What had happened to Pauline? Whose voice had I heard? Was it possible that we were about to accuse her of a crime at which the imagination reels? Had the child died, and was this the hour? I say that the minutes were a torture I would not live through again though Jehan Cavanagh's fortune lay at the end of the journey. And this was but the beginning of it. Our knock remained unanswered. We repeated it, listening together at the door, but she did not open to us.

"For God's sake tell me the truth!" I cried to him at last. "What has happened? What does it mean?"

He answered me very gently.

" She has saved my son's life, Ingersoll. She
may have lost her own in doing so. I hope that
it is not so. Do you hear anything? Is anyone
moving in the room?"

I listened, but my own heart beat so loudly
I could not answer him. Not a sound came
out to us, not so much as the whisper of a
voice.

" She is dead," I cried, but he held me there,
his hot hand upon my own.

" We must break down the door, Ingersoll.
I will call them."

He raised his voice, calling aloud in Russian,
and being answered almost immediately by three
of his own servants, the man Feodor at the head
of them.

" Break down the door," he cried.

They obeyed him instantly, and we entered
together. There was no one in the outer room,
the sitting-room which overlooks the garden, but
in the bedroom, which faces the south, we
found Pauline insensible in Madame Cavanagh's
arms.

CHAPTER XXXIV

THE MIRACLE

I HAVE heard it said that it is difficult to remember the little things which attend an event of great moment to us. This is not within my own experience. I have ever found my memory serve me well concerning those hours attended by great emotion. Nor does it fail me when I would speak of that supreme event at the Fen, so unlooked for, so amazing in its outcome.

Let me say first of all that the room was in much disorder. Even in the sitting-room the chairs and tables had been pushed about as though in a moment of some alarm. The windows were wide open, both the casement of the outer room and that of the bedroom. The light, I observed, was fully on, and Madame Cavanagh herself was dressed. As for little Pauline, she wore a long white gown tied about the waist by an Eastern sash, but the arm of it was now bloodstained and the shoulder of it blackened. These things I perceived in an instant, standing at Mr. Cavanagh's side. But how they came to be I knew no more than the dead.

I say that we had entered the outer room together, but here in the bedroom he pushed by

me and went immediately to Madame's side. To
this hour I can see her looking up at him with
wan, sad eyes, and then down at the pallid face
of my little schoolgirl. If I felt for the moment
that I had no part in such a scene, the pathos of
it is my justification. In truth, I seemed to stand
apart from them, my faculties numbed, my own
sorrow and anxiety expressed to none. For I
believed that Pauline was dead, and that the
long months of doubt had but this for their
harvest.

"Catherine! Why are you here, Catherine?"

Mr. Cavanagh spoke to the poor lady at his
feet, and she answered him in that sweet voice I
had heard already in the garden.

"There has been great trouble, Jehan. Please
send for Dr. Hanson."

He did not answer her for a spell, gazing at
her like one who has heard the voice of a dream.
When he did reply, it was to the man Feodor.

"Send to Kenton Park immediately," he said ;
"let Frederick go."

"Yes, yes," Madame added, "and Robiniof
may accompany him. It will be safer."

Again Mr. Cavanagh looked at her with those
amazed eyes.

"As you say, Catherine, it will be safer. Let
Robiniof go."

It was wonderful to hear him thus assenting
to the poor lady's will, but I think some miracle

of the truth already came to him as it had come
to me in the garden that morning. The curse of
madness no longer lay upon his house. Whatever the day had done for him, it had given back
to Madame Cavanagh her reason. This he understood but vaguely, as a man to whom some far-off
vision of a great joy has come. I saw the colour
mantling his hollow cheeks ; he breathed quickly ;
his eyes shone suddenly as though the light of a
great hope had fired him. And then he remembered me, and turning, he bade me come to
Pauline's side.

" Put your hand upon her heart," he said.

I stooped to obey him, and said that she still
lived.

" She has fainted," he rejoined ; " it may be
that her arm is broken. But she is very young,
Ingersoll, and we shall save her. By God in
heaven, I will save her—for you, Ingersoll."

This, I say, is my recollection of the scene.
Masterful as were the words I heard, I had an
answer to none of them. A dogged persistency
in the belief that Pauline must die to save this unhappy house had haunted me from the beginning.
Even the sure witness of her voice hardly robbed
me of that. For she opened her eyes at length
and looked up, and I knelt and kissed her, and it
seemed to me that this might be the last time
that I should ever do so.

"Please, Bruce," she said, so softly that I could
hardly hear her, " please do not touch my arm."

And what answer could a man make to such
a plea as that? Be sure that I did as others
would have done, desiring an inspired eloquence
to tell of all I thought and felt, and saying just
nothing at all. When Dr. Hanson came, he
found us thus, Madame and I by Pauline's side,
and Mr. Cavanagh still pacing the room, apart
with that great thought which had come to him
and must remain the miracle of this night. Nor, I
think, could any capacity for astonishment have
remained to a man who had learned so much as
Reginald Hanson of the secrets and the mysteries
of this house and its people.

We left him to the task, Mr. Cavanagh and I,
while Madame called one of the nurses to her
assistance. In the sitting-room adjoining it was
good to cloak impatience by some pretence of
interest in that which happened beyond the
windows of the house. Each knew that it was a
pretence—the lightness of our talk betrayed the
fact—but we entered upon it very willingly, and
tried to tell the story as Pauline would tell it if
she lived.

"You see," said Mr. Cavanagh, "it's written
in five lines. A man tried to get in at the
window — she met him at the casement and
drove him back. Well, what happened to that
man, Ingersoll? Can you make a guess?"

I feared to do so, and told him frankly. Nor
would I ask by what means Madame Cavanagh
came to the room. I have learned lately that he

had ever refused to impose upon the poor lady those restraints which her mental condition had demanded. A fine sense of fidelity to an image of the past forbade him, and he paid a heavy enough price for his noble chivalry. So I hesitated to reply to him, and while I hesitated he took me toward the open window and asked me to tell him what I saw there.

"Look yonder at the lake, Ingersoll," he cried, " what do you make of it ? "

" There are men upon the far bank," said I, " and they carry lanterns."

" Is there a boat ? "

" I do not see one."

" I remember ; we carried it up for safety. Do you know why the men are there, Ingersoll ? "

" I think that I could guess."

" Our old friend Dubarrac—it could be no other. He was coming in to kill my son, Ingersoll. And your little schoolgirl—but I must not think of it—not yet, Ingersoll. It may mean so much to you and me—so much."

He stopped abruptly and shut the window. I could divine the intention of that which he left unsaid, but I had no remark to make upon it. All my hope lay beyond the door which was closed to us. I could not conceal the fact even from him, and when Madame Cavanagh appeared, I implored her for God's sake to tell me the truth.

" Will she live ? " I asked her.

Her hand fell upon my own as a touch of rose leaves, and, her woman's heart speaking, she answered me :

" I could not bring you better news, Mr. Ingersoll."

But to her husband she said :

" Jehan, take me to my son."

I buried my face in my hands, did not dare to look upon them, as the angel of that supreme reconciliation breathed upon them both, and Jehan Cavanagh looked up and understood.

For now he must lay his burden upon the heart of the woman who had loved him, and this was the wonder of the truth as the new day bore witness to it.

CHAPTER XXXV

IT would have been upon the tenth day after we had good news of her son that Madame Cavanagh met me in the great library of the house and told me for the first time the true story of that which had happened at Baku.

Be sure that I am likely to forget none of the circumstances of a recital so unlooked for and in some ways so terrible. Day by day the conviction had been growing upon me that this gentle lady could make or mar my happiness, that my future lay in her hands, and that when she spoke I should now either be able to answer the world or must be judged by it. And now the momentous hour drew near. At the breakfast table when the others were gone, she begged me to accompany her to the library that we might speak of Pauline. I went there, knowing well that she had the secret. But what possession of it would mean to me, whether the beginning of a new happiness or the end of all that I had desired, this I knew not at all.

I shall tell you first that the old fable of the darkest hour had not been belied at the Fen. That night of miracle which lifted the veil from

330

Jehan Cavanagh's eyes had also brought to him
the news that his son would live. I can offer no
rational explanation of my own faith, but it seems
to me now that I myself had known this at the
moment of their reconciliation, and that nothing
afterwards robbed me of my belief. Upon others
the sun already had begun to shine. I remained
alone in that shadowland of doubt to which the
mystery had led me.

Of course, there was no more talk of plot and
counter-plot at The House of the Fen. The death
of Dubarrac, who had fallen from Pauline's
window to the terrace of stone below, this and
Mr. Cavanagh's instant resumption of his ancient
rôle opened the woods to us again and permitted
us to come and go as we pleased. An obliging
jury found an open verdict, a curious Press
related a fine tale of burglary and outrage, hint-
ing that the house had been watched for many
days, and that this daring attempt had been
frustrated by a woman's bravery. We read the
accounts and laughed at them. It was good to
ride out again and breathe the fine fresh air, and
understand that, whatever might befall us elsewhere, the House of the Fen remained a strong-
hold unassailable.

I write this foreword that I come with a
better understanding to the day when I found
myself face to face with Madame Cavanagh in
the library, and waited, as a prisoner for a verdict,
upon the story she must tell me. Still a very

beautiful woman, her long illness had not been
without its penalties ; but these were chiefly of
her manner, that timid, shy address which seemed
to say, " There is something in my life of which
I know nothing ; you know, but you are afraid
to tell me." This, I say, characterised her
attitude to me and even toward her husband,
whose devotion now surpassed all words. But
we believed that it would pass, and when she
met me in the library upon that fateful morning,
I observed already that a woman's confidence
was returning to her.

" Mr. Ingersoll," she said, inviting me to the
recess of the great eastern window, "you know
why I have asked you to come here, this morning ? "

" It is to speak of Pauline, Madame Cavanagh ? "

She assented with a nod of her head, and for
a spell gazed over the terrace below to which
they had carried my little schoolgirl, and where
she now lay upon a wicker couch, Jehan Cavanagh himself her sentinel.

" Yes, to speak of Pauline. It will be no
surprise to you, Mr. Ingersoll—there have been
many days now when you have asked yourself
why I did not speak."

" I first asked that," said I, " upon the day
when I met you in the garden."

" I was aware that you did, and afterwards
upon that dreadful night. You have thought

much about all this—I see how much you think about it—but has it ever occurred to you that it might be my duty never to tell you ? "

I looked at her, a hard question in my eyes.

"You are a woman and you will tell me," said I, " because you have loved."

She sighed and turned away her face. A band of sunshine fell obliquely through the casement upon her bent head, and, had I not known her, I could have said that it was the head of a girl. Indeed, this sense of her womanhood gave me a courage of which her words might otherwise have robbed me. I would not believe that I must hear from her lips a sentence which would rob me in an instant of all that new hope this meeting had inspired.

"You are a woman," I repeated, " and would do no unwomanly thing. Madame Cavanagh, I must know Pauline's story—I cannot live without it."

She was silent a little while, her face still turned from me. From the garden there came up to us an echo of young laughter. I heard Pauline's voice and then another voice, that of her own son.

"Listen," she exclaimed suddenly, turning to me and laying her hand upon my own, " if you loved a man and something that you knew might rob him of his happiness, would you tell it to another, Mr. Ingersoll, or guard your secret ? I ask

you that—a woman asks you. Would you keep
your secret or betray it?"

It was impossible to mistake the earnestness
of this or its meaning. As by an inspiration it
came to me that Pauline had been accused that
another might be spared. Was that other Jehan
Cavanagh himself? Good heavens! what a
thought!

"Would you keep your secret or betray it,
Mr. Ingersoll?"

I pressed my hands to my head and hid my
face from her for many minutes. Presently I
said:

"There would be another point of view. To
whom is the secret to be told, and how far shall
he be trusted?"

"I was going to speak of that," she said

"I can see," said I, "that the obligation
of silence has some claim. But two might be
conscious of it, and there being a good understanding between them and their aims being
mutual—but that goes without saying."

She nodded her head, following every word.

"There must be no more dark hours in his
life, Mr. Ingersoll."

"There shall never be one if I can spare him
that."

"I will not ask you for a promise," she went
on, "you have become as his own son. He has
told me so—he will never forget you, Mr. Ingersoll. If we cannot justify Pauline to him——"

"I ask nothing but this, that she shall be justified to me, Madame Cavanagh. Of course, I have never really believed her to be guilty. There were black hours at Bruges, and I am ashamed of them; but I have some excuse. They were all for the truth, and she herself confessed the crime."

"She confessed that her brother Georges might not be charged."

"Her brother?"

"Who married Adrienne Renaudier at Odessa."

I could not utter a word in answer to this, and she went on very quietly:

"There is much French blood in her veins. The family has always been spoken of as a French family at Baku. So the brother married a French woman. Then came the trouble. I remember it as one long night of terror and suffering. The people went mad. The oil wells were burned. They shot poor men down at my own door. My maid was killed almost in my arms. Of course, the Mamavieffs were suspected at such a time. It was easy to believe that Francis Cavanagh, my father-in-law, had been shot by one of them."

"Whereas?" I said, my lips so dry that I could hardly utter the question.

"Whereas he shot himself, Mr. Ingersoll."

A full five minutes must have passed before either of us spoke again. I could not tell her

what this meant to me—she had no need to ask.
The supreme joys of our lives are often the fruit
of the simplest issues. I had made a thousand
guesses at the true story of Baku, and not one
of them had touched the hem of this possibility.
But the spoken truth stripped the curtains of
that mystery as though a giant hand had torn
them down.

"He shot himself!" I cried at length. "And
you knew it, Madame Cavanagh?"

"I knew it ten days ago when Robiniof came
here from Bruges."

"Should I not know the whole story?"

"I must tell you—I owe it to you. Francis
Cavanagh loved Adrienne, Georges' wife. If this
had been known after his death, it would have
gone very hard with her—they would certainly
have suspected her or pretended to do so."

"I see it all," said I, "and this child lied,
firstly, to save her sister's life; then it may be at
the dictates of her vanity; and lastly—yes, we
come to lastly, Madame Cavanagh—that she
might spare your husband the truth."

She had not looked upon it in that light, but
I perceived it plainly enough. Oh, how simple it
all was! This Francis Cavanagh, a plausible
libertine, had been threatened with exposure by
the woman he would have dishonoured; little
Pauline was at the café door when he shot himself; clever friends got her away; she was afraid
that her sister would be accused, and she lied to

all the world. Did she not tell me at Bruges
that Jehan Cavanagh had been kind to her
mother ? I wanted no other argument ; I could
have run out for joy, crying to the very heavens,
" She is innocent ! she is innocent ! "

" Madame Cavanagh," I said upon an impulse,
" I will keep your husband's secret until your own
lips shall give me leave to speak."

She stood and put both her hands into mine.

" We will keep it," she said, " until he commands us to speak."

I assented, her hands still in mine. And that
was a promise I have kept—for to-day Jehan
Cavanagh himself commands me to write, and
this confession is that which he himself would
give to the world.

*   *   *   *   *

I say that he himself asked me to tell the
story, but much had happened before that came
about. And perhaps I should first make mention
of the quiet days which followed upon the great
event at the Fen ; sunny autumn mornings
and nights of sleep, and such peace upon the
house that its terrible story might have been but
a memory of dreams. Day by day now Pauline
began to recover her old spirits, and to insist that
we should share them. It is true that she still
carried her arm in a sling, and that there were
occasions when even the sunshine could not
bring roses to her cheeks ; but these became rarer

as the weeks went on; and one morning Mr. Cavanagh astonished me by saying that I must take her at once to the South.

"You shall have my yacht," he said; "spy out Algiers and Tunis, and then to Egypt, Ingersoll. Do not forget that she is born of the East. A winter in your own country is a penance you have no right to impose upon her. I have written to Greenwood, and he will have the boat in commission in a week. I need not tell you that you may go where you will. Here is a letter I got from our old friend Blondel, who is at St. Petersburg."

I could not read the letter, for it was written in Russian, but I imagined its contents very readily. And now I knew that Jehan Cavanagh had the secret also—if I had not guessed it many days ago. All the irony of that mad accusation must have come home to him these bitter days. But his mind rose above it, none the less, for he had found redemption at a woman's hand.

"And you, Mr. Cavanagh?" I asked him, turning towards him.

"I am going to the hills, Ingersoll," he said, with a light laugh, and then, "I am going to Canada. Have you never felt that your environment is too small, that you long for great spaces and the unbroken horizon? I shall go to the hills and look down a little while upon the world. But you will write to me often, Ingersoll—you will tell me of your wife?"

I suppose that I showed some embarrassment

at this, but he went on quickly to speak of greater
things, and I listened with bent ear.

"Canute would have kept back the sea, Ingersoll," he said, "but, after all, men have done
that since his day. They build walls and har-
bours ; they reclaim the land and plant it. That
which no man has done or will do is to keep back
the great flood of human progress, pressing on to
what goal we know not. Here's a sea whereon
also you will meet with storms. Ships will be
wrecked, Ingersoll, and men and women will
perish dreadfully. But it's a flowing tide, and
we who forget the truth will perish by it. I say
that human freedom needs even human madness
as its agent sometimes. No man sailing that
sea has the right to think only of his own poor
barque, and destroy others that he may live.
That's what I have been doing. I thought that
I had some title which my own conscience did
not give me, and I was wrong. Let the law be
to the law-makers. A society which cannot protect itself must perish—no man can save it, none
of his own volition. You knew this from the
first—your talk of the Individual sanction was
all cant, Ingersoll. But for what you did I thank
you—chiefly for your words at Madrid. There's
the peril of it—the blood-lust and the aftermath.
You saved me from that, and I am remembering
it while I live."

I made but an idle answer to this ; and, in
truth, it was a confession that needed no answer.

The finger of God had written the book for Jehan Cavanagh, and had written it so that all the world could read. I had nothing to tell him save the story of my own obligation and of the esteem in which I held him. But these were old sayings, and not to be dwelt upon.

And I recollect that we were riding in the park when the talk passed, and that presently the house itself came to our view, and the figures of two who waited for us upon the terrace. Here lay the gate of our city, and, without a word spoken, we quickened our pace and rode toward them. It was midday, I remember, and the sun at the zenith.

THE END.

PRINTED BY CASSELL AND COMPANY, LIMITED, LA BELLE SAUVAGE, LONDON, E.C.

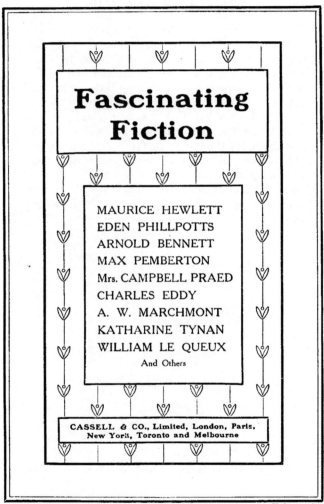

Fascinating Fiction

MAURICE HEWLETT
EDEN PHILLPOTTS
ARNOLD BENNETT
MAX PEMBERTON
Mrs. CAMPBELL PRAED
CHARLES EDDY
A. W. MARCHMONT
KATHARINE TYNAN
WILLIAM LE QUEUX
And Others

CASSELL & CO., Limited, London, Paris, New York, Toronto and Melbourne

Fascinating New Fiction

Below and on the following pages are given particulars of Cassell & Co.'s new fiction for the Spring Season, 1908. The best and most popular authors of the day are represented. Every lover of good stories, whatever his or her predilection, is fully catered for. In entrancing interest, vivid writing, and conception generally, these novels will be found unsurpassed among current works of fiction.

The Spanish Jade
By MAURICE HEWLETT
Author of "The Stooping Lady," "The Queen's Quair," "The Forest Lovers," &c.

With 4 Full-page Coloured Plates and End Papers designed by
WILLIAM HYDE. 6s.

MR. HEWLETT, that "mediævalised Meredith," as he has been called, tells a tale of the Spain of 1860—of George Borrow's day.

Contrasting the phlegmatic English with the passionate Spanish temperament, tragedy of a high order is achieved, and the end shows a renunciation complete, inevitable, yet not wholly unhappy.

Manvers, an English squire, riding through the land, comes upon a scene that revolts him. His English nature has just a touch of the Quixotic, and he interferes. The result is, he finds himself left with a beautiful Spanish girl to take care of, laying up for himself stores of unknown hate and love.

The plot quickens, the characters grow in number and depth of passion. Manuela (the Spanish Jade), Manvers' *protegée*, is driven to murder in defence of her own and her rescuer's life, and out of this murder emerges a story which reminds us of "The Ring and the Book," in its keen analysis of motives. It is told with all Mr. Hewlett's accustomed power, the vigour and colour and opulence of his style, his strong sense of character, race, and subtle feeling for the atmosphere of the country of which he writes.

The Statue
By EDEN PHILLPOTTS and ARNOLD BENNETT
With Frontispiece in Colours by W. HERBERT HOLLOWAY. 6s.

THIS novel will appeal to all lovers of the sensational. In it millionaires work the complex operations of European finance, and a Prime Minister and his Cabinet manœuvre to bring about a war between France and Germany. A huge statue is erected by a millionaire for certain mysterious purposes, which are not discovered until towards the end of the story. At the foot the owner is killed by another millionaire, whose trial is powerfully related. He is condemned to death, but for political purposes his sentence is commuted to penal servitude.

Prison life at Dartmoor is graphically described, and the reader is thrilled by a sensational escape by means of motor-cars. Altogether the book can be strongly recommended to those readers who like to have their thoughts taken away from the cares of everyday life.

CASSELL & COMPANY, LTD., *London, Paris, New York, Toronto & Melbourne.*

Wheels of Anarchy

By MAX PEMBERTON

Author of " The Diamond Ship," etc.

With Frontispiece in Colours by ROBERT B. M. PAXTON. 6s.

" WHEELS OF ANARCHY " is the story of an assassin told from the papers and personal narrative of his secretary, Bruce Ingersoll. Ingersoll becomes secretary to Jehan Cavanagh, the Canadian railway magnate, who suddenly decides to go to Antwerp to try to bring to justice Pauline Namavieff, the girl who assassinated his father at Baku. Thereupon follows a scene in which Mr. Pemberton's descriptive powers—his command of colour and his tremendous vim—are seen at their very best.

Next the scene shifts to Madrid, thence to Barcelona, next to Venice, and finally to England. All the time the wheels of Anarchy are revolving ceaselessly ; plot and counter-plot, and danger following danger, but Mr. Pemberton brings all these exciting events to a satisfactory and far from tame conclusion.

Mary Gray

By KATHARINE TYNAN

Author of " The Story of Bawn," " For Maisie," etc.

With 4 Plates in Colours by C. H. TAFFS. 6s.

SELDOM, if ever, has that very popular authoress, Katharine Tynan, written a more delightful love story than " Mary Gray." From beginning to end you are interested in the changing fortunes of the heroine, and you are led on to the last page by the skilful and fascinating story of her life. Katharine Tynan introduces you to a variety of interesting personalities and scenes. Now it is Mary Gray in the quiet home of a lady of title ; and next it is, under changed conditions, her work as a secretary. Finally, in deft hand, the threads of sentiment are drawn more closely, and we part reluctantly with a very attractive young lady as she is happily united in marriage to the man of her choice.

The Seven of Hearts:

Together with other Exploits of Arsène Lupin

By MAURICE LEBLANC

With 4 Illustrations by CYRUS CUNEO. 6s.

ARSÈNE LUPIN, the man with a thousand disguises, by times chauffeur, opera singer, bookmaker, gilded youth, young man, old man, Marseillese bagman, Russian doctor, Spanish bullfighter ! This is the man whose breathlessly exciting adventures when baffling Ganimard, the great detective, while bringing off his great coups, are related in an intensely dramatic manner. He is one of the most remarkable creations of modern fiction.

CASSELL & COMPANY, LTD., *London, Paris, New York, Toronto & Melbourne.*

Dragon's Silk

By PAUL HERRING

Author of "The Pierrots on the Pier."

With Frontispiece in Colours by H. R. MILLAR. **6s.**

"DRAGON'S SILK," the rare and exquisite fabric made in China, is a main thread in the plot, and a titled lady with great commercial ability endeavours to make a "corner" in this beautiful material. How this influences the trend of events which spring from a wealthy mother's ambition for a talented son, who loves the girl in Lavender Lane, is told by Mr. Herring with a spontaneous blend of imagery and epigram which is very refreshing. The young man goes out to China and almost falls in love with a charming and clever heiress, so that for a time it looks as if his mother's artful ruse against the girl in Lavender Lane has succeeded. But his memory of her breaks the other spell.

By Their Fruits

By Mrs. CAMPBELL PRAED

Author of "Christina Chard," "The Other Mrs. Jacobs," etc.

With Frontispiece in Colours by CHAS. PEARS. **6s.**

A FASCINATING story with twin sisters as the central figures. Aglaia-Pascaline, frivolous, a victim to the drug habit, immoral ; Pascaline-Aglaia, pure, spiritual, would-be saviour of her sister. Around these two characters the story is woven in such a skilful manner that the interest never flags for one moment.

To shield her sister the "good Pascaline" is ready to go to any extreme of self-sacrifice, whilst Aglaia shrinks from nothing to secure her own pleasure. The theme has been treated by Mrs. Campbell Praed in a manner that awakens the highest interest. There are incidents of intense dramatic force, and the dialogue throughout is bright and crisp.

Mrs. Bailey's Debts

By CHARLES EDDY

Author of "The Bachelors."

With Frontispiece in Colours. **6s.**

IN "Mrs. Bailey's Debts," Mr. Eddy tells with his usual verve the story of a pretty young widow's financial aberrations. She gets her affairs into an awful mess, from which even the gallant Dick, in spite of his devotion, cannot extricate her.

The young man's naïve but praiseworthy efforts to pull the chestnuts out of the fire are brightly recounted, and the pathos of the widow's situation is rendered all the more piquant by the Gilbertian element of amateur finance in the midst of the "bulls and bears."

CASSELL & COMPANY, LTD., *London, Paris, New York, Toronto & Melbourne.*

NEW FICTION

Concerning Belinda
By ELEANOR HOYT BRAINERD
Author of " Bettina Beguiled."

3s. 6d.

FOR something like thirty years the Misses Ryder had maintained a flourishing Select School for Young Ladies, located in the most aristocratic district of New York. They needed a teacher of English, and Belinda was panting for a knowledge of the world and success. She was " much too pretty and girlish," Miss Lucilla said; but as Belinda was willing to accept a very small salary, these disadvantages were overlooked. The subsequent episodes in Belinda's life as a Teacher of English and other things incidentally are described with excellent feeling, vivacious humour, and a sympathetic insight into the psychology of girlhood.

Betty of the Rectory
By L. T. MEADE
Author of "Julia," etc.

With Frontispiece in Colours by CHARLES HORRELL. *6s.*

BETTY is a veritable "Angel in the House"—one of the most charming characters created by Mrs. Meade. Burdened on the very eve of her marriage with the knowledge that her husband-to-be held a dread secret which she would not have him reveal, she bravely lives her life as the wife of a Rector. When the secret does come out she sets herself as bravely to fight the great evil which threatens ruin to her loved one and to her. How she fought and conquered, influenced and controlled the other characters forms a story that will take a worthy position among the other works by this author.

The Lost Millionaire
By LILLIAS C. DAVIDSON
Author of "The Great Dynover Pearl Case," etc.

With Frontispiece in Colours. 6s.

IT wasn't for the sake of a ransom that the baby millionaire was kidnapped, for none was asked. Now if a ransom was *not* the motive, what could have been the object of the plotters? On the face of it, they might just as well have kidnapped some other child if pecuniary gain was not their purpose. Again, how could such an audacious scheme as the misappropriation of the heir to over a million be successfully effected?

Well, there are mysteries, and Mrs. Davidson has woven them, with the craftsmanship for which she is well known, into a very exciting and convincing story.

CASSELL & COMPANY, LTD., *London, Paris, New York, Toronto & Melbourne.*

NEW FICTION

The Pauper of Park Lane

By WILLIAM LE QUEUX

Author of " The Spider's Eye," etc.

With Coloured Frontispiece by MISS L. SCHLEGEL.   6s.

MR. LE QUEUX'S powers in the realms of mystery and imagination are phenomenal, and "The Pauper of Park Lane," with its weird adventures in the East and West, its powerful love interest, and its remarkable portrayal of character, is undoubtedly his finest effort.

Max Barclay, the man in love with Marian Rolfe, is an inspiring character, and there is a spice of Oriental glamour and fascination about handsome, dark-haired Maud Petrovitch, daughter of the Servian statesman, around whose strange disappearance much of the interest of the story centres. A series of ingenious climaxes and problems lead up to a *dénouement* of astonishing power.

Vayenne

By PERCY BREBNER (Christian Lys)

Author of " Princess Maritza."

With Frontispiece in Colour by R. B. M. PAXTON.   6s.

UNLIKE its predecessors, "The Fortress of Yadasara" and "Princess Maritza," "Vayenne" does not introduce the reader to a mythical kingdom enmeshed in its web of petty intrigue, but the story deals with semi-private affairs, the fierce loves and hates, jealousies and tangled line of succession of the Ducal House of Montvilliers.

In the creation of the characters in the story of Roger Herrick, and the altogether unexpected *dénouement* caused by his coming to Vayenne; of fair Christine de Liancourt, and the tragedy of Jean, the great-souled hero, and all the rest of them, Mr. Brebner again justifies his reputation as a careful delineator of character.

The Enchanted Ship

By R. ANDOM

Author of " We Three and Troddles," " Four Men with a Van," etc.

With numerous Illustrations.   3s. 6d.

IN his new story this popular humorist has taken a fantastic idea which is frankly impossible, a fact which, in his merriment, the reader will doubtless forget before he has read a dozen pages. Laughter is an excellent tonic, and those to whom the comic side of things makes a wholesome appeal will find that Mr. Andom's fun is as exuberant in the present book as in any of its predecessors.

CASSELL & COMPANY, LTD., *London, Paris, New York, Toronto & Melbourne.*

A Millionaire Girl
By A. W. MARCHMONT
Author of " The Man who was Dead."
With Coloured Frontispiece by H. R. MILLAR. 6s.

" A MILLIONAIRE GIRL " deals with the machinations of a gang of high-class criminals under the direction of Gilbert Merridew. Mrs. Merridew, Gilbert's mother, also claimed to be the wife of Parmenter, the dead millionaire, whose daughter was engaged to Jack Fenwick, son of Lord Belborough. Her father's fortune therefore passes away from Olive; but Mrs. Merridew, in order to " make assurance doubly sure," does her utmost to bring Olive to marry Gilbert.

The disappearance of some Government papers for which Jack Fenwick was responsible brings the reader to the first stage in the unwinding of the *dénouement.* Olive discovers that the theft is the work of the Merridew gang. Thereafter the release of Purvis from prison complicates the Merridews' policy, until at last the gang is unmasked, and Olive achieves her heart's desire—the proof of her father's good name.

Her Faithful Knight
By W. BOURNE COOKE
Author of "The Horned Owl," etc.
With Frontispiece in Colours by CHRISTOPHER CLARK, R.I. 6s.

MR. BOURNE COOKE'S new novel is a story of romance and adventure, of love and battle, the scene of which is laid in Nottingham and Leicester between the years 1641 and 1645. The heroine, Oriel Deane, an orphan girl of great wealth and beauty, is a charming personality, fascinatingly delineated. The ardent struggles of her two cavalier lovers to win her hand, the stirring episodes through which they pass to achieve their purpose, and the many romantic and thrilling incidents with which the story abounds, are forcibly related.

Flaming June
By MRS. GEORGE DE HORNE VAIZEY
Author of "How Like the King," etc.
With Frontispiece in Colours by F. C. DICKENSON. 6s.

THE heroine of this story is an American girl with unconventional ways and pronounced American characteristics. On her way to England she becomes acquainted with a family of unscrupulous adventurers, and against the advice of her friends accepts an invitation to stay with them. Fate gives her the companionship on the journey of Captain Guest, whose friendship deepens into love. He is able to win her gratitude by helping her against the attempts of the adventurers to rob her by forging her name. Readers who like strong love interests in their stories will find all they desire in this novel.

CASSELL & COMPANY, LTD., *London, Paris, New York, Toronto & Melbourne.*

Recent Fiction

The following Novels have met with striking success during the past season. Their continued popularity among fiction readers, as evidenced by the unabated demand, is distinct proof of their merit. They cover every field of style and interest, and the tastes of all novel readers are fully satisfied.

Kate Meredith
By C. J. CUTCLIFFE HYNE. 6s.

The Slanderers
By WARWICK DEEPING. 6s.

Caleb Conover, Railroader
By ALBERT PAYSON TERHUNE. 6s.

Golden Morn
By H. A. HINKSON. 6s.

The Admirable Davis
By RONALD LEGGE. 6s.

The King of Kerisal
By MAYNE LINDSAY. 6s.

Bettina Beguiled
By ELEANOR HOYT BRAINERD. 3s. 6d.

The Spinning of Fate
By AGNES C. MITCHELL. 6s.

The Lord of the Dyke
By WALTER WOOD. 6s.

The Heiress of Densley Wold
By FLORENCE WARDEN. 6s.

Through Wintry Terrors
By DORA SIGERSON SHORTER. 6s.

The Dainty Lady Lucy
By FOXCROFT DAVIS. 6s.

The Call of the Drum
By HORACE WYNDHAM. 6s.

The Plains of Silence
By ALICE & CLAUDE ASKEW. 6s.

An Experiment in Perfection
By MARION T. D. BARTON. 6s.

A Wingèd Victory
By ROBERT M. LOVETT. 6s.

The Coming of Isobel
By HELEN WALLACE. 6s.

Four Men with a Van
By R. ANDOM. 3s. 6d.

A Hole in the Coat
By CHARLES EDDY. 6s.

The House of Murgatroyd By C. C. ANDREWS. 6s.

Not George Washington
By HERBERT WESTBROOK & P. G. WODEHOUSE. 6s.

The Throwback
By A. H. LEWIS. 6s.

The Immortal Light
By JOHN MASTIN. 6s.

The Diamond Ship
By MAX PEMBERTON. 6s.

CASSELL & COMPANY, LTD., *London, Paris, New York, Toronto & Melbourne.*

Further Reading

On the Trail of Arthur Conan Doyle:

An Illustrated Devon Tour

by Brian W. Pugh & Paul R. Spiring

"Its succinct account of Conan Doyle's association with Devon and with George Turnavine Budd and Bertram Fletcher Robinson is invaluable, and just to follow the Devon Tour on paper is fascinating."

The Sherlock Holmes Journal

(Spring 2008)

Further Reading

Bertram Fletcher Robinson:

A Footnote to The Hound of the Baskervilles

by Brian W. Pugh & Paul R. Spiring

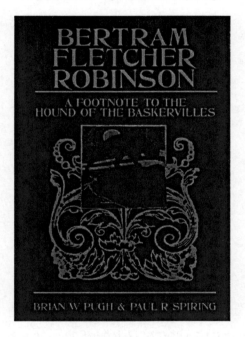

"A full scale biography of Fletcher Robinson. Being first in their field allows the authors a virtual blank canvas for their word painting, and this they use to no little effect."

The Sherlock Holmes Journal

(Winter 2008)

Further Reading

Aside Arthur Conan Doyle: Twenty Original Tales

by Bertram Fletcher Robinson

Compiled by Paul R. Spiring

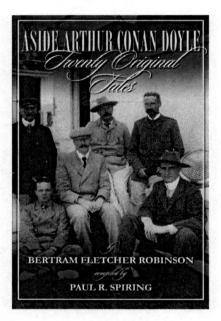

"The collection proves that Fletcher Robinson was more than capable of producing good work and would probably have gone on to greater things had his life not been cut short."

The *Weekend Supplement* of the

Western Morning News

(14 March 2009)

Further Reading

The World of Vanity Fair

by Bertram Fletcher Robinson

Compiled by Paul R. Spiring

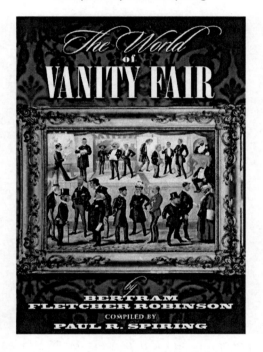

*"Every now and then, you come across a really sumptuous book,
where just turning and looking at the pages takes you into
another world. Such is the case with this one."*

The Bookbag

(May 2009)

Further Reading

Bobbles & Plum: Four Satirical Playlets

by Bertram Fletcher Robinson and PG Wodehouse

Compiled by Paul R. Spiring

*"The discovery of four satirical 'playlets' by PG Wodehouse, seen
by the public for the first time in 100 years this weekend, prove
that the humorist – who is often viewed as apolitical – had a
strong interest in public affairs from his youth."*

The Observer

(26 July 2009)

Further Reading

Rugby Football during the Nineteenth Century:

A Collection of Contemporary Essays about the Game

Compiled by Paul R. Spiring

Introduced by Patrick Casey & Hugh Cooke

"There have been some cracking rugby history books down the years, but never have we been treated to rugby writing by the men who were there at the time. Until now."

Rugby World Magazine Book of the Month

(June 2010)

Further Reading

Panto for Beginners: Just When you Thought it was safe to go back to the Theatre

by Hugh Cooke

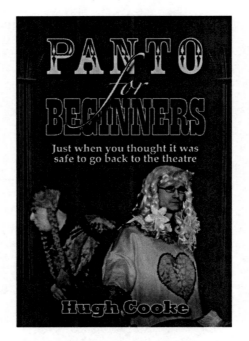

"If you are creating lesson plans and want something interesting and fun this book is very helpful. Rather than just tell you how to create a pantomime, it also includes several that you can easily change. Very practical."

Amazon.com & Amazon.co.uk

(November 2010)

Further Reading

Arthur Conan Doyle, Sherlock Holmes & Devon::

A Complete TourGuide and Companion

by Brian W. Pugh, Paul R. Spiring & Sadru Bhanji

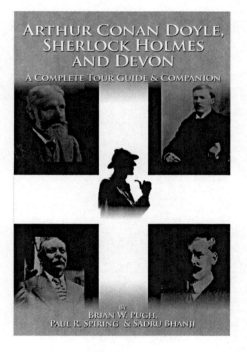

"A short review cannot do full justice to this book...The authors are to be congratulated for bringing so much intriguing and enlightening information together in one book."

Transactions of the Devonshire Association (Vol. 142)

(January 2011)

Lightning Source UK Ltd.
Milton Keynes UK
19 December 2010

164558UK00001B/6/P